Also by J. P. Donleavy

Novels
The Ginger Man
The Beastly Beatitudes of Balthazar B
The Onion Eaters
A Fairy Tale of New York
The Destinies of Darcy Dancer, Gentleman
Schultz
Leila
Are You Listening Rabbi Löw
That Darcy, That Dancer, That Gentleman

Novellas
The Saddest Summer of Samuel S
The Lady Who Liked Clean Restrooms

Nonfiction
The Unexpurgated Code: A Complete Manual of Survival and Manners
(with drawings by the author)
De Alphonce Tennis: The Superlative Game of Eccentric Champions
J. P. Donleavy's Ireland: In All Her Sins and Some of Her Graces
A Singular Country
An Author and His Image

Plays
The Ginger Man
Fairy Tales of New York
A Singular Man
The Saddest Summer of Samuel S
The Beastly Beatitudes of Balthazar B

Stories
Meet My Maker the Mad Molecule

Autobiography
The History of the Ginger Man

THOMAS DUNNE BOOKS
ST. MARTIN'S GRIFFIN
NEW YORK

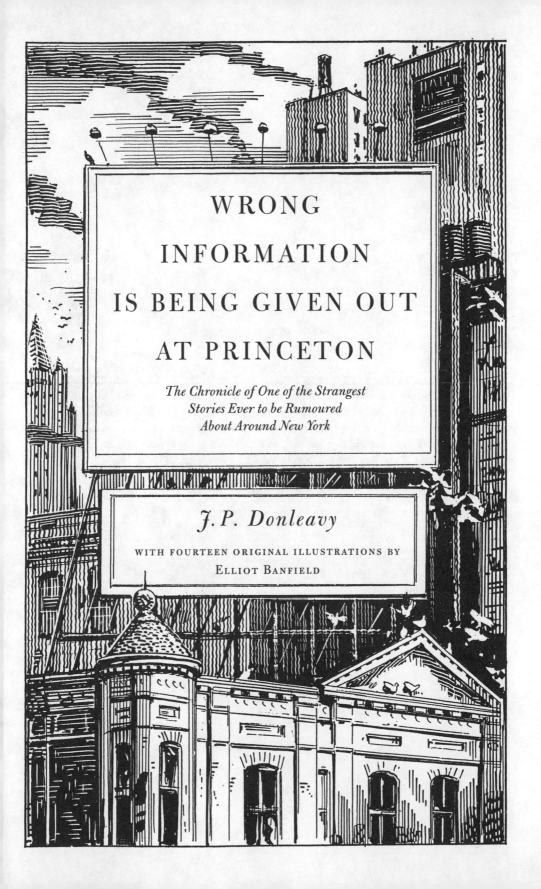

WRONG INFORMATION IS BEING GIVEN OUT AT PRINCETON

The Chronicle of One of the Strangest Stories Ever to be Rumoured About Around New York

J. P. Donleavy

WITH FOURTEEN ORIGINAL ILLUSTRATIONS BY
ELLIOT BANFIELD

THOMAS DUNNE BOOKS.
An imprint of St. Martin's Press.

WRONG INFORMATION IS BEING GIVEN OUT AT PRINCETON. Copyright © 1998 by J. P. Donleavy. Illustrations copyright © 1997 by Thornwillow Press, Ltd. All rights reserved. Printed in the United States of America. No part of this book may be used or reproduced in any manner whatsoever without written permission except in the case of brief quotations embodied in critical articles or reviews. For information, address St. Martin's Press, 175 Fifth Avenue, New York, N.Y. 10010.

Production Editor: David Stanford Burr

Library of Congress Cataloging-in-Publication Data

Donleavy, J. P. (James Patrick).
    Wrong information is being given out at Princeton / J. P. Donleavy.
        p.   cm.
    ISBN 0-312-19372-6 (hc)
    ISBN 0-312-24499-1 (pbk)
PS3507.0686W76   1998
823'.914–dc21   98-19411
                                                                         CIP

First published in the United States of America in a handmade edition limited to 175 copies by Thornwillow Press, Ltd.

First St. Martin's Griffin Edition: December 1999

10 9 8 7 6 5 4 3 2 1

WRONG
INFORMATION IS
BEING GIVEN OUT
AT PRINCETON

P EOPLE WERE ALREADY BEGINNING to forget we were veterans after the Second World War and that the government no longer owed us a living. Face-lifting, hair replacement, and breast enhancement hadn't yet come into vogue and people still believed there were other kinds of contentment. Especially when television was just beginning to pleasantly paralyze the nation. The forces of commercialism and survival were hard at work doing a lot of us down, and I was at the time at a loose emotional end, as you might say, when she came into my life in the cold blue winter before Christmas. There'd been a couple of big snowfalls and icicles were hanging down from people's windowsills.

It was a Sunday afternoon and I was standing in a friend's ramshackle West Thirty-fourth Street apartment in a gray and dingy Garment District around the corner from one of the city's biggest hotels, the New Yorker, and not far from the entrance to the Lincoln Tunnel that went out westwards under the Hudson River, starting a high-way all the way to California. I was always fond of know-ing where I really was in New York, right down to the bedrock and subsoil. There wasn't much heat in the building and the friend, whom I had got to know while we were on the same ship in the navy, had a log fire going in his fireplace and I was glad to be somewhere warm. Her name was Sylvia and her girlfriend called Ertha, and both arrived enclosed in a bunch of thick heavy sweaters. Sylvia's top was in green and her friend in blue. Both were advocates of modern dance, and even with all the thick wool over them you could see they were athletically curvaceous.

My friend Maximilian, who had after a brief marriage and divorce come back east from Chicago to make his fortune in New York, was already gaga over Ertha, having met her at a modern dance recital, and was now giving her his further line inviting her into his bedroom. To show her, he said, the rare fragile beauty of his seashells he'd collected on the Sagaponack beach out on Long Island. I took the opportunity to chat a little with Sylvia, who, with long brown hair tied in a ponytail, told me she was as an abandoned baby adopted by parents who were rich. She had attended fancy private schools and then a liberal girl's college where the affluent students could indulge being radical. Growing up, she took an interest in music and classical ballet but finally, when she'd grown too tall, switched to modern dancing. When she found out during her last year at college that she was adopted, it was like a fuse on a bomb that had been lit as she went off delving into a mysterious obscurity, to search for her natural mother and father.

Anyone who was rich in those days about five or six years after the Second World War, or had in any decent way a pot to piss in, was immediately embraced in friendship and given the most comfortable orange crate upon which to sit. When I pointed to the best crate, she suddenly swept around in a circle, singing and repeatedly said hi right at my face by way she said, of an Iroquois Indian greeting, and did I want to go with her and spend the sixteen hundred dollars she had right there in her purse. I felt she was being the way some people briefly get before the real big hammer blows of life fall. Having served in the navy, I calculated I was about five years older, and had been a petty officer second class gunner's mate on a battleship letting off sixteen-inch guns inside a turret. And here she was already taking command of the situation.

"Hey Sylvia, whew, give me a moment to think."

"Sure. Think. You got five seconds."

I moved back to lean against my friend's new griller his mother had sent from Chicago for him to be able to cook steak and lamb chops in his apartment and in two seconds said to Sylvia, "That's a lot of money." Having removed two sweaters, she said, "Sure it's a lot, but let's spend it." At the time I could have lived on sixteen hundred dollars for the next six months, but to achieve some rapport I pathetically tried to say, "I guess that's what money's for," but she said it first. As indeed she's said or tried to say everything first ever since.

I had a couple of times in my life thought I was in love when I'd find I'd get a magnifying glass to examine every tiny scrawl of a girl's handwriting in a letter to see if it would reveal some mystical character hidden deep in her soul. And on a couple of occasions in doing so, and just when I thought I had the girl under my thumb, in the next letter I found I was gently but nevertheless ignominiously being brushed off. And the denouement—hey, what the fuck did I do wrong—was always severely painful and depressing. Anyway, in growing up in a large family your need for emotional attachment to other nonkindred people isn't too great. But now I was out of the blue trying to assess my prospects with this attractive girl who had the most wonderful tits I'd ever seen in a sweater. I then sat on the orange crate myself and promptly crashed my way through it ass-first onto the floor. She continued in circles around the room, only now she was bent over double holding her stomach, convulsed in laughter.

"Forgive me my mirth, but the dumb way you just sat down was really funny."

I should have realized right there and then that I was getting involved with a deeply spoiled bitch. Albeit whose ever-ready attraction was her astonishingly attractive body further revealed in her ballet practice gear, and the animalistically sensuous way she chose to move or pose to stand. She had said she was only privileged by proxy. Because from the vague hints she heard of her real mother

5

and father, she was probably from the wrong side of the biological tracks. And suddenly during these speculations, she would put her hands on her hips, flexing her left knee forward and with her right buttock expanded, ask,

"Hey you don't say much. Now why don't you tell me all about you."

"Well, except that I am a composer, there's not too much to tell."

In fact there was a goddamn massive lot. But to fit in a little bit with her own imagined underprivileged social estimations of herself, I invented a few romanticized ideas about how my own background had been deprived. Like I was disadvantaged growing up in the middle Bronx, and right from the cradle was denied any real opportunity to step choo choo choo on the big gravy train as it pulled out of the station, No Wheres Ville. But in fact our house in the Bronx was in Riverdale and isolated in the middle of a suburban contour of similar houses and was spacious enough with thirteen rooms with one of them housing a concert grand piano. And my first-ever composition as a composer came from tinkling the ancient Steinway. Outside it had a knoll of trees and outcroppings of rock and even a garter snake or two. I also had at least been to a couple of decent prep schools and after a couple of expulsions, finally graduated from one of the lesser-known ones in New Jersey. Plus, the rumor was that my own large very Irish family of seven children had been fairly prosperous bootleggers who still owned a couple of Bowery saloons as well as one in Hell's Kitchen and a bit of city slum property. We even had a cook and a couple of maids. And it was when Sylvia saw me wipe the snow off the windshield of her car with the elbow of my jacket that she said it was a sure sign of being privileged.

"And hey, not only that but you seem to go do exactly what you want."

And I guess that that was more than a little bit true because then, early after the war on the GI bill, I headed to Lawrence College out in Appleton, Wisconsin. I learned about dairy cattle and the chemistry of paper and a coed blew me out in the middle of a cornfield. And in the sylvan collegiate pleasures there, I got to thinking the world should have more dance and music. So after only a year I took off to attend the next two years at a music conservatory in Italy. Living in Europe and traveling a bit, I developed a social consciousness about the upgrading of the underprivileged. That they should enjoy the better things in life. That everybody, despite color, creed, or race, should be entitled to getting a square deal. But returning to America and arriving back in the land of the free and the home of the brave, I began to find that not all Americans were on my side in this conceptual concern. In fact I found that when I posted up a sign, EQUAL OPPORTUNITY FOR ALL, some of these bastard neighbors flying the Stars and Stripes on their front lawns shouted they were tax-payers and were shaking their goddamn fists at me and wanting to kill me. And then along with all this I was having more than a few of life's blows fall. My favorite and so beautiful sister I dearly loved and with whom I often exchanged our concerns, one evening, anguished after discussing her unhappy marriage alone with me at the kitchen table, fled the house in her nightclothes and rushed out in front of a truck on the nearby highway.

Back then upon that cold blue winter day there was already enough said between Sylvia and me to reach a sort of understanding, especially that I was on the side of the underdog, and it had us both thinking that we were suddenly in love at first sight. We giggled holding hands down those dark ramshackle stairs of Max's apartment, leaving him and Ertha examining the seashells in his bedroom. Jumping into her nifty but chilly convertible car which I helped push out of the snowdrift, we sped off up Eighth Avenue to get on the West Side Highway. Crossing the George Washington Bridge to the top of the majestic Palisades along by the Hudson, we had warm new questions about who we thought we were and where we came from. And I was telling her that you could so easily be that way in America. Invent yourself moment to moment. Because in Europe, if you were anybody, it was already carved on a building, printed in a book, or remembered by somebody somewhere all over the goddamn place.

Sylvia said there was a lot of secrecy about her being adopted. And she didn't, despite four years of searching, yet know who her real parents were but had nightmares that her father might have been a pimp and her mother a prostitute. Even growing up on a big estate with a farm and even learning how to milk a cow, she felt her life with her real parents would have been in a shack by the railway tracks. She often reminded me of being able to milk a cow, which I pretended to her was not a totally useless skill. Especially a few times later in our relationship when I found her exercise of the practice pleasurable. But her obsession with who her real mother and father were became bleaker and deeper. And she took to chanting a little song she wrote.

Keep your muscles strong
Around your asshole
Keep your muscles strong around your brain
That way too much shit doesn't get out
And stops you sounding insane

Her adoptive parents had a property way up in New York State in the mid-Adirondacks, and in that direction is where we headed, driving north breaking the speed limit on the scenic highway. Stopping once along by the Hudson on a promontory, we looked back at the distant silvery thin skyscrapers sticking up out of Manhattan Island. Then farther north past all the passing wilder-

9

nesses, where I had the fantasy of cheaply and healthfully living in a tent where I could with a piccolo compose and in order to eat, hunt with bow and arrow. It had just grown dark when we were finally driving through the tree-lined streets of Albany, and one took pleasure from the somber comfort of all its Edwardian and Victorian framehouses and their little lawns where nobody yet was standing shaking a fist at me. Then there were these small kind of hick towns she knew well. With names like Sabbath Day Point, Ticonderoga, Pottersville, and Sodom. And where she said folk talked in a twang and you knew if you asked them if they smoked, they'd say, "I ain't never got that hot."

Her adopted parents also kept an apartment of sumptuous sprawling rooms full of Impressionist masterpieces back in the city at Sutton Place, overlooking the East River. But here up in the country she said we should stay well away from her adopters, whose too-close proximity put her under strain. Fast driver that she was, she sure had me under strain as we whizzed around and especially as we reconnoitered a few curving miles of the adoptive parents' estate wall and fence. And finally, at my insistence, slowly driving past the big iron front gates that led into their thirty-two-room mansion with an indoor swimming pool, tennis and squash courts. And as Sylvia described, a dozen French doors opening onto that many different brick terraces screened in summer and glassed in in winter. From a high point on the road and through the trees, you could see in the distance the front gable and tops of four Doric columns holding up a porte cochere. We then had a whole week of hilarity racing around town to town visiting a few of her friends who rode horses and played lacrosse, and who also had estates, one with a polo field, and others with formal gardens and imported statuary, and all the ladies seemed able to heave a football farther than you could believe and make you feel you needed a Charles Atlas course.

I didn't want to be too nosy, but sometimes you really want to know where such nice things as her adoptive parents' obviously lots of money came from. And where there could be so much at once that it never stopped coming. But she would never say where exactly, indeed if she even knew, but vaguely mentioned a couple of ranches out Utah, Oklahoma, and Montana way and utilities in one of the bigger midwestern cities, plus the land that a couple of midtown cross streets of New York City were built on. And reference to Palm Beach, Paris, and Rome were never far from her lips. However, as I was fairly broke, why worry about geographical details when she was paying the expenses as we stayed in a couple of pretty nice roadside inns. And dined plentifully on steak and knocked back some really nice dinner wines from around the Finger Lakes. But having to obey a sense of frugality in my life, I was tempted to complain about the size of the tips she made me leave. Her out-of-control extravagance making her sixteen hundred dollars disappear fast. And once she even grabbed a bunch of bills right out of my wallet when she said she needed some change. But again, aside from snatching a few bucks from me, what the hell, why intrude my parsimonious attitude, it was her money.

The nights got freezing cold and all the places we stayed were practically empty of other guests. Nor were the managements killing themselves making an effort to send heat up into the radiators of the bedrooms. In one place, the coldest, as well as the architecturally grandest, we danced alone on a dance floor where, with no other customers, the guy playing the piano at midnight, after dinner, suddenly stopped and was closing his piano and taking a bow. Then coming out onto the tiny stage from a side door, a guy looking like a Mafia don threatened to fire him if he didn't get back strumming the keys. It was embarrassing, as then we had to go on dancing, and the guy looked so downtrodden glum as he went on playing in the empty room. Sylvia, obviously recognized as local gentry, said it served him right, but since I caught a snatch of marvelous Berlioz he played out of the *Symphonie Fantasique* while we were eating dinner, I thought this was cruelty to one's talented fellowman and that the guy, if he already didn't belong, should go pronto to join the musicians' union.

"Sylvia, let's go upstairs, and let the poor guy go home, and if he's got any, to his wife and kids."

"Sure. Your behavior is what I'd expect from someone full of warmth, understanding, and sympathy for his fellowman."

As it was a cold night, I let the remark pass and instead felt her ass as she climbed in front of me up the stairs. And even though we were freezing in the bedroom, she divested of her woolly warm covering. With her nipples as hard as little acorns, she gyrated, cavorted, spun, and whirled through a half a dozen dances. A boogaloo and bolero, a bunny hop, a frug, and a Charleston. Then ending with a minuet. My God, she knew how to send me into a delirium even in the ice-cold bed and even when she got in between the sheets in a nearly frostbitten condition. The full moon seen out through the frosty window spun like a fast Ferris wheel and the stars exploded. Wham, bam, boom. Even as an atheist, I was wondering why does God do things like that to us. Impose enslavement. Putting one fatally in the grip of carnality.

"Stephen, I have a few other things I'd like to do, too, you know."

"Honey baby, you just go ahead and tell me. I'm ready."

"I want you to whip me with your belt."

Holy cow, what's new next. And although she didn't specify, I got the impression that she'd seen her adoptive

13

parents at this antic. A few nights in bed later, in, thank God, a somewhat warmer bedroom, she said she was also a little bit of a sadist and would I mind being a masochist for a while. She said with my straight black hair combed back flat, I resembled Rudolph Valentino, only that I was a paler shade. And when she asked for it, I gave her my belt. As if to make it more supple, she pulled it back and forth in her hand. Then in nearly a frenzy, before I could stop her, she whipped the living hell out of me. The lashing was excruciating and her glee alarming. Like a scalded cat, I jumped up out of the bed. She was with the belt still raised over her shoulder, in midlash.

"Hey Jesus Christ honey, I'm only human flesh. Take it easy will you."

"Hey, gee, I'm sorry. I guess I got carried away putting welts on that beautiful beatific pink ass you've got and I guess I just like drawing blood and inflicting pain."

"Well, what do you say, honey, if we just skip this next round while my wounds mend."

The blows hurt more higher up on the back, but the welts left all over my rear end made it nearly impossible and painful to sit down. I especially was concerned and didn't like the grin that seemed to stay on her face. I thought any second her whitely beautiful canine teeth were going to enlarge into yellow fangs and sink into my neck. At least it was a lesson learned not to agree to everything she suggested. But what she suggested next happened back in the city and nearly before I knew it.

14

"That's right, I want to get hitched up. And you make an honest girl out of me."

We went to take blood tests to make sure we didn't have syphilis, and who knows whatever goddamn other things we might not have, and a few days later we were married at City Hall. Max and her best friend in the big blue woolly sweater, to whom Max showed his seashells, both were there as witnesses. She carried a yellow rose. While I had a big lump in my throat wondering about supporting two when I was still not yet on the verge of supporting one. I thought to myself, Hey, what the hell am I doing. This could be incarceration for life with a vampire sadist wielding a cat-o'-nine-tails and with my future freedom paid for by alimony till merciful death do we otherwise part. And looking in the mirror before the wedding, I was getting less resembling Rudolph Valentino in a hurry.

"Gee Stephen honey, you look so pale."

"Well honey, maybe it's because I am."

Lordy sakes alive, what the hell do you do if you're a composer with artistic sensibilities and have a deep compassion for your fellowman and in a country where the underlying ethic is to make a dollar and let dog eat dog. And what is worse, where no one wants to know you when you have no job, no income, and with the responsibility of marriage thrust upon you so early in life.

"Come on Stephen honey, has the cat got your tongue. Don't look so goddamn glum."

She was right. The thoughts were getting even worse when we came out into City Hall Park, walking a gray day through the pigeons with snow slush splashing up from passing cars. Each of us chewing on a slice of pizza, which was temporarily serving as the wedding reception. Across the street from the park I could see the lighted windows of the Barber College, where, I cataloged for future reference, you could get a nearly free haircut from the trainees for practically nothing other than maybe a gap left in the hair here and there or a little slice taken off an ear. And while I was watching, I stepped deeply into canine *merde* with my commando corrugated shoes. Another omen I thought, of odoriferous things to come. My little heart didn't know what to do, save to go on baffled and beating.

"O God Stephen, I am insatiable for your seed. We're going to be so happy. So goddamn happy."

She tugged me by the arm and flagging a taxi, we all went back to her girlfriend Ertha's apartment on Waverly Place in the Village. My first financial embarrassment was not having enough money to pay for the cab. My second chagrin was having Max buy the couple of bottles of champagne we had with the canapés. Then I started to choke on some of kind of gristle or something and Max slammed me on the back so hard, I fell face-first into the champagne bucket. The force Max used was explained when he said he didn't want me to die in his girlfriend's apartment with a whole lot of fuss with ambulance and police squad cars arriving and people writing down notes on pads like they were agents of the Internal Revenue Service. And especially where his own wife, whom he had married last year and just divorced, could find out he was holed up with the present lady of his affections and trace him to collect her alimony.

"Hey old fella Steve, sorry I hit you so hard between the shoulder blades."

It did almost seem as if everyone was taking a turn belting the hell out of me. But what worried me most were the debilitating blows my nonfat wallet was taking. I never saw money disappear so fast. Present circumstances being what they were, I did perforce harbor a thought or two about Sylvia's rich adoptive parents coming to the rescue who were giving Sylvia an allowance that would at least help keep her four-fifths in the manner she'd been accustomed to. But with fortune hunters everywhere, the parents were furious to hear of the marriage to which they weren't invited, and a month went by before there was any sign of relenting, when we were finally invited for afternoon tea at the mansion in the country, where I learned a little more about what Sylvia was accustomed to. The Doric columns were ten times bigger than I first imagined. Every inch of the house polished and gleaming.

"Welcome home, Lady Sylvia."

It was the butler called Parker, with an English accent, receiving us at the door. And with the adoptive parents just arrived back from Paris and still on their way up from the city, Sylvia gave me a quick tour of a wing or two of the house. Then took me to see her bedroom and about fifty different bath salts in glass jars all over the bathroom. She clearly lived like a princess with her silk embroidered chaise longue piled with pillows, and a spacious desk with iron claw legs clutched deep in the floor of her carpeted sitting room. Not that I was going to bust a gut over it but Christ, how did people get and stay so goddamn rich.

Then, as the parents still didn't arrive, Sylvia said we should stay overnight. Parker dancing attendance, we dined in the candlelit sumptuous dining room, knocking back with roast duck a couple of fabled vintages of claret, the like of which I thought could only be served in a sommelier's heaven. After having an ancient aged brandy and chocolate in the Pavilion Room, we then in Sylvia's bedroom knocked off an exotically acrobatic piece of ass. As I was about to sleep, I had to dissuade myself of foolishly thinking that the world could go on just like this. Then realized it could if someone dumped a few million bucks on you. That not being likely soon to happen, I fell asleep and dreamt I was running to catch a train and tripped over someone's briefcase left on the platform and fell on my face. It was Sylvia belting me awake with a pillow.

"Wake up you sleepy Irish bastard and fuck me."

Strangely pleasant in the dawn to look out the window on a forested countryside and to have breakfast in bed. Then to perform ablutions on the warm tiles of the bathroom and following another fiercely fought fuck, to go taking in great lungfuls of the fresh clean country air as we then on this blue-skied sunny day walked out on the grounds and over grassy vistas. Sylvia twirling and executing balletic moves through the formal gardens of boxwood hedges. Then we went along a narrow trail into the woods, Sylvia's mood seeming more solemn as she headed us along a disused path through thick foliage and saying that the snakes were safely hibernating. Under towering trees in a clearing, we came upon the back of a small lodge with a pitched roof of cedar tiles. Going around to the front, a veranda with two shuttered windows. Steps up to a porch approached by a straight, long pebbled avenue flanked by a strip of lawn and bordered by the woods. Sylvia taking an ornate golden key from a gold chain around her neck.

"Well, if you've ever wondered what this key is for, it's for here, the Doll's House and this door I'm about to open."

A music box sound of tinkling "The Bells of Saint Mary's." A gaily carpeted room across which the woven shapes of dolphins cavorted as if alive, swimming in a sea. Seated on shelves, teddy bears and dolls balefully looking out. A desk. A pink tutu and pairs of ballet slippers. Pho-

19

tographs of ballerinas. A little library of books. A large stone fireplace. A variety of straw and felt hats hung adorning a wall. Berets and boaters, sombreros and sunbonnets. Framed children's drawings and pictures. In a corner an enormous Georgian doll's house, full of a perfection of miniature furnishings. Right down to a dining room table set for dinner with the tiniest candles in silver candelabra. I felt something woefully sad as I listened to the litany of Sylvia's descriptions.

"This was always my cherished safe and secret place of refuge.

"This is where, while my parental usurpers were away, which was mostly always, I nearly spent my life as a little girl. My favorite haven in the whole world. Cool in the summer. Heated in the winter. At this little table I had tea with my governess in front of a fire at four. She taught me to play chess and honeymoon bridge. And, if I were alone, to sing, and I'd never feel lonely. On the record player we'd have Beethoven's Adagio from his Piano Concerto Number Two. And if you ever wondered sometimes why I'm able to tolerate you when you're intolerable, my governess was Irish. Guess she was designed to stop me becoming too much of an American. I still come here to be alone with myself. In there, that was my little kitchen where I could cook and bake cakes. See my little real dishes. All these pots and pans. And in here. My very own little bathroom. Tub, basin, and shower. And in this bedroom my governess could sleep. I loved it here. And

if you've also wondered how I ever got so musically sophisticated. Here's my collection of records. Beethoven, Bach, Mussorgsky, Handel, Bizet. My big radio could reach all the way to Europe. My skis are there. My snowshoes. And in here my bedroom, where, when I didn't have a governess anymore, I was allowed to stay with that little girlfriend you see me holding hands with in that photograph. The two of us, when we were older, would go up those stairs to a little attic loft lookout window from which we could watch what the deer, possums, squirrels, and chipmunks were doing out in the woods. An enormous owl lived not far away in a tree. And sometimes on the hot summer nights you'd hear the big black snakes slithering over the leaves."

Tears in her eyes as the Doll's House door closed and was locked behind us. As we stepped back down the steps and walked away on the front-approaching drive, Sylvia's eyes cast down, looking at the ground. And her little friend with whom she played as she grew up had mysteriously disappeared hiking across the arctic wastes of Alaska. Only later did I learn that the longing she felt for the world of all her small treasures of childhood, among which she had lived in this cozily lavish little hideout, was while she didn't yet know that she was adopted and someone else's child.

"Thank you Sylvia, for showing me."

"Well thank you for the way you really looked and responded to everything. I'm beginning to think you're really a softhearted and kind person. But God, look at the time. It's time to meet the folks. Parker will have a writhing fit if we're late for tea. He's always harping on about the vulgar lack of manners and punctuality he suffers in America. Later I'll show you the pool and tennis courts."

In the drawing room, called the Pavilion Room, Parker had laid out cucumber sandwiches, scones, clotted cream, and imported black cherry jam to be scoffed back with a choice of India or China tea. Leaving the innocent with a plethora of urgent decisions. And what gave me a further few moments of contemplation, if not panic, was Sylvia's slenderly tall and otherwise elegantly good-looking adoptive mother, Drusilla, her hair marvelously coifed back from a stunning profile, and who had a tic in her left eye which I could not have known, unless told, made her unpredictably wink. And stupid dunce that I was, made me once wink back. And bleep bleep, instantly returned were her two winks. I could feel the blushing blood go all the way out to the edges of my ears. Then the father turned up. I stood up to shake hands. The son of a bitch seemed to try to break my fingers. Perhaps not surprising, as I was crouched over like a cripple in a hopeless effort to disguise, despite all its recent use, a god-awful erection.

To escape my dire embarrassment and my tumescence adjusted as best I could painfully down my thigh, I took up her father's invitation to go have a look at the horses. About at least thirty Arabians in a palace of a stable. Even the sawdust was spread like a palatial carpet, and the boxes were like luxury hotel rooms. I said wow, gee and gosh, to get me through the viewing. And pretended to know the difference as to what is meant by a fetlock or a pastern. I must have succeeded, for before we left, he asked to go have a drink with him at his club. My God. An emolument perchance, as I'd already been dropping hints to Sylvia. Or at least the opportunity to explore if one could be in the offering. I was finding that the difference with me, and anybody else in America in the circles in which I presently moved, was that I thought the world should be and maybe could be, a better place than it was. But all these people, having a mountain of money, seemed to like things just as they were. And above all to keep them that way. Nevertheless, I would adhere to my principles. That if composing music achieved such a purpose of bringing a little happiness to mankind, the composer's goal was achieved and he should be applauded and aided without being subjected to snide remarks, such as could come unpredictably out of Sylvia, that while helpful could also be amusing.

"Hey, Chopin, here, take this. It will get you back and forth to Carnegie Hall and buy you a couple of beers and pretzels."

I had an important meeting with a prominent conductor at Carnegie Hall and to take an odd taxi these days and have leftover spending money, Sylvia slipped me a twenty-dollar bill always got crisply new from a nice bank that looked like a country mansion on Madison Avenue. I objected to being called Chopin but found if I made an issue of it, it would mean taking the subway. Anyway, the son of a bitch prominent conductor who wore too much jewelry and pointy-toed shoes didn't show up and I ended up having plenty of beers and tons of pretzels in the nearest bar. Indiscreetly of course, one took up a conversation with a nearby girl, who repeated that usual observation.

"Hey you, don't you look a bit like Rudolph Valentino. Buy me a drink why don't yuh."

There were no more twenty-dollar bills for taxis for a while, but taxis were less necessary as nobody seemed that anxious to commission music or make appointments with me anyway. We'd now been living since the marriage in a temporarily borrowed apartment belonging to one of Sylvia's girlfriends on West Sixty-eighth Street, from where I strolled into the park each day, looking around the skyline of the city, which, if you didn't stare at it too long, was an inspiration. It was also a ready reminder of, holy cow, look at all the competition there is lurking behind every window you could see. Where people living on trust funds and investments just like Sylvia's parents were ensconced amid their priceless antiques, filing their fingernails, powdering their asses, or else giving themselves pleasant enemas. Although we were living modestly comfortably on Sylvia's allowance, I was also looking hard for somewhere to rent cheaply, heading downtown beyond the Village to reconnoiter around Little Italy. Meanwhile, I was starting to express the idea I had already more than hinted at to Sylvia that when I met her father I might suggest a stipend in the way of substituting for some kind of fellowship or grant repayable in full, which could allow me to give full time to composing. She smiled as if she had my principles at her mercy and whispered, "Hey, handsome kiddo, let me put you in the mood for groveling. Drop your drawers and let me give you a couple more swats on the ass."

Listening to these further snide, demeaning remarks, I now understood how wife beating could come about. And it was also significant enough to stir up the past terrors of beatings in one's life and those done in my Catholic grade school by Sister Shirley Sadist, the most stern disciplinarian in America, who with yard-long rulers belted the shit out of us in ninth grade or whatever numerical it was that designated her attendance upon us. The stings and yowls to high heaven of these trembling figures lined up in front of a whole class, suppressing their screams of pain, still haunted me. Sylvia also could be a bit of a card when she wanted, and when I told her of the school beatings, she suggested she dress as a nun to give me my next swatting across the ass. The trouble was the other things she wanted to do and have. Her total, undivided independence, she said. And that women should be as promiscuous as men. I caught her up short once when I said sure, good-bye, see you in the reincarnation. She didn't like that kind of adieu much and said she'd stick around and be temporarily satisfied with steady boring fucking. Meanwhile, I took up the appointment to go have a drink with her father. While she went to have a beer or two with an always groaningly salivating admirer who wanted to marry her after she divorced me and then give her a two-hundred-foot yacht, a grass-roofed palace in Mexico, and open accounts—which, as it happened, she already had—in the best, most famous fashion stores in New York.

"He's an international banker. Has fingers in all sorts of pies. He loves me and would do anything for me. Don't you understand. And you're yet to be somebody."

I was of a mind to tell Sylvia to tell her friend to take his finger out of one of his pies and shove it up his ass, or indeed her ass, as she frequently requested me to do. But I demurred as my appointment with her father loomed. His club was a massive gray stone outfit on Fifth Avenue, with its own driveway in and out on a crosstown side street. It even seemed to get more massive inside, with a room like a football field and a ceiling so high, it seemed outdoors. But even with the size, you could get the impression the echoes could make everybody be aware of the subject, if not actually hear your conversation. I was still fumingly angry at Sylvia for suggesting I was some kind of panhandler trying to blackmail somebody and that I'd be groveling. And as if to remind me of my status, she shouted after me as I left the apartment.

"It's the rich what gets the pleasure, it's the poor what gets the pain."

This was a little European song I'd learned and had been foolish enough to sing for her. The remainder of the vocalization being, "It's the same way the whole world over. Isn't it a fucking shame." Anyway, there was no shortage of further intimidation. The adoptive parents, I found, minus Sylvia, were listed amid a lot of other similar surnames in the *Social Register*. Well, I might not own much of it, but this was my country, too. I fought for it when other foreign ethnics were doing us down, my eardrums and brain getting concussed in a turret of sixteen-inch guns. But having spent an hour getting ready with the right clothes and avoiding anything too much resembling casual dress and in the only thing I owned remotely suitable for a funeral, I even thought for a second I might, in this somber club chamber, be going to be arrested for being Irish Catholic and once an altar boy who thought that Jesus Christ's flesh and blood were being eaten in the white wafer they gave you at the altar rail for Communion. Although he wasn't onto my secret religious thoughts, I could tell he knew more about me than he first let on. I was planning, so I could appear courteously knowledgeable and bullshit a little, to ask for an imported beer. Then I forgot every goddamn brand there was, and ordered tomato juice. He didn't beat around the bush.

"Nice to see you again, Steve."

"Good to see you too, sir."

"I understand you want a handout."

"I beg your pardon."

"I don't want to hurt your feelings, but I think you heard me, a handout."

"I wouldn't put it that way, sir. I believe the expression is an honorarium or bestowment."

"Well, who do you think you are, other than being married to Sylvia, to be so deserving."

"I might not yet be a Wilhelm Richard Wagner perhaps, who was worthy of getting help from King Ludwig of Bavaria, to whom he accorded much heavenly rapture and ecstasy and whose *Schloss* residence—Neuschwanstein, to be specific—on the Rhine is the wonder of all of Europe. But I must admit I thought I'd be at least meriting some kind of sympathetic emolument in the form of a dowry in the manner of an appanage, as it were, to contribute to the continuation of my musical studies and be able to work variously on a symphony, a slow stately dance, waltz, a gavotte or minuet, and also of course to help keep Sylvia more in the manner to which she has been accustomed."

"Hey, you're not a pinko, are you."

"What is that."

"Hey, come on, you know what it is. We've got a prominent senator broadcasting every day about it. A Red, a Commie. An enemy of our free country."

"I do not deny that I admire the principles of socialism, but I am not a Red or a Commie."

"Well then, Steve, I guess you've got the gift of the gab, but I don't have to remind you we're not in Europe now, where these old customs, if not liberal niceties, may prevail, but you can take some consolation in the fact that your charm and sincerity rates one hundred percent."

"Thank you, sir."

"And I'm also impressed by your compassion, especially for the continuation of Sylvia's welfare and maintenance of her living standards."

"My top priority, sir."

"Well, that's swell, because I just stopped her allowance."

"You what."

"You heard me, Steve."

"Sir. I consider that very unfair."

"How is it unfair, when you're her husband and you just said supporting her is your top priority."

"Well, priorities can have their way of being sequential, and stopping her allowance sir, does rather stultify the lifestyle we would wish to maintain."

"What, are you kidding. West Sixty-eighth Street was bad enough where you were living, but now Chinatown, down nearly on the Bowery with a bunch of alcoholic hoboes and derelicts all over the place."

"Well sir, yes, there may be these persons discarded by society but who were once, many of them, citizens trying to do their best. However that area has many historic buildings and people of noted distinction to boast of who previously lived there. As well as many examples of Chinese artifacts and culture. And where can be obtained ingredients beneficial to health, such as ginseng root, dried sea horse, deer's horn, and preserved bear's testicles."

"Hey don't try to be funny with me, Steve."

"I'm not, sir. Merely demonstrating that the area of Pell Street is not an habituation of the down-and-outs. Plus, it carries the name of a most distinguished family, the Pells."

"Hey, what the hell are you. Some kind of social climber."

"I am a delver into all aspects of the historic matrix that has played a part in forming possibly the greatest metropolis the world has ever known."

"Well, okay. I'll buy that bit of spiel. You seem to know quite a bit about this little old city of ours."

31

"Plus, sir, such knowledge as I have, if I may be so blunt as to mention, prompts me to think, sir, that you might want to avail of an opportunity for you to become a munificent patron of the arts."

"That's more pedantic speak."

"But honestly spoken, sir."

"Well, I think if you take the trouble to look into as much as you have about the Pells, you'll find my family name already well represented all over this island of Manhattan as a contributor to the arts. While your family seems to own just a couple of beer joints, a hangover from speakeasy days, in what some people might regard as the wrong part of town. I hear, however, they do okay business. But having had you personally checked out, your own financial status and prospects rate zero. Sit down. Don't get alarmed. I would, in giving you a handout, only be giving you more financial quicksand to sink in."

"I'm not looking for a handout. And I'm not sinking."

"Well, I'll admit that maybe you're not, because with your kind of sales pitch you might get a job down Wall Street in a brokerage house speculating in Confederate bonds."

"Sir, I'm not giving anybody a sales pitch. And I regard your statement as an insult not only to me but to the southern gentlemen who gave their lives in the cause of the Confederacy."

"See what I mean. Gift of the gab. Next you'll be telling me you grew up in Opelousas, Louisiana."

"As a matter of fact sir, I have ancestral kin there."

"Well, glad to hear that. But my word, let me look at my watch, and excuse me, I'm afraid I've got to rush. Just got time to get over to a backgammon match in exactly ten minutes. But stay where you are. Finish your beer. Oh, sorry, it's tomato juice, isn't it. Well, I've enjoyed our little informative chat. And it's true what Sylvia says. You do look a little like Rudolph Valentino who, I believe, was also a little impecunious and did a bit of dish washing before he became a star. Pity acting is as tough to make a living at as composing. But good to meet you again, Steve. And if there is any way else I can help, outside the financial, that is, don't hesitate to keep in touch. Good-bye."

As Jonathan Witherspoon Triumphington III departed out his club's front door, Stephen O'Kelly'O was left standing, having as he came to his feet pushed over his chair in the solemn silent emptiness devolving upon this place, the sound seeming to echo out to Fifth Avenue. And then the overwhelming need to take a nervous pee. Relieving the bladder lessens the stress. Head to the gents. I should have hit him. A goddamn social upstart. The O'Kelly'O's were kings in Ireland when that fucker's ancestors, somewhere obscure in England, were wiping their asses with fig leaves. And this while the O'Kelly'O's were from their own carved stone lavatory seats shitting

34

from a height up in their tower houses, and pulling a bell rope to make musical warning to everyone below to get out of the way. Although being hit by an O'Kelly'O turd was considered good luck. Now move across this vast room, through all these empty tables. But holy cow, I was shot down in flames before I was even airborne. Had a good mind to tell him I got twice awarded a Purple Heart. The fucker, a lieutenant commander in the navy, having a good time in Washington, D.C., during the war, probably sailing up and down the Potomac drinking cocktails on a yacht that one of my sixteen-inch guns could have blown out of the water with one salvo. He has the nerve to shake my hand vigorously. Then smiling, leaves me to finish my tomato juice with a couple of pretzels while he goes to play backgammon at another snooty club. Clearly the sort of person starving the cultural life of the United States, and wouldn't between his polo matches know George Frideric Handel from Albert Einstein.

Stephen O'Kelly'O pushing open the door to the gentlemen's rest room. The sweet smell of embrocations and the polished ceramic surfaces. A bottle of toilet water. Just of the sort one would expect a smooth socially registered fucker like Jonathan Witherspoon Triumphington III, with maybe fifty trust funds drenching him daily in dollars, to use. The son of a bitch is handing out worse blows than the blistering swats already landed across my ass from his adopted Sylvia. I'm sure its against a club's rules to leave someone, a nonmember, unattended like me, a stranger who could then go start stealing books or magazines from the library or the toilet paper and bay rum from the gents. Where, Christ, right now I'm shaking in such rage that, holding my prick, I've already pissed all over my goddamn shoes.

At the coat check, O'Kelly'O retrieving his soup-stained overcoat, a button missing. Struggling with it half on and half off. And the sound of ripping echoing all over the vast room as another big tear splits the lining down the inside of the sleeve. The hatcheck gentleman, instead of calling the enforcement arm of the *Social Register* to have me apprehended, handcuffed and gagged, bowing a pleasant good-bye. All such thoughts a sure sign that my paranoia was going out of control. Miracle I have enough self-esteem left to hobble to and out of the front door. Time to reinvent myself. Famed linebacker on his prep school football team. Wartime naval hero slightly concussed, of noble Irish lineage, now foxhunting across the countryside of New Jersey. And soon to conduct his Fifth Symphony at Carnegie Hall.

With the light turning green, Stephen O'Kelly'O, collar up, tweed cap pulled down tight on his head and hunched in his coat, crossing Fifth Avenue. Yellow stream of checkered taxicabs roaring by, splashing up slush. Don't give a good goddamn what they do to pedestrians. A secondhand phonograph record and book seller freezing his balls off on the corner. At least there's a sign of some cultural dedication and concern for those impecunious who can't afford new books or classical records. But somehow one feels he'd do better with a begging bowl. My occasional momentary inferiorities are busting out all over the place. A big cold sore beginning to erupt on my lip before I even got down the three or four steps out of that club. Be a relief now to go mingle awhile amid the more sympathetic animals in the zoo. Whose pleasant roars and screams won't be accusing me of social climbing or looking for a handout.

The sun a red cold ball in the sky, sinking down somewhere over Nebraska. The light fading over the zoo. The sudden strange beauty of this city alerts you to its majesticness. Until some kid is screaming he's lost his balloon floating away up over the hippopotamus house to disappear into the pink chill of the New York heavens. Once saw an eagle soaring up there over the apartment rooftops of Fifth Avenue just north of maybe Eighty-first Street. Still free in nature. And down here on earth in the zoo, the squawking, squealing seals knocking their way around the ice floes in their pond. An aqueous furore as the keeper arrives with a bucket of fish to toss in. Walk over to where the big outcropping of rocks are and see how the polar bear is psychologically coping pacing back and forth, claws clattering on the cement. Or maybe is content that he can luxuriate in the chill weather. Make a day of it here uptown before I go home downtown and face any more ignominy. Go check on the monkeys, who in their own rent-free hot house can go ad-lib amusing themselves scratching their asses, and shoving pricks into holes that take their fancy and then grinning obscenely out their window at the miserable spectators.

Darkness falling. Heralds danger in this city. Walk over through the winding little paths of the park. Have fists clenched, ready to bust the first marauder in the chops who's at large trying to mug you, get your money, stick a gun in your ribs or a knife in your guts. The skyscrapers looming out of the cold mist along Central Park South. Lights on yellow and warm in the windows. Snow beginning to fall. Sweeps and whorls down out of a leaden sky. To whitely annoint the shoulders of the lonely. Strauss waltz comes through the air from the skating rink. A voice on a loudspeaker announcing to clear the ice. Sylvia said she went there to skate when the rink at Rockefeller Center was closed.

"George the chauffeur, until he fell madly in love with me, would bring me. My figure skating always drew a watching crowd."

Talk about the privileged rich. With nothing better for the soul to do than to go shopping, get facials, and have their hair done. On the Triumphington's estate a dozen different designed bathrooms all over the monstrous house. And way out on their miles of lawns, they have a couple of handkerchief trees, specially shipped all the way from China. Blooms like a bunch of snow white handkerchiefs. All just so you could get excited at the full moon, seeing the white fluttering going on during a windy night. And maybe be reminded to blow your nose. Just the value of one of his Arab horses or couple of polo ponies would have been more than enough to see me through to the completion of my first concerto for flute and harpsichord and full orchestra.

O'Kelly'O emerging from the park. Crossing the street to walk under the marquee lights of the hotels. The little groups of strangers in town. From way out west. Texans in ten-gallon hats and cowboy boots. Their wives in fur coats. Waiting for taxis to take them to Broadway musicals. Doorman holding open doors and spinning those revolving. Saluting from the peaks of their caps as they are handed folding-money tips. At least it all looks bonhomie. And Sylvia said why didn't I go see a very rich lady and noted patron of the arts who lives at the top of the Hampshire House on this Central Park South and is dedicated in her love of music and was known rarely to ever refuse a worthy cause, and might contribute to mine since she knew her. And here I am venturing to the doorway to look into the guarded lobby and have already got cold feet at the intimidation. Because like one of the rats living in their millions in this city I've already gone back down into the subway and some son of a bitch is glaring at me until I glare right back and make a goddamn fist in his face. He gets off at the next stop. If he didn't, I would have killed him. No wonder there is murder, with people not minding their own business. To allow the citizens of this city to have some dignity in public and to otherwise ply their lives in the decent pursuit of peace and content-ment, which doesn't look like the case in a picture in the evening newspaper the guy's reading across the aisle. A man committing suicide jumping out the window on the twentieth floor of a hotel and landing on top of a passing car, kills the driver and the car, out of control, kills two pedestrians. And just as you might expect as I reach what I now call home in Pell Street, some guy just finished piss-ing in the doorway invites me to join him in genital stim-ulation. Shake a fist in another face. And the masturbating desecrator goes mumbling off. Then up in the apartment just as I remove my overcoat and take the rest of the whole goddamn lining out of the sleeve, Sylvia in her leotards, who had worked up a sweat while exercising with her weights, laughs and thinks it is a big goddamn joke that my clothes are coming to pieces. Then when I tell her a little of what happened at her father's club, it doesn't take her long to embellish the embarrassment further.

"Well, what did you expect in bringing up a subject like that. You're lucky he didn't have you to drink at his other club, where he was going, which is even snootier and would have made you really feel like something the cat dragged in. And where if they let you get that

40

far, someone might jump up from a backgammon table and say your more than slight deshabille was a distraction to their game and want you pretty quick dragged out again."

"Well, by the way in bringing up subjects, he stopped your allowance."

As a reminder of all the thousands of lonely miles across America, you could hear louder than usual traffic chugging by on its way to and from the Manhattan Bridge. The next day, Sylvia beat it uptown over to Sutton Place. And as the snow kept falling, the chill days went by getting chillier. To play the piano while composing, I wore gloves with the fingers cut off. Sylvia said that among other confidential reasons I couldn't come to see her and luxuriate on Sutton Place was that her parents had important guests staying. This news cheered me up a lot. But at least with Sylvia gone, I could do something serious in cutting down on groceries. Walking down the Bowery to buy cheap vegetables and over to South Street, able to get fish from the Fulton Fish Market, whose motto was exactly suited to folk like me.

TO SUPPLY THE COMMON PEOPLE
WITH THE NECESSITIES OF LIFE
AT A REASONABLE PRICE

And until the rent had to be paid, one was surviving, just. Then one suddenly unseasonably sunny, balmy afternoon dawned. I was on my way back to Pell Street, faintly smelling of fish from the market because the Italian grocer where I had just bought a loaf of his delicious bread said he could always tell by the piscatory perfume when someone had been down on Fulton Street. He'd customarily give me a few free olives to taste and sing a few bars of Vincenzo Bellini's opera *Beatrice di Tenda*. He had a beautiful voice, which astonished in the setting of vegetables, wine, and salami and always left a broad smile on my face. Which I was still smiling as I came around the corner of Pell Street and the Bowery. And there approaching me was a tall and sinewy lady in a red hat and green coat with a silver fox–fur collar, who came to a full stop directly in front of me. Both stopped in our tracks as we stared at each other. Her skin shone the silkiest shiniest black. I smiled an even bigger smile. And she uttered her first pleasantly unforgettable words.

"Hey, you know, I ain't never seen such a beautiful smile on anyone's face before. You, honey, I want to fuck."

On such a cheerful note and not wanting to appear unfriendly, one naturally invited her for coffee back in the apartment so conveniently close by. Suddenly it was looking better than Sutton Place, and in the hall and up the stairs she had her clothes off the moment she stepped inside the apartment's front door. As I followed her into the bedroom, I could now think of a thousand more confidential reasons why I wouldn't be visiting Sutton

Place. And glad the telephone wouldn't ring because it wouldn't be installed till tomorrow. Her name was Aspasia. She said it meant "welcome." Out of the Deep South, she'd sung in a gospel choir. Her father was a preacher. She'd studied at the Art Students League up on Fifty-seventh Street, in the Fine Arts Building designed by Hardenbergh. She even knew her architecture. When she found I wrote music, it seemed like we had a lot to talk about, but instead, in a bout of savage fucking we broke the bed and it fell apart on the floor. Teeth marks all over me. And as I realized I had desecrated my marriage, I hear Aspasia's words.

"Hey, composer man, that was a true honey fuck and you done justified my desire. Nothing good is ever going to come to you by itself. You have to go out and forget that's what you're looking for."

Aspasia was both a jazz and opera singer. She could go through four octaves like Yma Sumac. Dressed, as she was about to leave, we started kissing again in the doorway, got undressed again and went back to the bedroom. She wouldn't tell me where she lived but said I was going to be a burning ember in her life and that if I got a message to the Art Students League, she'd leave a message for me about when and where we could meet again.

"Hey, composer man, I better get the hell out of here before your wife comes back."

After Aspasia had gone, my gonads glowing, I opened

43

up the window to let some nice new fresh fumes come from the passing traffic. For some days I had been further intensifying my study of the fugue. And taking deep solace listening to my heroes in the world of music. Especially the great swelling melodic choruses of Gounod's *St. Cecilia Mass*. Which I had once traveled to Paris to hear when it was being performed in the church of Saint Sulpice. A sacredly remembered day in my life. The waves of sound and voices still sweeping through my brain and throbbing in my ears even as I would walk along a noisy avenue. And heard myself saying, "Praise be to you, Gounod."

And then opening up the window even wider, I played the record and turned up the volume. The orchestral sounds and the voices of Gounod's *St. Cecilia Mass* thundering out again to the uninitiated passing in the street. Not a goddamn person ever notices. How dare they be uncomprehending and not stop and listen. How dare they not let their souls be uplifted with the sound. Push up the window even wider. Further turn up the volume. Shout Gounod, Gounod out over the street. Listen, you bastards. The choral voices are roaring *"Sanctus dominus, sanctus dominus."* And you, you philistine fucker in the lumber jacket on the curb with your big stomach sticking out. Who the fuck do you think you're shouting at.

"Hey, somebody call Bellevue, will yuh. A guy's gone crazy up there in the window."

"Fuck you, you infidel barbarian scoffer. Get out of here before I come down there and bust you one."

A little group had formed and a gang of kids collected. As well as the passing garbagemen, who stopped. Even one who had his face busily buried in the *Wall Street Journal* studying his investments, looked up. Lean out, shake my fist. Could make me look like someone who can't take this city anymore. And lead to maybe any second an ambulance or paddy wagon coming to take me away to a padded cell in that building euphemistically referred to as "Bellevue," with barred windows on the East River. Or if I bust one of these bastards in the face. Or worse if they shoot me, take me to Bellevue morgue, where the hundreds of bodies lie unclaimed. Sylvia could identify me on two sides. Either with the scars she's left on my arse. Or by the size of my Irish big prick.

"No need to roll him over. That's him."

The hopeless obtuseness of it all. Except for the advent of Aspasia, how can one's creative desires be unleashed to soar. The indifference to be found in this city has no equal. Makes you want to jump from the Brooklyn Bridge into the murky East River waters. Instead, all you can do is weep. Boo-hoo. But then one might as a pedestrian venture somewhere in the city and pass, totally out of the blue, some roving minstrel which would restore hope and optimism. Only yesterday I was elated as I stopped to listen to a man playing the concluding bars of Giovanni Pergolesi's Concerti Armonici for strings. The quality of the playing astounded. And one was inspired by the total fortuity and happenstance. I removed my cap and swept it in a bow at the last fading chord. And although I could not afford it, I dropped half a dollar in this outstanding instrumentalist's hat.

And this day as I was about to slam the window shut and go down and beat the shit out of the infidel barbarian scoffer, suddenly the music stopped. Just at the words *"Benedictus nomine domini"* sang out and ended, *"hosanna in excelsis."* I turned around and there was Sylvia. Standing there in the middle of her exercise space in her flowing mink coat. Hands on her hips, lower lip tightly drawn across her mouth, and surveying me."

"Who's been here."

"What do you mean, 'who's been here.'"

"I mean, whose goddamn cheap nasty perfume am I smelling. The bed is broken. Blankets on the floor. Those are teeth marks on your neck."

"I was having a nap and a nightmare. And the marks are legitimate indentations caused by my own fingernails dug into the skin."

"Like hell you were having a nightmare. Hanging out the window and music blasting out all over the street and I had to sneak in the downstairs door."

"I was dealing with uncouth infidels."

"You were dealing in the bedroom with some bitch who has been here. Look at this, big sloppy gobs of lipstick on a cigarette."

46

"Well, I don't want you to assume that I am the composer of the hour but if you must know, it was an opera singer auditioning. Someone who is to sing soprano in Gounod's *St. Cecilia Mass* at St. Bartholomew's Church, where there is a very good chance I may be invited to conduct. Its parish has a musically discriminating and sophisticated congregation."

"You fucking liar, you couldn't conduct your way backing assward out of a wet, broken paper bag. You couldn't even meet a raving queer conductor to kiss his ass and get somewhere, as he didn't turn up."

"Hey, you just wait a minute. I've been dealing with enough graceless reprobates in the street and other hindrances in my musical work to want to hear any more crap. Why don't you just go back to Sutton Place and stay there."

Horns honking down in the street in a traffic jam, as Sylvia, her fur coat flying open, pulled off the wooden arm of the broken chair and sent it sailing across the room. The piece of walnut shined with elbows, bouncing off my upraised arm with the sound of something that could be broken. Or something so goddamn bruised, it was beyond being used for squeezing again. As she huffs off through the kitchen, sweeping pots and dishes from the shelves, dismounts a pan cooking on the stove, and disappears into the bedroom. More sounds of flying objects and breaking glass. Life, as it does with a moment of bliss and promiscuous carnality, conspires then to bring

47

every goddamn worry upon you. Not only attempted murder and a possible fractured arm but also the clap. Or worse, the syph. Or some other goddamn fatal affliction. That I may, if I've now got it, now give. Cerebral anguish that would drive you into buying a television set. Or attempting to climb a tree or get into heaven. Or best of all, to go get a ticket on a ship back to Europe. But she's back before I can even get out the door.

"That's right, look at me with your amazed look, Chopin."

"Why the hell did you do an unladylike thing as that. Potatoes that I was boiling, all over the floor."

"Since I've paid for everything in here, why not. After all, it's merely the sort of primitive peasant vegetable your ancestors used to dig out of the ground."

"Hey, you cut out that ethnic slander."

"It happens to be an anthropological fact. I may have engaged in consensual gang-banging in my time, but you're not going to bring someone into where I live to screw."

Holy Christ, she stands there readmitting her carnal past. Knowing of the wounding it gives and the sour wrench of distrust it sends convoluting through one's guts. When such should be interred to remain in her graveyard of memory. In which it probably won't be long before the indiscretions of yours truly reside. But I was a total innocent victim of an unpremeditated carnal incident, whereas women always plot and plan and always like having a few reserve pricks they can fall back on, even when the present one they're enjoying stimulates them. And they never forget a shape or size. Plus, the more pricks hanging out around them nearby, all the better. I want similar freedom. And not be a poor innocent who encounters a moment of healthy carnal gaiety and ends up suffering a dusting-over and the apartment gets visited upon it even worse. Such goings-on could predict that one might never again have peace on earth. Never again see Aspasia's big innocent doe eyes, hear her pleasantly raucous laughter, or feel her silken soft lips or incredible elliptically enticing tits.

"I want to know who the hell you had in here."

"I've already explained I am auditioning."

"Yeah. To fuck somebody. What's the shade doing down in the bedroom."

"How dare you impugn my professionalism and make such a crass and entirely unfounded accusation."

"Boy, you sure can be a real hoot sometimes."

Sylvia returning to the bedroom. Closet doors slamming. A suitcase flung on the broken bed. Holy cow. She's just pulled the godamn shade down off its roller. What kind of a disagreeably goddamn future is this. After the warmth of a so freely giving, soft enveloping Aspasia. So wonderfully conspicuous in her red hat and silver-fox collar. And so stunningly naked in her shiny dark skin.

49

Black enough to provoke white racial slurs against us in this bigoted land. As I hunger and yearn now to hear some Gregorian chant the Adorate Deum of the Introitus. The faster I get up to St. Bartholomew's Church in a hurry, the better. Where I have often gone to quietly listen to their choir. Now knock on the rector's door. Please, will Your Esteemed Graciousness allow me to conduct old Charlie Gounod's *St. Cecilia Mass* in your most beautiful Byzantine church. Of such richly salmon-colored brick and Indiana limestone that it stands as an oasis in the sea of glass and exaggerated modernity hereabouts on Park Avenue. Vouchsafe that I be able to approach through your elegant bronze doors depicting scenes from the Old and New Testaments. My baton polished and ready. The New York Philharmonic and your church's choir ready to enjoin in rapturous harmony, and Aspasia to make her guest appearance. Just as Sylvia makes hers clearly on her way somewhere.

"Where are you going with that suitcase."

"None of your fucking business. I'm leaving. Lover boy. Out of this hellhole and removing myself perhaps even farther away."

"Have you no regard for someone telling the gospel truth."

"That word *gospel* should be bullshit. And big-time conductor and Romeo, if you want to go on with that phony story, it's best you know that it just so happens that my nonbiological mother and father are members of St. Bartholomew's congregation, with their name reasonably readable on a pew. And I've been there more than a couple of dozen times, to perhaps be reminded that maybe my real parents were Jewish, Italian, or who knows, God forbid, even Irish and that I was lucky to be allowed in the church."

"I'll overlook that inference to being Irish, but it's eminently understandable that your mother and father should want to indoctrinate you to religion."

"Don't you ever, ever call them my mother and father. Do you hear me. Never. They're not my mother and father. Whom I am forced to adopt as parents. They're my goddamn adopted mother and father. My real mother and father are someone else."

"Forgive me. For clearly, as one might aver in French, *j'ais commis un impair*."

"And don't give me any of your fucking fractured French, either."

"I have merely said in entirely linguistically correct French that I've made a tactless blunder in conversation."

"And maybe that right now reminds me that I've made a blunder in marriage. I'm tired of not having any money while you take solace in the so-called great music of the so-called great composers, which seems to provide you with a curtain of insulation to shut out the unseemliness in your life, like a landlord coming around here pestering

51

for rent while he's trying to make passes at me. And by the way, I bought and paid for that Gounod record, not you."

"Are you finished."

"No, I'm not. Away from here, I won't have to listen to any more of your bullshit. That one day you shall be richly recompensed standing on the podium in front of your awaiting orchestra in Carnegie Hall. Ready to receive Rubenstein. Who comes onstage with a roar of clapping, and, as he sits at the piano, the audience suddenly silent, he holds out his arms and then, at the anointment of your baton, with a flourish of his fingers descends to the keyboard to begin O'Kelly'O's Nocturne Number One."

"How the fuck do you presume to know how Rubenstein's fingers will descend to the keyboard."

"I don't. But to such an unlikely event you can bet I'll wear my tiara. Just make sure on the occasion your big cock is not hanging out. If whoever was here is in the audience, they might want to rush onto the podium to give you a blow job."

"I reject your vulgar aspersion as grossly insulting."

"What's vulgar about sucking an old-fashioned prick. You're so goddamn prudish. Meanwhile, I'd really still like to know what, between your big-deal concerts you conduct with equanimity in your imagination, you'll be doing for food, since my adopted father, who may never have been guilty of doing a generous thing but sure knows how to live on other people's money, refuses to donate to the furtherance of your career."

"I shall emulate the tradition already established by many of the great classical composers who precede me and who without patronage have had to diet."

"Well, one thing is certain. My adopted father could be accused of doing the stingy thing but never be accused of doing a stupid thing, like giving handouts to jerk-offs."

"Who do you think you are to talk to me like that."

"Oh, you're not going to give me a punch in the jaw."

"I have never struck a woman in my life, but maybe I might start."

"Well, Mr. Potential Wife Beater, you just try it. My adoptive father was right when he said you were given to pedantic speak."

"Well, in any kind of speak you want and in any language you want, you can anytime you want to get the hell out of here."

"Well, I am. But just remember, I did once in a while try to be accommodating to your career. You could have gone as I suggested to see that rich lady I know living up in the top of the Hampshire House on Central Park South. Who could have been a help. But composers, for God's sake, half of them are queer cocksuckers or deaf neurotics or both. Not that there is anything wrong with healthy God-fearing cock sucking. I mean, who's to know for certain if those notes you're scribbling over there are ever even going to get heard, never mind change the world. So far, all your musical compositions have done is lose me my allowance. The only one who seems impressed by your being a composer is my eye-winking adopted mother, who by the way, before I got here, asked me to ask you to come for a drink at the apartment, which is why I'm here, and if you want to take the trouble to change your clothes, I'm supposed to bring you there. You might even get a free meal of it."

Horns stopped honking in the street. Sylvia waiting in the strange silence for an answer. Look out the window. A policeman directing traffic around a stalled car. Sylvia cleaning up the mess of my potatoes. Arguments seem to end as suddenly as they begin. But leaving me still suspected and unforgiven. Every clash between us always revealing some new fact of her life. Bitter to be adopted. Are her real parents maybe immigrant. And maybe even worse than Irish, Italian or Jewish. Without estates or trust funds. Ghetto dwellers in their litter-strewn streets. But who, if only they could have a chance to listen, could have respect if not love, for great music. And for whom I can and must win. Against all the adversarial odds. Rise up to be recognized out of the thousands of composers in this city alone. In their studios, testing notes on oboes, pianos, and harps. Hold tight to my nerve. Tinkle my harpsichord. Struggle on. I will change my clothes. Look respectable. Head uptown on First Avenue in a taxi to see my adopted mother-in-law. Maybe humming a song I've just thought of.

> *How deep is your affection*
> *Tell me soon so I'll know*
> *Is it skin-deep, oceans-deep*
> *Or shallow like a piece of glass*

As darkness attempts to descend upon this city, the lights as they always do, light and glow back up high into the sky. And I did go try impromptu again to meet the lady in the top of the Hampshire House, but they wouldn't let me in without an appointment. Even though their attitude suggested that by the look of me it was inconceivable that I might try and steal one of her valuable paintings. And now on the corner of Canal and Mulberry streets, a yellow-and-black-and-white Checker cab squealing to a stop. Sylvia, minus her suitcase, climbing in. As I follow. The destination eliciting a preferred polite attitude from the driver. His ears alive to the silence of our conversation. Up and over to First Avenue. Through the Gashouse District, once a neighborhood of shabbiness and grime where the Irish once lived later joined by the Germans and Jews. At Twenty-sixth Street, passing by block after block, the massive grim complex of Bellevue Hospital. Treating the sick and injured, who on stretchers pour in its doors. And where, along its massive corridors, the dead under their white sheets are wheeled away into the cold silence of the morgue in there beyond the windows. Without a relative or friend, unmourned, get given to a private embalming school for practice. No sorrow so deep nor anguish so torn. The living screams inside the barred psychiatric wards. Where each face must desperately look to find a kindly smile. The kidney of New York ridding the city of its waste. A derrick lowering unclaimed bodies and amputated arms and legs into a barge moored on the river. Taking them to Hart Island for burial in a pauper's grave beneath the legend HE CALLETH HIS CHILDREN BY NAME.

The taxi turning into these emptier streets, where the rich live on Sutton Place. And other socialites calleth by telephone. The windows of the buildings polished, gleaming. The acolyte doormen who adorn their entrance lobbies. In this my city. My town. My streets. Where I was born and grew up. Defiled by these pretentious interlopers with their sacks of gold hidden somewhere, who use precious space as a dormitory to come and occasionally play in. I detoured one day up the wide steps of the New York Public Library to find out more. And, heels clicking along its great marble halls, went to inquire how this street we now headed for had achieved its mystique of becoming such a bastion for the elite. Where the residents came to sit in quiet composure to defecate and ladies to urinate in the carved marble toilet bowls. In the vast reading room of the library and sitting an hour at a desk, I read in the pages of *The New York City Guide* for 1939 that this so unobtrusively situated location on a rocky high overlooking the swift-flowing East River was named after Effingham Sutton, an owner of a line of clipper ships. Here the East River briefly widened and yachts were moored, and the slum children came to swim from a wooden pier at the end of this dead-end street.

The taxi drawing up at the front entrance of this somberly elegant building. Sylvia, who complains of no money, giving the driver one of her new crisp twenty-dollar bills from the bank built like a mansion over on Madison Avenue and, after handing back a big tip, stuffing all the change in a secret side pocket of her mink coat. Follow the rich. As I do in trepidatious anticipation as one approaches the mausoleumlike solemnity of this entrance. The chiseled stone. The perfume scent. The polished brass. The green-uniformed doorman holding open the door.

"Good evening, Miss Sylvia. How nice to see you. Good evening, sir."

No recognition of our marriage in his greeting, you bastard. Or that Sylvia had ever recently been staying at Sutton Place. At least he didn't say, Hey, bud, where do you think you're going. And don't try to steal the flowers off the marble table in the lobby. And why don't you get your zoot-suit shoes shined.

The elevator operator smiling at Sylvia and at least a little more polite, nodding his head at me. Takes the shiny brass knob in his white-gloved hand and turns it downward. And upward we go. In the darkly paneled chamber smelling of lavender wax. Past doors on each floor. And so that New Yorkers can avoid bad luck, no thirteenth floor. And no need to worry, as we're not going that high. Slowing gently to a stop. At the Witherspoon Triumphingtons' private entrance on their private floor. Step out into the glowing light of this domed vestibule. With its pillars flanking marble busts in niches around the wall. Philosophers upon their plinths. Drusilla standing there. In the center of this white marble area.

"Why hello. Didn't expect you quite this early. But come in."

Sylvia flinging her fur onto a chair. A stooped white-haired butler in a crimson brass-buttoned waistcoat emerging from the shadows. Takes my torn overcoat and Sylvia's mink. Drusilla, a long ivory cigarette holder waving as she leads along a long hall to a vast drawing room. She'd only very occasionally smoked but always liked to have something in her hand. Just walking on the gleaming parquet from the domed entrance hall, you could see in the different directions, all the doors, and that ten families could easily live here and squeeze in a few more families

of their relatives, and still have room for family wars. And with every architectural nuance to make you uncomfortably feel you were something the cat dragged in.

"Sylvia, I know, hates daiquiris. Even though she has them. But you'll have your usual grapefruit juice, won't you, my dear. What would you like, Stephen."

"I'll have a beer."

"Gilbert does make wonderful daiquiris. He will be along in a moment. Poor old fellow, he's only just recovering from the flu. He is, you know, rather getting on, takes an afternoon nap. I'm having a daiquiri."

As we sit surveying the array of canapés in the sitting room, the stooped-over Gilbert ferrying in his tray of drinks. Out of his black coat and now in his white, the light flashing on the brass buttons of his crimson satin waistcoat. These Witherspoon Triumphingtons have a butler in the country, a butler in town. The hoot of a tugboat on the river below. Out the windows, the lights of Brooklyn in the distance. Walls along the hall decorated with etchings and glass cabinets full of snuffboxes. And in this room one or two fabled paintings I have actually seen pictures of in books. A portrait of a woman in a great black hat and black gown holding a small bouquet of purple flowers and a hound on a lead in front of her.

"Ah, Stephen, I see you're looking at that painting. Are you perhaps a connoisseur."

"Hardly that, ma'am. But, as the saying goes, I know what I like and I like that painting. Might it by any manner of chance be a Boldini."

"My, you are a connoisseur."

"Well, I have now and again visited a few galleries and looked at a few auction catalogs."

Drusilla stands and moves to serve canapés. A curvaceously stunning figure revealed in a long dress of raw silk. Décolletage exposing the gentle outline of her creamy soft breasts. The delicate fragrance of her perfume. One's own mother, by dint of a large family, always seemed to smell of her kitchen and had no choice but to be in an apron all her life. Sewing and mending, she further enveloped herself with her children, keeping them around her like a great protective cloak. And was never to be found in restaurants for dinner or in nightclubs all night for champagne. The Irish always like to say they worked their fingers to the bone and endured every sacrifice for their progeny. Certainly my mother's hands were calloused and certainly were less tapered and fingernails less long than this elegant Drusilla's, upon whose wrists diamond bracelets glitter blue-white and bright.

"Now tell me, what have you two lovebirds been up to downtown, or rather, especially you, Stephen, whom we haven't seen for such a good long while. You know, you musn't ever think we don't always want to see more of you. Do you play canasta. I'd love to invite you, you know."

"Well ma'am, I don't believe I've ever played canasta. I've been under pressure with work with a deadline."

"Oh, now that is good to hear. How many people do we know who are under pressure with work with deadlines. Who I do really think should be, you know. And how refreshing to hear that someone is. Solitude must really be so meaningful to you. And what are you working on now, Stephen. I know that can be an infuriating remark, for its not always a genuine question, but is often asked by way of saying you've never done anything yet and if you do, it will equally be of no importance. But I mean the question in its best sense."

"Well ma'am, yes, it is kind of you to give me the benefit of the doubt."

"There you go again, so damn formal. Why haven't you done something about that, Sylvia."

"Well, he's not always that formal."

"Then Stephen, please call me Dru. As in the past tense of *draw,* as with pen and ink. And so if I may so inquire, what is it you're actually working on now."

"Well Dru, I'm presently composing a minuet. And also I'm rehearsing conducting in the Russian manner."

"Oh. I didn't know there was such a manner."

"Well, yes, there is. As one might imagine can happen with some of the more temperamental Russian conductors such as Nicolas Slonimsky, who is, as it happens, a foremost champion of contemporary American composers. Some Muscovite conductors can be too bizarre and behave like they are big birds, arms flapping as if to fly them off the podium. As indeed did happen once to one of them in Saint Petersburg conducting the explosions at the end of the *1812 Overture*. It blew him in an arc right off the podium."

"Oh my dear, I don't mean to laugh, but how funny."

"He landed feetfirst, going through a kettledrum being kept in the well of the stage. And wore it like a hula-hula skirt. And then did a rumba."

"Ha, ha. How utterly rich. Well, I sincerely hope you're not going to end up doing that, Stephen."

"Well, of course one does eschew the conducting of some of these prima donnas. Imperceptibility is called for in one's movements and not too much of this jumping up and down unless the music absolutely demands it. Then it is best done by a certain flexing of the knees. Calls for one always remembering to do one's deep knee-bending exercises."

"Ha ha, I never would have thought conductors had to be so on their toes. How wonderfully interesting, and it must for you, too, Sylvia."

"Yeah, it's pretty fantastic. To stand around and watch prodigies springing up from nowhere to become major virtuosi playing at bar mitzvahs and weddings and Italian picnics. And all they need in the beginning is to be in their underwear, up on a reinforced orange crate, practicing in front of the mirror, bowing to the wall, shaking imaginary hands all around them and then doing deep knee bends. And then falling off on their ass."

"Oh, that sounds rather more than a little impatient of you, Sylvia. Someone not knowing you would even say spiteful. Stephen is going to look very nice on the podium, and indeed, although I'm not familiar with the Russian manner of conducting, I'm sure once mastered it's extremely effective. Stephen, let me replenish you. Do, instead, have a daiquiri. You've hardly touched your beer, and you must be a thirsty boy."

"I don't mind if I do try a daiquiri, ma'am."

Drusilla pressing her little ivory servant's button. Gilbert swaying in with another tray. Pouring out the drinks. His shaking hand an unsteadiness giving the impression old Gilbert was, by way of testing their strength, sampling the absolutely powerful daiquiris. The ambience beguiling as one sat on the down-filled pillows. Sylvia at one end and I at the other of what had to be a Louis XV gilt-wood sofa. Resting back and breathing comfortably amid the splendor everywhere. The carpeting, the statuary, the tapestry, the wonderment of the paintings. One's eye changing focus. From the silver bronze figures to the other myriad objets d'art. Silkily soft napkins around the bottom of drinking glasses and coasters featuring foxhunting scenes on the polished, gleaming tabletops. Preserve above all the patina from the potential devastation of where one might place the moistured bottom of one's glass. Should, of course, the napkin not have absorbed such wetness. Water puddles on your finer things could be as lethal as acid. At least I'm thinking that's what propriety and good manners are all about. Don't fuck up, if you can avoid it by decent behavior, another's property. And no fear, that wasn't the way it was growing up in my house. Every surface fucked up beyond restoration or redemption. But not in this outfit on Sutton Place. To which, as the alcohol seeps into my brain and knocks my neurons for a loop, I must confess I am taking an inordinate liking. Anything here could be shoved into an auction house to be bid upon and the proceeds support me through the writing of at least five major symphonies. And who cares if they are played at bar mitzvahs and weddings. Although I'd prefer the Italian picnics, quaffing red wop wine and sausages. And then when I've put my last note upon paper, and the last tremulo comes out of the string section of the last orchestra ever to play my minuet, and I hear my last standing ovation, then there would still be enough money left to support me, retired in Fort Lauderdale, Florida, in luxury for the rest of my life.

"And Sylvia, you must keep on nibbling on a little something, you know. And you, too, Stephen."

"Thank you, ma'am. I think I might just try this little sliver of smoked salmon."

Sylvia's adopted mother did, as she then passed the canapés closer, brush her hand over mine. Nor could one take one's eye off a strange fanciful sculpture nearby on a side table, depicting, of all people—for there he was, absolutely, his head atilt, dancing the tango with Natasha Rambova—none other than Rudolph Valentino. The legs of the figures on point in the attitude *croisée* and their sculpted faces ivory white. Which whiteness seemed in contrast to remarks always made of his reputed darker-shade resemblance to me. The two of us both sure looking white tonight. A nice thought to contribute to the conversation, which, stilted as it was, was distinctly not the most stilted of all time. For on every occasion of Dru waving her ivory cigarette holder as she drawlingly spoke, she also winked and further stiffened my most uncomfortably situated cock.

"Well, since one hardly gets anything of news these days out of Sylvia, perhaps Stephen, having already brought the subject up, do tell me now is the minuet you are working on presently what one would term a 'serious work.' I mean, of course it's serious. But I mean in the sense of its being something like a score, as part of a much larger work like an opera or a symphony. Perhaps for a special performance."

"Well, ma'am—"

"Stephen, if you call me 'ma'am' again, I think I shall raise my voice in not-so-mild protest."

"Well as a matter of fact, Drusilla—"

"Dru, please."

"Well, Dru, I do not eschew operas or symphonies but often prefer to work on something light, short, and perhaps even sweet. Preludes, mazurkas, impromptus, and scherzos. But for the moment, and not being too embroiled in a creative panic, the minuet has, as a musical form, overtaken my attention."

"Oh, how nice."

"One looks for a certain perfection of tonal combination and pitch, occasionally dissonant, to be performed by a major virtuoso on the concert platform. I'm also trying to instill in it a certain quality inspired particularly by the majesty of Russian choirs in singing their wonderful folk songs. Availing of the soulful sadness and clarity of their voices in chorus. It is so marvelous when one of their voices breaks exquisitely loose in solo performance to permeate the air. In effect, the musical nature of what I should attempt to emulate."

"Oh isn't that marvelous. To hear this. To know firsthand as to how the artistic spirit works. That when bestirred by inspiration, it immediately takes pen to paper, the notes flying onto the page. Don't you think that's spirit stirring, Sylvia."

"Yeah. Maybe."

"Oh, dear Sylvia, considering that we are talking about Stephen's work, that is a singularly unenthusiastic response."

"Well, yeah, why not. I haven't heard the minuet yet."

Solemn, sulking Sylvia. As I once called her. And multiorgasmic, as well. Crossing her exquisitely tapered legs, which these days kept inciting a vision of the gang-bang guys of her college days for whom she had expressed so much enthusiasm. Beer-boozing, water polo–playing fraternity brothers with their Green fraternal letters emblazoned in lipstick across their chests. Seven of them. They stood in a row, because if they stood in line, they'd be poking their pricks up one another's asses. And all of them foaming at the mouth, ready in turn to jump on her and shoot their wad, as she said, one after another. It was, she said, after she said it was true, a phony story she invented because if it happened, she didn't want to ever know who might be the father of any child she might ever have. It sounded too damn true to me not to be enraged, and I shook my fist at her. Somebody else could be the father if ever she got pregnant. She said, "Waiting to be a mother isn't driving me nuts yet, but when it is, it's my body, my ass, my mind, and I'll do what the fuck I want with them. And you can take your squeamish Catholic bullshit morality and shove it as far as constipation will allow up your own ass."

"Well now, my dears, are your daiquiris all right. Oh, sorry, I altogether forgot you're not having daiquiris. Oh, but you are. Both of you. Do have another, Stephen."

"Thank you, Dru. It's having an effect. They sure pack a wallop."

"Ah, that sounds better. So good to see you two young things together. Jonathan is away now so much and one is more than one likes these days on one's own. One does get sick of playing bridge and backgammon and uselessly gossiping away at cocktail parties and dinner parties and balls. Saying the same things over and over again. I ought to go visiting downtown, where you are, where all the action is."

"Well, Dru, it's pretty much besmirched down there near the Bowery, with a bunch of bums hanging around all over the place, you must be warned."

"Well, I know I should be simply charmed. But what a lovely word, *besmirched*. I had thought of going to Paris for a few days. But hardly know enough people there anymore, and the ones I do know are getting old enough to die. Hey, what's with you two saying nothing to each other Sylvia. What fucking well gives. If I may be so bold as to inquire in an old-fashioned vernacular."

"Nothing much fucking well gives."

"Well, Sylvia, you do don't you, as I'm sure Stephen does, like your Verdi. And such weeping sound as is found in passages of Puccini's 'Nessun Dorma.'"

69

"Christ, I hear plenty enough already of the abstruse about music in my dancing classes without wanting to go into any more of it just now."

"Well, I guess that signals our move toward dinner. At least I know you like Italian food. Stephen, you've nothing against Italian food."

"No, ma'am. Sorry, I mean Dru. I love Italian food. And excuse me a moment. If I may inquire where the nearest men's room is."

"You may inquire. Just out and down the hall, third door on your right."

A nice long wink and smile from Drusilla as one stands up. One, too, did get a shock both of recognition and surprise at the use of the word *fucking* coming from this most elegant woman's lips. Who was ready with a sledgehammer to break the ice of our overly polite conversation. And then finding that she knew more about music than she let on. Especially as I was aiding and abetting her every wink coming now, which made my already-rigid prick stiffen even more and made it feel a few inches longer. And after half a beer and three daiquiris consumed, left one more than desperate to take a pee. And as I got up to stand, I knew, Christ Almighty, that Drusilla knew I knew she was staring at my crotch as I headed to open one side of the double mahogany doors. And go counting to the third door, foot stepping on this glowingly golden carpet, and enter this exquisite little powder room off the hall. A dozen face towels, embroidered with the initials WT, hanging on gleaming hot rails. Scents and toilet waters. Soaps and powders. The washbasin in the shape of a great pearly shell. Unzip my fly. Can't get ahold of my prick. Which I know is in there, because it's busting to get out. Holy cow. In my emotional backlash panic down on Pell Street, after busting the bed with Aspasia, and changing my clothes, put my shorts back on, back to front. Leaving even less space for my hard-on and no space at all to get it out to take a pee. Before I piss in my pants. Have to take them off. And to get them off, because of the slight peg in the cuff of the leg, I have to take my god damn shoes off as well. Everyone is going to wonder what am I doing to be gone so long. Casing the joint to steal valuables. Well, standing in my socks, I'm looking at the unfunny cartoons on the wall, for a start. And I'm waiting for my prick to detumesce so the urine can flow. And I've just pissed, missing the toilet bowl. Momma meeo. Soaked my smelly long-unwashed socks in the puddle on the marble floor. And into which puddle, now to wipe it up, must go the most pristine towel I have ever laid eyes on in my life. Turned a butterscotch color. Sorry, Dru, I just pissed all over your house and just tried to do a little wiping up. And even as I rinse out the towel, it's going to remain soaking wet. Will leave Gilbert, the butler, or who-ever cleans up in here, wondering what the fuck hit the place. As I squeeze the piss out of my socks. And spin them in the air to hopelessly dry. Christ, and put god-damn spots of drops on the mirror and the rest of the fucking towels. And no time left to obliterate, never mind clean the piss-tinted desecration or to lay my socks for an hour or two on the hot rail along with the warm towels, which now also need a washing. This is all just perfect to lead to long-term psychotic manic depression. To which I suspect I'm already prone, with my recurrent bimonthly relapses conducted at myself in the mirror, which results in frenzied foaming at the mouth driving me into making accusatory assaults not only on myself but on the surrounding air.

Stephen O'Kelly'O shuffling back along the hall. To the raised voices in the drawing room. And Sylvia shouting, "Don't you fucking well tell me what to do. I know how to lead my own goddamn miserable life." Now silence as I, Stephen O'Kelly'O, ever so gently with the hanging handle open one side of the mahogany doors. The ladies arise as I enter. Sporting my wet anciently unwashed socks. Sylvia's and Drusilla's faces flushed. And we all proceed to the domed front hall to get coats, with the pervading stink of my feet following. What a figure Dru has, and a fantastic ass watched from behind. And whoops, another wink from her as she holds my miserable piece of apparel up for me to put on as she asks, "Well, Stephen, what about the weeping sound in Puccini's 'Nessun Dorma.'"

"Well, I am very much taken with the emotive content found in the singing voice telling a story."

"You know, Stephen, I should one day so very much like to hear you play. You must come and try our Steinway in the music room. What about I give you a tinkle."

As we three of us went by taxi to an Italian restaurant in a quiet street in the mid-Fifties, I thought, well, since you've already given me a hard-on, Drusilla, why not a tinkle. And it would be a little less embarrassing. It was one of those casual crosstown streets you walk along in New York, hardly noticing anything and noticing everything. And finding a couple or more of lifelong inhabitants still lurking behind the jumble of doorways and windows. And with nearly my last few dollars, I paid the fare. Not to suffocate us with the stink of my feet, I kept the taxi window a little open. But now, my God, if the proprietor, Jesepo, who is flapping his hands and uttering hosannas at Drusilla's appearance, gets a whiff of me, I'll be thrown out the door. Thank God waiters are scurrying around wielding their napkins to clear the air in front of us, ushered as we are to, as Jesepo said, her usual discreet table. Be just as well if my squelching feet continue to smell to high heaven. As we at last sat down, there is poured and placed before each of us a tulip glass of vintage Charles Heidsieck champagne. Poured from its bottle, taken from an elaborate bucket on its stand by the table. Jesepo, before putting his towel to the bottle, twirling the bottom rim on the edge of the bucket to rid it of excess drops of moisture. Drusilla raising her glass, proposing a toast.

"To you two, or at least one of you. And Stephen, here's to your minuet. I really know it's going to be wonderful and have all the critics in town impressed."

"Thank you, Dru. And this is such marvelous champagne."

"I'm so glad you like it. You know, collecting napkin rings and ice buckets, I fear, are two of my real weaknesses. And Jesepo keeps this crested one for me. I've always felt the best champagnes deserve the best silversmith's buckets to keep them chilled."

One waiter pouring the last of the bottle into the ladies' glasses as another waiter opens another bottle of champagne. One's mind floats free on the alcohol, back north to the Bronx, where, as a member of a large family who did not observe the democratic and American God-given principle of weekly pocket money, it was only occasionally that I could afford to ask a girlfriend out to the movies and for an ice cream soda afterward, especially as sodas had gone up to fifteen cents from a dime. And one bottle of this champagne tonight could buy a hundred sodas at the old price of sodas. If ever I get anywhere in life, I will leave a legacy in a few printed words of advice. Despite quaffing marvelous champagne, wet socks in one's shoes makes one feel at a distinct disadvantage in elegant company. Only a little bit less worse than if one had a conspicuously fatal disease. And following the toast, one excused oneself to repair to the men's rest room. For in my last hysteria taking a piss, I repressed much of my pee.

"Ah, please do excuse me, if you will, ladies."

As I walked rearward in the restaurant, one lady in six rows of pearls and wristfuls of diamonds sniffed the air as I passed her table. And my God, what a nice new nightmare it was in the men's room. Some son of a bitch in black tie, tassels on his black loafers and looking me up and down, and mostly down, was, as I reached for the bay rum, already reaching for it, and had the nerve to say as he grabbed the bottle, "Do you mind. I'm rather in a hurry to get out of the disagreeable fumes in here."

Amazing how deeply one takes personally ridicule, insult and humiliation and starts blending them all together, and what you've got when you sum them all up is a chip on the shoulder the size of an Egyptian pyramid. I merely told the guy, "Well fella, anchors away. You better hurry like hell. A fart like you can really stink." Holy Jesus, you'd think I'd insulted God, the way this guy reared up in outrage. His head looked ready to explode off the top of his neck. I thought my remark was a reasonably clever riposte to his own implied insult, although I suppose he wasn't to know it was me with my wet rancid socks who was stinking and providing the disagreeable fumes. But what I had objected to most were those words—"Do you mind"—when the fucker grabbed the bay rum. Of course I fucking minded, you stupid supercilious bastard. If you had any sense of good breeding, you would have let go of the bottle and said, "After you," and I would have said, "No, after you." And for a few minutes, out of that stilted rejoinder, we could at least have left the bottle there untouched.

Stephen O'Kelly'O exiting from the men's room into the sound of voices, tinkling glass and laughter and aromatic enticingly appetizing smells, returns to the table. The menu produced in the glowering silence. And one could forget the men's room for a minute. I was surprised at the prices, for there were none. Recalling Sylvia once saying that she did not grow up in the school of hard knocks. But then she went on to say it was much worse. That she got just one big knock, which smashed her psyche. To have found herself in adulthood misplaced among the sort of people who, all they have to be is who they are. And being who she was, she wasn't one of them. Having gin and tonic before lunch and daiquiris before dinner. And over dinner, talk about horses, dogs and candlesticks and never, God forbid, should the human condition or a question that it wasn't wonderful, ever intrude into the conversation.

But then when I'd first returned to the table, what was

absolutely stunningly amazing was to come out of the men's room and find that the fucker was not already assembling other tassel-shoed confederates to assault me or at least to have a couple of dozen lawyers ready to serve me with a summons. And there he was, with five others. At a table not that far away, clearly contemplating revenge. And as he gloweringly watched me rejoin my table with Drusilla and Sylvia, he spoke to his friends, who cast glances in my direction, and these friends seemed to speak back to him all at once. And imperceptibly, his manner utterly changed, and when he next looked in my direction, he actually nodded at me and smiled. And I, being a charitable sort, nodded and vaguely smiled back. But which made me wonder why his sudden change of attitude. Perhaps with their three ladies sent home, the tassel-shoed gang of them would be waiting outside to wreak vengeance in the usual New York manner.

Sylvia toyed with her food, leaving each course nearly untouched on her plate. Whereas I had an excellent appetite, scoffing down a really wonderful piece of fish in a magically delicious sauce and worthy of originating from the Fulton Fish Market. The vino was a superlative Sancerre. And we finished up with an exotic peach dessert with a Château d'Yquem which was beyond what one ever imagined wine could taste like. Or indeed could ever cost like, as whatever this was, I found later, maybe cost as much as twenty thousand ice cream sodas. Then outside, ready to enter a taxi Jesepo had called, we heard gunshots echoing in another street and then sirens of a dozen police squad cars converging on cross streets and screaming up and down the avenues. Sylvia taking it upon herself to refuse us both an invitation to return and have coffee and liqueurs back at Sutton Place.

"Oh, no thanks, Drusilla. But thanks. Stephen and I have to be up so early."

Drusilla in her own ankle-length black tweed coat lined with chinchilla fur, climbing into the taxi and waving what I thought was a kiss as it pulled away. Someone I just caught sight of in a window across the street, with a pair of binoculars, watching us. Another taxi coming around the corner approached and was flagged down to stop. Sylvia announcing she was going on her own way alone, downtown to Pell Street to get her suitcase, and that she and I were parting ways on this chill sidewalk. And then she was going somewhere where I didn't need to know. I watched the flexing of her calf climbing into the cab and she stopped halfway in and turned around, stared a silent second, and began shouting.

"Rehearsing in the Russian manner, are you. You're looking for a certain perfection of tonal combination and perfect pitch to be performed by a big-time vituoso, are you. You've got a deadline, have you. Well, you're a bull-shitter. Who the fuck has ever heard of you. Nobody. Nobody. And nobody is ever going to hear of you."

Drawing her mink tighter around her, I thought I could see tears in her eyes. And better than the daggers that I thought were there. And just as she nearly had the taxi door closed, she said something to the taxi driver and opened it again and said her final parting words.

"Well, whoever it was, in the Russian manner you were fucking, you were pumping your personal genes into her. Well go ahead, pump some more. All she'll beget is a fucking nonentity like you, who's so prurient he gets a hard-on over a horny old hag like my adoptive mother. And don't you ever think you're ever going to get a penny of my money that you married me for. You Irish bastards always think you're the cat's meow. Good-bye. And meow, meow."

Left standing there, the harshness of her words ringing in my ears I watched her taxi disappear around the corner onto Fifth Avenue. And found myself saying to myself, Hey gee, kiddo, you poor goddamn fortune hunter, you need a fucking break. I walked the few blocks up and over to Fifty-seventh Street to the Art Students League. Looking up at its darkened windows, the building seemed closed. It sure didn't start with Butterfield 8, but I scribbled my less revered, newly installed telephone number in a note to Aspasia to call me in the morning, and found a place to put it in the door. At the nearby late-night grocery store I bought a tub of walnut ice cream. Walking down Seventh Avenue my feet now feeling frozen cold, I stopped and looked into the windows of the crowded Stage Delicatessen, remembering and reminded of the sharp smell of sauerkraut on the air in the zoo, as two figures came out, talking.

"You know, Sidney, always remember I'm ready to show the way. You're an upper-echelon-type person. But I wouldn't want your perfect sense of culture to be like an obstacle and slow you down in commerce. Otherwise, I'm convinced you're outstanding."

"I'm glad you said that, Arnold, because you're sincerely the kind of person in whose direction I'd like to travel."

Listen and you can hear sensible words spoken by these people who could be composers, playwrights, or actors. Scoffing back over a beer their massive thick corned beef sandwiches swabbed with mustard and dipping their forks into mouthfuls of coleslaw. Ticket brokers to the big Broadway musicals. Stagehands who shift the sets backstage. On their momentous salaries replenishing their energy to be able to go sit with the newspaper and study their investments on Wall Street. Some pretentious fucker just the other side of the steamed-up window, shooting his cuffs with gold links the size of mountain boulders and a big round diamond ring on his pinky finger. Showbiz habitués. Cigars in their mouths. Shiny fabrics on their backs, fancy shoes on their feet, and shirts pleated down their chests. Who keep the serious composer down. Before I shake a fist through the window at the inmates and leave before they call the police, I stop to wonder. And remember that just tonight I overheard Sylvia shouting at her adoptive mother, as she now calls her, back at Sutton Place and she was shouting, "Don't you tell me what the fuck to do." It was in reply to Drusilla's quieter words, spoken first.

"Is there any way you can think of to treat him well. He might then be your liege man."

"Why. Are you going to treat him well."

"If you don't Sylvia maybe somebody else will."

Now left friendless on the street this could be my life. Heaped upon one the burden of someone who thinks you are a failure. Sneering and running off to better things. Away from a nobody. Well who the fuck isn't a nobody. When you finally end up at best a name on a stone in a cemetery. She asked me to marry her and then turns around to tell me I married her for her money. What was I supposed to do, throw a tantrum, say I can't marry you because she was rich. But all that's happened is I've got poorer. She didn't like it when I said that in the glow of glory the igniting spark of disaster always lurks. Boy did that little aphorism stop her to think for a few seconds. Hard now to recall that we had in the earlier days of our association done impromptu things like to actually go for an ice cream soda. One day I even prevailed on her to take the subway. Because she didn't take subways. Because the Witherspoon Triumphingtons didn't take subways. And had never been on one in her life. So I blurted out. Holy Christ millions do it every day. Let's go to Coney Island. Which sports its slogan as the sand bar that became the world's largest playground. She was both suspicious and amazed. And stunned silent on the subway train one could see she was wondering which way to go and what to do to get out. Any second I thought she might jump up from her wicker seat and run for it. And finally we got out at Stillwell Avenue, Coney Island. We went munching hot dogs along the boardwalk and on the hard sand washed by the gray green ocean. I showed her the shell of a horseshoe crab thrown up on the shore and hoping to make an impression said it was one of nature's most ancient creatures. From the top of the Ferris wheel we could see for miles to the horizon and the distant ships at sea. And turned upside down in the Cyclone, we could see the ground. Then on the roller coaster they called the Gravity Road she was as cool as ice in the front car and grinning as it plunged on its tracks like a stone and seemed headed into oblivion and it scared the living shit out of me. On firm land again, I yawked up my frankfurter and sauerkraut while she tried not to be seen to laugh. We visited the freak shows, the penny arcades and went on the carousel, the folksy music of the organ throbbing away. Screaming squirming children and every nationality passing by. It turned out to be both the happiest and most miserable day I ever spent with her. Sylvia saying, "Holy gee wizz, hey, has all this been here all this time way out here beyond Canarsie. It's real humanity in all its forms, flavors and colors."

Coming back on the train between the Eighteenth Avenue and Ditmas Avenue stations, we were assailed by some kids in an empty car. I was standing looking at the map, reading the subway stops and without making too much of a nightmare of it I was trying to work out how to take the free transfer on the Culver shuttle to the Fourth Avenue line in order to get off the subway at a stop near Pell Street without a nightmare of taking the wrong train and ending up in Canarsie. I felt a poke in my back, and as I turned around, a long-bladed hunting knife was pointed at my heart. His associates grinning behind him, a spokesman kid in a black leather jacket adorned with a skull and crossbones now pointed the weapon lower, at my crotch.

"Hey daddyo I'll cut your balls off if you don't give us all your money. And the lady's money, too."

"Hey kid, hold it a second, let's talk."

"You don't talk, daddyo. I talk. I give the orders."

"Kid, why you wasting your time. You could be running a big business with your gang there behind you."

"I said shut up, daddyo and give us your money fast, or I'll cut you."

"If you so much as move a muscle, kid, I'll knock your head off."

The kid moved a muscle. Jabbed out the knife. Caught me in the shoulder padding of my jacket as I side-stepped and grabbed his wrist. The knife blade cut through my sleeve. But my fist landed on his jaw so hard, it sent him on a fly halfway down the train. His brave jeering associates retreating just as we were pulling into the Ditmas Avenue station. The knife wielder minus his knife, scrambling up off his back, his face spouting blood as he ran, following his confederates out the train door. Nearly knocked over a woman getting on the train, who screamed. As the train pulled out I could see the gang through the window, racing toward the exit on the platform. One of them had enough theatrical flair to stop, and his thumb stuck in his teeth, made a Mafia curse sign at me. Then the darkness again of the tunnel as the train continued on its long way toward its final destination in the northern Bronx. And I missed the free transfer on the Culver shuttle. Sylvia sat silent all the way back to Manhattan and Delancey Street, where we got a free transfer back downtown to Canal. I thought she'd been left in shock. But it slowly became evident she was on the side of the marauding gang. And showing that, despite wanting to avoid rubbing shoulders with New York's subway millions somewhere buried in her psyche there was a strong streak of sympathy for the criminally minded downtrodden.

"You should go to jail for hitting that young kid."

"Is that right. Because he was going to rob and kill me with a knife, I should go to jail."

"Yes. That's what's wrong with this country. Big bullies like you beating on the oppressed."

And on this night after midnight of the lavish dinner in the Italian restaurant, I now walked alone down Seventh Avenue to Broadway and Forty-second Street. A girl cousin who took care of me when I was small and taught me to watch out for shooting stars said Forty-second Street and Broadway was the center of the world. Where people would come from Nebraska and Arkansas and even from farther miles away, to just stand, marvel and stare. The latest global news broadcast up in lights, the words passing like a train in front of your eyes. And as I arrived there into its glow of neon illumination, steaks being barbecued in windows, flapjacks being tossed in pans, one needed only to look down to see the sidewalks covered in crushed cigarette butts and blobs of chewing gum. It maybe could be the nearest place to hell. A traffic of strangers. And others. Pickpockets waiting for pockets to pick. Lurking pimps and prostitutes in the doorways. Loitering little groups of shady characters, crooks and drug dealers. For the prurient, movies to see. And for sale, the array of lewd, salacious and vulgar periodicals, pictures and books. In big numerals, the time and temperature. Smoke rings blown out of a mouth on a billboard. And as I went down the steps into the Eighth Avenue subway I felt that the peaceful soft white flakes of snow starting to fall were an anointment of cleansing refinement. At least before the flakes reached the ground and turned to gray slush in the gutter.

Stephen O'Kelly'O plugging his nickel into the turnstile. As smart kids growing up in the Bronx, there were always these dreams of how to constantly make a lot of money if everyone who went past you had to plug a penny into your personal turnstile. Or if you could install a revolving door in a big department store on the understanding that you could sell the electricity you generated from the revolutions. Thoughts to think while on this platform where someone is kicking a vending machine to pieces that didn't deliver their chewing gum. And while the train is noisily roaring under the Garment District back down to Pell Street keep an eye out for knife wielders. Emerging back up out of the subway again I had the prolific composers Vivaldi and Handel on my mind. Then along the roadway came a tottering drunk shouting out, "Fuck God and the Holy Ghost." I stepped into a doorway and listened to this itinerant iconoclast. Words that one might hear free of lecture charges.

"Be the reality. I was on Iwo Jima and Okinawa. I am the fucking maverick at large. What are the fucking issues. The fucking issues are Wall Street. They have us by the balls. Moral values are fucked. The wrongdoers with something to hide are behind their closed doors on Park and Fifth avenues. Skeletons are clanking in their closets. All over this city it's the idle rich getting the pleasure and the goddamn working poor getting the pain. Those are the goddamn issues. There's no question about it."

I nearly stepped out to follow the man to hear more. This war veteran bringing back memories of the war. But as he walked farther away, he stumbled upon and fell headfirst into an empty garbage can. The roaring and rumbling passing trucks drowned out his voice. Then, as he picked himself up and on his way once more, I could just hear him singing "It's a Long Way to Tipperary." Then these leviathan vehicles coming out or going to the Holland Tunnel under the deep waters of the Hudson River, finally obliterated his voice. I wanted to go shake the hand of this lonely tottering figure and at least say the word *friend* to him. He could have been in one of those amphibian assault boats which wasn't blown to bits, hitting the beach. And now instead he is falling drunk into a garbage can. Turn my key in the door and open it into the stale smell of the hallway. Climb the rickety stairs. Open another door to the emptiness of the apartment. Switch on the light. And the cockroaches, goddamn bastards, scatter everywhere to hide. On the record player was left the French national anthem, the "Marseillaise." If Sylvia isn't eating crackers and drinking soda pop driving her car all the way to California, then maybe she's on a ship first-class crossing the Atlantic to go to Paris.

Stephen O'Kelly'O checking through the apartment. Drawers, shelves, and closets. Her ballet books gone. All her notes she kept on Isadora Duncan, whom she would emulate in a toga while floating about spouting out Greek and Roman ideals. Dust-free space left where her jewelry box once rested. Full of gold chains, bracelets, and pearls. Crossed my mind once to ferry them all to the pawnshop. But keeping my dignity meant more. In the bathroom, where there is only room enough to stand along with her toothbrush, the toothpaste gone. Another expense to reckon with in order to keep the teeth white and bright. Plus, disappeared from the rusting medicine shelves are all her expensive creams and cleansers. Nightly to caress her smooth summer-tanned skin with the oil of this and oil of that. In the bedroom closet, a crumpled hat and her old raincoat and a couple of dresses. Vamoosed. Shipped out. Perhaps to Cincinnati, Ohio. To Milwaukee, Wisconsin, or to Kansas City. As she's done previously in search of her real mother. She didn't even know where to start to find her real father. But one guy said no I'm not your father, but come in I'd like to kiss you as if I were.

Wild-goose chases to no avail. To go knocking on a strange door waiting for a strange face to say no I am not your mother, get the hell out of here. And she would go away from such doors racked with sobs. Back to some anonymous hotel. To next day fly back on a plane to New York. Then to vanish somewhere into the luxury of her own life. Emptier than it was before. Now she's speeding far away from the poverty of my life. "Who the fuck has ever heard of you." she said. "You're a nobody." And so was Vivaldi at the end of his life. But while he lived, he was one of the finest violinists of his day and a composer of dazzling warmth and verve, who only in death lay in utter lonely obscurity in Vienna. Just as Stephen Foster died impoverished in this city. The ignored end of great men's lives leaves a cold clutching hand on the heart.

Stephen O'Kelly'O easing himself beneath the blankets of the broken bed. Staring at the ceiling, trying to sleep. Cold spell descending on New York. Radio warnings of a blizzard. Snow falling through the night and still falling in the morning. Flu epidemic raging throughout the city. One out of five going down. Suicides going up. Short on food and I've never felt healthier. In the navy, the most hated food was candied parsnips. And best liked was peaches in syrup poured on muffins as a dessert, which would make one take a five-second positive view of staying the navy. Force myself now to remember the

pleasant taste. And my sailor-tailored bell-bottomed trousers. That Maximilian Avery Gifford, just to give a few of his Christian names, and the only friend I had in the navy, said I should get made to give the ladies a thrill. Wonder how such tailoring would go with a pair of tasseled shoes. Worn as a true sign of being a member of the tasseled-shoe club. Maybe someone will think that I am someone who is someone. Meanwhile look out the window. No tasseled shoes for sure in this neighborhood. Heat is at last tingling up through the pipes. Next the landlord will send a shiver of pain up my ass when he starts fist-pounding again on the door for the rent.

At dawn, hungry pigeons landing on the windowsill. Stephen O'Kelly'O putting out scraps of bread. Have breakfast. And give the pigeons some. Avoid electrocution while cooking up coffee in the old percolator. A couple of stale rolls, heat them in the oven with butter and save my two cinnamon buns. Today for lunch have some tomatoes, spinach and celery. Pizza pie for dinner. As mesmerizing time passes, play and compose for as long as I can. Put on another sweater and lumber jacket. Lace up my old woodsman's boots and zip up my lumber jacket. Go to the store. Buy some nourishing cheese. Man who takes care of the garbage cans of the building next door is out chopping up the ice where he has cleared the snow from the sidewalk. He's in the same thick brown jacket and black hat and earmuffs he always wears. For the first time as I walk by, he speaks.

"Hey, I found out it's you who plays piano. I like the music. I can hear it a little bit down here on the street, between the traffic."

"Thank you very much. It's always nice to have my work appreciated."

"Hey, that's your music you composed."

"Yes."

"I like it. My father was in a symphony orchestra. Played oboe in Prague. He came here, fought for this country, got killed in the First World War. You think we needed a Second World War. I'm now like the refugee he used to be. That's what's wrong. No appreciation for anything. They don't respect genius. They don't care. That's what's being celebrated in America today is mass stupidity. And kissing asses of celebrities."

A single small word of praise lightens and quickens the step through the snow. He heard me playing part of my minuet. Brightens the infinitesimally tiny glow on the horizon of the future. For the darkness in one's soul gets so dark and so bleak that one's fingers and hands struggle to feel and claw the way out. Folk brushing the snow from their automobiles. Shoveling to dig out their tires. Guy with his car hood up, recharging a battery. Grocery boy with a heaped box of groceries, wheeling it by on his bike. It could be like a little village in France or Italy. At least for eight seconds, until you wake up and know you're only a stone's throw away from the Bowery, the last and hopeless refuge of the defeated and forgotten. Now pass this doorway which has always looked suspicious. Two fat, dark, short men, one holding the other by the lapels, shouting into each other's face. Then they are silent as I walk by, but start shouting again at each other when I've gone past. Woman bundled up wrapped in rags and coats, has a place cleared of snow on the sidewalk to sit. She is picking up and squeezing lice between her begrimed fingers.

One seeks for pastoral and civil places away from the wild energy of New York to induce musical ideas and relaxation. And the snow comes a great blanket of temporary silence. Wasted as I merely have lain late in bed. Let the lonely days go by. Forced in the chill to wear the gloves with the fingers cut off in order to play. Even the warmest of melodies fails to loosen the stiffened keys of the piano. Then at noon trudge out through the new drifts to the grocery store. To stack up with beans, potatoes, and the cheapest vegetables money can buy with what is left of my sixteen dollars and eighty-six cents. The rent to pay. One hundred and sixty-four dollars owing for two months. The gas and electricity could soon be cut off. My last steady money was as a war veteran being unemployed and looking for a job and accepted as a member of the Fifty-Two Twenty club. Twenty dollars a week for fifty-two weeks was at least survival until Sylvia came along. I ate all the potatoes she threw on the floor. Then as a last desperate measure, went over to the family-owned saloon farther uptown on the Bowery. Feeling like a begging leper. Warned by my parents never to be seen there. Sat in a darkened booth in the back like a wino. Had a couple of free bottles of beer, a pickle and a roast beef sandwich swamped in gravy. Bartender could have been a little more friendly. A big shiny cockroach ran across the table. To kill it, I took an empty beer bottle, smashing it down on the table. Missed the cockroach, broke the bottle, and left busted glass all over the place. Message will go back to my family I was unruly and maybe even drunk.

My long walks now each day took me north on Broadway. Past store after store selling everything on earth. Rugs, peanuts, hip boots, dresses, trusses for rupture, luggage, Halloween masks. And if I were hungry I could buy a salami sandwich with extra relish at no extra cost. When I reached Fifty-seventh Street, I left another note for Aspasia. Then to eat as cheaply as I could, went to Horn and Hardart. Opening up the little glass doors, pushing nickels into the slots. Pulled out a cheese sandwich and a piece of blueberry pie. Shoved a glass under the tap and pushed the lever for an exact glass of milk to pour out. As I sat eating at a table up in the balcony, a guy my age, and draped in a long raincoat buttoned up to his neck, goes with intelligent poise from table to table, taking the dregs of coffee left in cups and pouring one into another to make himself a full cup into which he puts masses of sugar. And then pours red gobs of tomato ketchup on his collected crusts of bread. And finding a newspaper to read he sits down to his free lunch. So well manneredly eating. Watching him he suddenly nods at me. It must be in affirmation that we both do what we've got to do to survive.

Then Jesus Christ. Someone has just walked in to announce that that is who he is. If it isn't someone proclaiming they're the Redeemer then nearly everyone else, and everywhere else you look in the corner of or behind something in this city, there is something or someone profane. A man in a large overcoat is lurking over a balustrade of the balcony, watching a woman in her tight white uniform below collecting dirty dishes while he's pulling his prick. Then when you go out to walk across the park where within the shadows of the thicker shrubbery, guys are loitering with erections, and while they pretend to be pissing, they are instead conducting their own public den of iniquity. But even with all this disgraceful behavior, maybe it's safer uptown. Because last night, a Mafia don with a cigar half smoked in his mouth just got gunned down in the local Italian bistro. He was ordering his fettuccine and about to taste a glass of wine. Always a nice little reminder that anywhere, just sitting or stepping out for a pleasant stroll on the street, or just as it was on the train from Coney Island, suddenly everything can turn into a fearsome battle for your life. Or sometimes you don't even get time to battle. When a bullet instead goes through your brain. And your neurons get sent into the centuries yet to be invented.

Back on Pell Street where I hoped every moment there would be some good news, the phone had yet to ring. All seemed a desert wasteland where I wandered lost. No one is ever going to give me a commission to write an operetta. Or announce, Gee, Mr. O'Kelly'O, your minuet is the ten-thousand-dollar winning composition. Good to have reached you on the telephone, we've been finding it hard to track you down in order to inform you that the New York Philharmonic is practicing playing your wonderful opus prior to its gala performance. Of course meanwhile we will emolument you at the rate of one thousand dollars a month until your next masterpiece is completed, with the usual use of a concert grand Steinway in the isolated cabin in the Connecticut woods, and so as not to annoy you, all the other composers and commissioning agents will be kept at their distance. Three meals a day delivered to your door. And what you do in private with the female fans lurking in the woods, and over whom we have no control, is your own secluded and personal business.

Then the daydreams of glory vanish as quickly as they come. Sink back into depression. Unused hours to go by. Relive the misery of all the parting words Sylvia said. Unable in my despair to compose at the piano. Each day wrenching myself out of the apartment, to merely set out and walk again north along Broadway, through these canyon streets. Until dressed now in a jacket, shirt, and tie in order to frequent the better hotel lobbies. Pass by Broadway Central Hotel once billed as America's most palatial hotel and greatest of all of New York's hotels. Still there and long faded from its glory. I went in to stand and survey its large and once most fashionable lobby. I even looked at a room when a most civil gentleman manager inquired if I'd like accommodation. And then, cheered up by this courteous attention I continued on, as I did this day, tramping all the mile after mile of city blocks. Through the bleak streets of the Garment District, cutting across to Hell's Kitchen, where the most secret of the family's saloons was located and where the Irish gangs used to scare the shit out of the Italians. Then back through Times Square and onward to Columbus Circle. Ranting speakers on their soapboxes. So many cowed dark figures. Almost seems as if everyone has given up and is too tired to insult each other. Remembered the feeling throughout the war of dreaming when it would be over. And the life of freedom one could look forward to. Lazing about on a beach drinking mint juleps. And here it was. The war was over. And the dreams shrunk to a struggle to stay clothed, housed, and fed. The main things of life survival that one took for granted in the navy. And

complained about. Three meals a day. And no longer having to swing in a hammock but given a canvas bunk
tiered one on top of the other but at least a dry, warm
place to sleep and comfortable so long as someone wasn't
trying to stick a prick into you. Now it seems like the last
act of desperation to hope that one might even run into an
old prep school chum who could ask me if I needed any
money and invite me for a week to his mansion up farther
north on the Hudson and well out of the Bronx. Or even
someone, a gunner's mate I knew from my turret on my
ship, who's made it big on civvy street. Or best of all,
Max, who married Sylvia's closest friend and trans-
planted in total silence to big big money in Texas. But my
thoughts got all different as I finally detoured on reaching Fifty-ninth Street, to walk east along the conspicuous
elegance of Central Park South. Thinking of the rich, like
the Witherspoon Triumphingtons. And all these other
folk who passed me as I loitered on the steps of the Plaza
Hotel. Then I went in, walking through the marble halls,
past the Palm Court to the Fifth Avenue–side lobby to
further loiter. Doing the same thing was a pleasantly eccentric tall, dark-haired woman in an ankle-length black
Persian lamb coat, thick gray socks and sandals. She
elaborately wiped off the seat before she sat down. And
then suddenly getting up again and in retrieving a discarded newspaper, she came back, and as she sat, missed
the chair and landed on her ass. I nearly gave a guffaw, un-

til I saw the look of humiliation on the woman's face, and I rushed to help her up, and there were tears of appreciation in her eyes.

But nobody I knew was to be seen on my walk. The exhilaration and hope I first felt in taking my ambling strides now faded and died as I took the subway back downtown. I went to drink three beers in Minetta's in Greenwich Village and could overhear these artistic bullshitters in their cashmere sweaters talking about the nobility of art. And then I walked the remaining blocks to Pell Street. Past the buildings that had now become familiar. As I entered the apartment, the telephone was ringing. Such was my haste to answer that I tripped over a chair and nearly ripped the phone wires out of the wall and the earpiece fell off the hook. It could be a commission. Or at least Sylvia saying sorry she left and wanting to come home. But it was instead a deeply growling, hostile voice.

"You white cock-sucking motherfucker, I'm going to come there and cut your balls off and then your prick. You go fucking my woman, you hear, you honky cock-sucking motherfucker."

The phone hung up. And later, Aspasia rang that she was hiding out up in Harlem on Sugar Hill and in the Florence Mills Apartments on Edgecombe Avenue. At least one had the consolation of the apartments being named after that wonderful musical-comedy star. Her boyfriend broke her door down and threatened to choke her to death to get my telephone number I wrote on the piece of paper I'd left at the Art Students League. And now her boyfriend was looking for me to cut off my balls but didn't yet know my address. And if he didn't kill her in the meantime, she would call me again. I growled my own few angry words that I'd break his ass and blow his fucking head off if I saw him. Meanwhile as deaf as Beethoven I spent the rest of the day sitting with my head in my hands and my balls spiritually in a sling. That night I propped a chair against the door and stacked milk bottles to get knocked over to alert me from sleep. I slept with the carving knife, part of a canteen of cutlery I planned to soon pawn, from Sylvia's adoptive parents. My hand gripped to the handle under my pillow. Waking up bleary-eyed, it was a struggle to go out to buy something for breakfast. Heading downstairs, I had to look in every shadow to see if anyone lurked there. Standing then looking left and right to see if the way was clear in the street. But I already had in my hand a letter from the mailbox. My name written in flowing beautiful script on an elegant cream-colored envelope. A gold-edged card inside, and beneath the Butterfield 8 telephone number were a dozen brief words.

As promised instead of my tinkle
my card.

The Steinway awaits.
Dru

Boyo boy I mean it, did I in one goddamn hurry dial Butterfield 8. And those words I heard on the other end of the phone. "Come right over, why don't you." And I nearly broke my ass in the speed with which I took a shower. Ripping the shower curtain down as my feet slipped on the soapsuds in the bath I crashed on one buttock and one elbow and banged the back of my head. It was a wonderful feeling. Even with my broken ass trembling I was elated and as if I were on the stage of La Scala in Milan I sang an aria from *La Bohème* and looked at my naked form in the mirror. Not bad. And looking trim. Then putting on my clothes and trying to find clean underwear, socks and an ironed shirt. New York became a different city as I rode north on the BMT line and got off at Fifth Avenue and Central Park South and now I didn't give a good goddamn how sad the look was on people's faces. Or maybe I did but they were now too crushingly dismal to contemplate. Also any second I expected some black bastard to come charging at me with a knife, screaming, "I'm going to kill you, you white bastard." But at least for a moment or two, I had somewhere to go in life and play music. I walked east on Fifty-ninth Street, stopping off in the shoe-repair store, where, from one of their efficient team of shiners using about a dozen different creams, I got a badly needed shine. And here I was, all the way from Pell Street. And on these quieter pavements of Sutton Place again, that you would believe was another and nicer world. In which my presence produced a slight suspicion and then surprise in the eyes of the doorman, who pretended not to recognize me and had stepped back behind his desk, his finger already pointed at names in a book.

"Are you expected, sir."

"I'm expected."

"And who may I say is calling."

"Alfonso Stephen O'Kelly'O."

"Oh, yes. Listed here as Stephen O'Kelly'O. One moment and I'll announce you."

The elevator operator kept glancing down at the slight peg in my pants and then at my shoes which were before getting a shine, a little worse for wear. I felt more and more inappropriate as we rose up through the elegant floors of this building. Even old Gilbert forgetting he ever saw me before and, at the door, giving me the once-over. But recovering his powers of recognition as I made no bones about my identity.

"Oh, of course, Mr. O'Kelly'O, nice to see you again. I'll take your coat. Madam is awaiting you in the music room, then if you'll follow me this way."

Another hallway exiting in another direction from this domed-ceiling lobby. The feet silently tread in the serene peace across these carpets. And then make noise on the parquet. The faint smell of wood smoke. And something not noticed before, a curving staircase sweeping upward to an indoor balcony. Dare one ask how many rooms and how many floors this joint has. No. Don't dare. Just carry on. Let all knowledge arrive freely. A left turn and then a right through two double mahogany doors paneled in green baize, the doors closing over one another and opening into an enormous, somber if sumptuous room with prints and gilt mirrors on the walls, picture windows, a small terrace, and far below, on the river, a tug boat hauling barges, its bow afoam pushing its way through the ripples and waves. And there, across the golden carpet, the ebony concert grand piano, its top ajar ready to be played. Flames licking a brace of logs in the fireplace. But not to be ignored in the soft hues of light and seated at a small table in another of her white clinging gowns, her hair gleaming and drawn back from her face, Drusilla. And by her elbow, a dish stacked with a variety of cookies, and from within an elaborate silver ice bucket peeked a golden-topped bottle of champagne, and on a side table a tray with pink tulip glasses and canapés.

"Ah, the moment I've been waiting for while I've been playing my game of patience, with cards of course, as you are a little later than expected."

"Forgive me, ma'am."

"Oh please, no."

"Sorry. I mean Dru. I had to find clothes to wear."

"Well, I had a perfectly awful thing happen. So your later arrival has given me further time to recover my composure. Join me in a drink to help wash away images. You will, I hope, have some of my favorite champagne."

"Yes, thank you. What a wonderful room."

"Yes, originally two enlarged into one. Entirely soundproof. Well, there it is, the Steinway waiting for you."

"Nice to feel one has no worry concerning any protesting neighbors."

"And it is so nice to see you, Stephen, it really is. And I'm so so sorry about the situation. It's not, of course, for the first time that Sylvia has run off and disappeared."

"What would you like me to play."

"Well, I'd love to hear your composition."

"I might perhaps warm up my fingers on some composer whose music already possesses proven greatness."

"Oh, you *are* modest, aren't you."

"Well truth be known, yes I am. Possibly because when I first used to play piano, growing up in my house, among my unappreciative family, only my dog Chess, appreciated my playing. And he would sit up, trying to balance on his hind legs out on the driveway below the living room window, howling always in perfect pitch."

"Well then, would you know something perhaps by Rachmaninoff."

"Yes, I believe I would."

"Then Rachmaninoff."

"How about some passages from his Piano Concerto Number Three in D Minor."

"Oh, yes, that has such marvelous bursts of romanticism. And the climaxes arise so splendidly."

Stephen O'Kelly'O massaging his knuckles and fingers, advancing to the piano. Turning to gently bow back to his smiling hostess. When about to sit to play, always the moment to set the scene. With the utmost seriousness in one's posture, stand perfectly still, count to thirteen. Then be seated, look upward, as if seeking spiritual inspiration from above. Hold outstretched the fingers above the keys. For a moment, hold them as if to cause levitation and the whole piano to rise to the ceiling. Contract the fingers ever so slightly. Then. Now. Bring them down. Strike. Fingertips concussing upon the ivory whiteness. Usher into the world this exquisiteness of sound. What a pity it can't escape across the fast flowing, shimmering water of the west channel of the East River. And thence pass over the gloomy shadowy buildings on Welfare Island to Queens and thence across to the distant lights of Brooklyn. And, in traversing the ether, even reach a sympathetic ear in Brownsville and Canarsie. To quaver, quiver and tremble their euphonic sensibilities as one's fingers touch the keys and reverberate the strings strung across this cast of iron. And most nobly best of all. To have as well, as I strike the last chord upon the keys, the appreciative warmth and joy of an admiring listener.

"Stephen, that was wonderful, wonderful. Oh, you do play so beautifully. So marvelously easeful. Without being extrovert. Yet youthful. And with such forward surge. I can't imagine why you're not on the concert stage giving performances."

"Well, having undergone a rather long stale stretch in the navy, where there were few pianos to be found to play, I have I'm afraid missed the boat. Very little privacy to pursue musical interests within a gun turret aboard a battleship."

"Oh, you poor you, you. Did you make big bangs. Here, let me replenish your glass. And then, although I'm aware it's not entirely finished, you must play for me your minuet."

Stephen O'Kelly'O rising from the piano. Crossing the room, tripping on the carpet. Gaining his composure, a hand held over his heart, a broad grin on his face. Taking up his glass and drinking deep into the delicious grapey substance. If there were any condition and moment mankind could undergo that could be termed that overabused word *happiness,* then this was it. Amazing how with just a little admiration one is tempted to strike a Napoleonic pose and behave like a prima donna. And of course meanwhile wondering when old Jonathan Witherspoon Triumphington is going to jump out of a closet or from behind a door or come swinging into view off a chandelier with a .38-caliber pistol aimed at my head. And make his own big bang for my being here playing his piano and drinking his champagne and desperately now wanting to fuck his wife, who hasn't even winked once since I began to play. Which I again return to do. The world premiere performance of my minuet. Bow. Beseat oneself to play. Totally and absolutely inspired. Improvise and embellish chords and harmonics. Fingers going wild, produce integral multiples of fundamentals up and down the octaves. Then dulcet passages on this dulcimer instrument. Tears welling in Drusilla's eyes. Her hands folded still in her lap. Which, as I struck the last faint key, she raised to clap. A diamond on a finger glinting along with diamond-encrusted bracelets on her wrists. She stands and crosses to me. A kiss on my brow.

"That is simply so wonderful. So sadly delicate at the end. I'm so glad I worked up all my nerve and invited you to play."

"And I'm so glad that you did and that I played."

"Well you are brilliant. Come and let's finish our champagne. Oh, but you're limping."

"A fall in the bath taking a shower in my rush to get here."

"Poor boy, you must show me where it hurts. I believe in the laying on of healing hands. But now I do have a question or two, of course. Is your first Christian name

Alfonso. They called from the lobby as you were coming up in the elevator."

"In fact, yes. But I only use it to achieve people's attention."

"Ah. And question two. And I must warn you, I am incurably and insatiably curious. And I must ask. When last here, whatever were you doing in the loo, if I may use the British slang. Gilbert thought there had been a burglary, or at least a pipe leaking."

"I did wonder when you might venture to ask me that. I suppose it was a damn silly business. But I was conjuring up to compose a march of pipes and drums."

"Dear me, in the loo. How interesting, although I do hate and despise the word *interesting* and all those who use it throughout these our United States. But I do so love your pedantic speak."

"Well as a matter of true fact, it comes from a slight impediment I have in the use of English, not that I speak French and Italian that well. However in the loo I had rather an insufferable situation. An accident. Or rather, discovered I had mistakenly put my shorts on back to front."

"Oh my God. Forgive me. I can't help finding that just a little bit droll. No wonder my dear fellow, that you had to pee. And your march you were conjuring up, pipe and drums. Did you compose it."

"As a matter of fact, in my panic, I didn't. But being

also enamored by the lute and harp I instead put together a little bridal hymn."

"Oh, did you. How sweet."

"Well I'm afraid it's not exactly sweet. Despite my classical tendencies, I do synchronize on the downbeat."

"Oh, do you."

"Yes. For hepcats. But I guess on the occasion in your powder room, I would have been better occupied composing something a little more akin to a dirge with muffled drums."

"Oh, you mustn't say that."

"Well except for tonight in your wonderful presence, I've only met thus far dissent, opposition, and rejection in my efforts to enter the public forum, and to be recognized for my work. I eschew the barren and trite minds consumed with their pose of cultural omnipotence and pretense at original creativity, who by their very existence make the dedicated composer's life such a misery."

"You know, I have a solution. You must come out to Montana. I have a little ranch out there. Mostly wilderness. A grizzly bear or two. Buffalo, moose. And I suppose it might have more than a few rattlesnakes. But I've never seen one. Otherwise completely possessed of solitude. No one but me, a ranch hand or two, and the caretaker need know you were even there. I could have a Steinway for you. And I know you could work quietly in peace. Why do you not answer."

"Well, I'm trying to remember all the languages that I can say yes in. *Oui, sí, da. Igen.*"

"And *a'iwa,* I believe, is Arabic."

"And *ja,* I believe, is Lettish."

"You have such exquisite hands, Stephen. I'll bet you were lionized by the girls when growing up."

"Well again, as a matter of true fact, I wasn't. As a relatively poor boy of a very large family I could never ask anyone out on a date, even to the movies. With hardly much change left out of a dollar and ice cream sodas gone up to fifteen cents in the sweet shop where once they were only ten cents. And where some of the kids hung out who could afford it."

"Oh, how sad for you."

"Well, there was a little kid we could bribe for a nickel who cleaned up the candy wrappers and Popsickle sticks inside the movie theatre. Who would open up a side emergency fire exit to let us in, but I thought it an inappropriate entrance for an invited young lady."

"Oh dear, I would have thought that so sweet and exciting."

"Well I'm afraid young girls in the neighborhood were a little too conscious of what kind of an impression they were making. Their dignity and esteem and their reputations to uphold I'm afraid took precedence over the carefree."

"Oh dear. When I was that age, before the war living

as we did in Paris, where on Avenue Foch there were no neighborhood cinemas, no ice cream parlors, I remember I was always dying for something carefree and American like a pineapple soda and a jukebox crooning out something like 'I'll Never Smile Again.'"

"Pineapple's my favorite too. Well I hope you weren't, had there been sodas then in Paris, short of an extra franc or two."

"Well as a matter of fact, I was. Very short indeed. I'm afraid my frugal parents did not believe in children's allowances. The only entertainment to be found for me as a young girl was a nearby street named Rue Rude, which I always laughed at, thinking that if you walked there, someone would be discourteous to you. Although I suppose, for all my parents' parsimony, one might say one lived in rather ornate if shabbily genteel circumstances amid treasures. And as the saying goes, the beauty of which give their owners so much joy. But to a juvenile girl just wanting desperately to find someone to love her, gilt-wood consoles, rock-crystal chandeliers taken from the imperial palaces of Saint Petersburg, even a few pieces of silver furniture belonging to Louis the Fourteenth which he hadn't melted down to finance his wars, were of very little consequence. And frankly, I always thought we were always very poor. To the degree sometimes that I shudder having to give someone a dollar."

"Well Dru, I'd be glad to lend or give you a dollar

anytime you feel nervous like that. And if I may gently say so, it's not half-bad the way you're living here."

"Well, perhaps I exaggerate a little. Owning divine things is how people cling to life, I suppose. And especially at the time the end of their own lives inexorably approaches. Ah, but how morose one is. Time to fill our glasses. Do have a cookie. We are still alive. But I did, before my own unpredictable demise may come, delayed as it may hopefully be, simply have an overwhelming urge to hear you play. And I would so like you to stay and play some more but I have to go meet Jonathan due soon at Penn Station off the train. He hates flying. He's been duck shooting out west. He does rather have a fixation on his shooting, claret, and cigars. And he hates not having someone meet him. But I shall see you soon again, shan't I."

"Yes, for absolute sure."

"You know I often watch along with the numerous seagulls, faithful pigeons fly together past and below the window here, their wings almost touching and it sends a wrench through me. And I do think I can talk about anything under the sun with you and circumstances permitting, think I might want to know you better. I am, after all, I do believe, still your mother-in-law."

"Yes, ma'am. Sorry, that keeps slipping out."

"Well, I'll keep forgiving you. And I know that it may rather seem I've propositioned you, but you will think of

Montana, won't you. You have, you know, helped to set my mind at rest. After a totally unsettling experience just before you came. Gilbert was otherwise occupied and I thought I heard a noise outside the service door at the larder end of the kitchen. Opened it, and there was the grocery boy with a delivery but with his trousers open, pulling upon himself and at the crucial moment insisting I watch, and I thought he might have a gun. It made one flush with rage. Then he, pale with fright, poor boy, burst into tears. And said he was so ashamed. An altar boy at his church. I felt sorry for him. Then had to let him get the groceries in, two enormously heavy boxes. And before sending him on his way, he was in such a state and so shaking, I gave him some whisky and strictly advised him not ever to come back. Do you think I did the right thing in not calling the police. I can of course, be such a sentimental old fusspot."

"Dru, I know this may sound like pedantic speak but allow me to say that there should be inaugurated as soon as possible in this town a devout society dedicated against the total indifference to the erosion of the human spirit. Enormous amounts of which are clearly present in your own heart."

"I must kiss you for saying that. I must. Just a peck."

Stephen O'Kelly'O taking his leave, formally bowing to Dru at the elevator door, kissing her hand in the European manner as clock chimes on two different clocks rang ten. Nightlife in New York starts to wake up. Not that the day life ever dies. Departing empty-handed. Tempted as I was to have stuffed a few of the delicious canapés into my pocket. And to have put my arms enveloping around her. The sound of the elevator coming. And the warm inner nature of this woman. As she suddenly rises on her toes, leaning forward to again kiss me on the brow. So close. Smelling so sweet. So welcome to the nose. As there is no worse or more unforgettable smell on a battleship than cordite and the stink of half a dozen sweating men.

Stephen O'Kelly'O walking with a limp along Fifty-seventh Street. Go by, one after another, the massive apartment houses. Somber with their many windows. And spaciously spaced inside where souls dwell, self-existing on private incomes. Doorways with their doormen stationed within. Suspicious eyes peering out. And I go step by step across this tall city. Passing a pharmacy and a discount store selling rugs, paintings. A hardware store selling locks. Another selling brass bathroom fittings, that the citizens struggle to own. A dark dingy brick building there with no windows but has a sign.

INTERBOROUGH
RAPID TRANSIT CO.
SUB STATION NO. 42

The pedestrians thicken westward across First, Second, Third, Lexington, and Madison avenues. And in this city of fervent aspirations, finally to Fifth Avenue the geographical center of wealth. And farther on where it begins to fade, turning into the stone bow-fronted elevation of Horn and Hardart. This old faithful emporium for the cheap square meal. For a dollar bill getting change of twenty nickels strewn out on the worn piece of marble. Twenty times you can read "United States of America. Liberty." A buffalo bent ready to charge on one side and the noble profile of an American Indian on the other. And the settlers beat the holy shit out of both. But when plugging enough nickels in the slot, a hamburger, glass of milk and piece of blueberry pie come out.

My old pal seen last time I was here is now over there, halfway across the room, collecting his usual dregs of coffee, cup by cup, and with what looks like a script of some kind tucked under his arm. Gives me an acknowledging smile as he ladles out the ketchup on a goodly sized scrap of bread and munches away. Amazing how one can so immediately recognize a kindred spirit. Even though everyone is pulling his prick in this city and shooting each other with guns and stabbing people with knives, it's still, with its flowing heaving tides of raw humanity, a wonderful democracy. And with a vengeance capable of leading to murder, everyone free to despise, resent and hate everyone else.

Thought of Drusilla all the way back to Pell Street, subway noise roaring in the ears. The faint blue veins of her hands, long-fingered and strong. A glittering bracelet covered in diamonds on both her wrists. Turn now to catch a peek at the rogue's gallery of somber faces across the aisle. Each one looking as if he's committed a recent murder or is about to get murdered. Although I had to rake up leaves and cut grass, I had a thirty-five-cents-a-week allowance and poor old Dru had nothing. But in my present poverty there is a vast chasm between our lives. The poor who want advantages and the rich, who don't want to be taken advantage of. And her wealth, married as she is, wearing her golden handcuffs. Linked and locked up to a rich, rich man. Sampling her luxury makes the confines of Pell Street feel ever more gloomy. And dangerous. As later that night, Aspasia called again. Asked if I got the recording of her singing she'd left against the wall downstairs under the mailbox. I said I'd go and see and that it would be a miracle if it hadn't been stolen. Said she told her boyfriend I lived on the corner of Fifth and East Sixty-first Street. She knew it was a house she had walked past many a time when she worked wheeling out an old man down the street, and which always looked empty. And now the boyfriend was foaming at the mouth to get there, with a knife longer than she had ever seen before. God help anyone answering the door without a baseball bat to knock the fucker on the head.

As a good citizen, I skipped downstairs, found the record, and went out and made an anonymous call to the police. Mayhem expected at Fifth and Sixty-first. Crazed, berserk, mentally ill and frenzied man rabid and foaming at mouth, armed with a big knife and screaming he is going to commit murder. Please try to save the lives of all the decent people you can. Then I returned to the apartment slightly happier, indeed delighted that justice might be served on Fifth Avenue and Sixty-first Street and put Aspasia's record on the phonograph. And listened. My God. The exquisite beauty of the melodic golden sonority so purely rising from her throat. A voice reminiscent of the great Russian sopranos. What if they don't get this son of a bitch and I were ever conducting and she were a soloist at St. Bartholomew's. Dru and her husband there. And Sylvia on the steps outside, smoking cannabis and snorting cocaine up her nose. Then Aspasia's boyfriend, if he hasn't already been arrested by a couple of dozen policemen jumping out of half a dozen squad cars, rushes in with a war cry and foaming at the mouth, charges up the aisle with a knife. My back turned, he has his stiletto raised ready to plunge in between my shoulder blades. The congregation knows I'm a Roman Catholic, so none of these Episcopalian Protestants will deign come to my rescue. And because of the thunderous voices of the chorus, no one hears folk shouting, "Hey, conductor, watch out."

Waking this next morning in Pell Street unstabbed, alive, and hungry. The sun briefly out from behind the taller buildings shone as it did for exactly eleven minutes on the bed before it disappeared for good for the rest of the day. Exhausted by my dreams of a Steinway somewhere out in the wilds of Montana, I lay between the yellowing sheets and went back to sleep without anything to eat. At lunchtime, resurrecting to go out to buy my matters of survival, a bagel, cream cheese, an orange, and splurged on a croissant and the *Daily News*. Brewed some coffee in the old percolator, a comforting sound as the dark liquid spurts up. And then as I sipped my first cup, I turned over the newspaper to the front page and nearly keeled over in a faint. There a picture of a marauder brandishing a nine-inch knife and surrounded by a dozen police, guns drawn. Son of a bitch black bastard looked like a giant. With an equally massive headline.

MENTALLY DISTURBED MAN
ATTACKS FIFTH AVENUE MANSION

It was as if the whole world now knew everything about my life and that on any line as I read down the page, my name Alfonso Stephen O'Kelly'O would be revealed. Aspasia's boyfriend luckily described as incoherent and disarmed after a struggle, was apprehended by the police, arrested, and arraigned. And he could fi-

118

nally be brought to prison on Rikers Island just up the East River and through Hell's Gate, only a short canoe ride from Dru's. And I could have been playing my minuet to send him on his way. A sort of tickling sensation to be at last part of the conspicuous activity in this city, even as a remote root cause, and maybe not so remote and safe, from some mad son of a bitch trying to kill you.

Spread open on the kitchen table I read the caption and the brief story a dozen times. Some black bastard gets a knife and goes out to kill a white bastard and in less than five-minutes activity gets his picture all over the newspaper. While I struggle for months to get a tiny plug for my minuet for immediate release, maybe in a parish magazine. And the only recognition I have to show is my name published on my mailbox. To take immediate delivery of an electricity bill. It's the pigeons who have the best time in this city. Flying where they want. Roosting and cooing and shitting from on high all over the goddamn place. And just as I was imagining hearing Liszt's Hungarian Rhapsody No. 2 in my mind, the phone rang. Sending a shiver through me. Because I owe the phone bill. Pick it up. Wait for a growl. Or now an interrogation by the police. And hearing the Chicago drawl of a familiar voice, sigh with relief.

"Hiya kid, old buddy. Remember me. It's your old friend Maximilian. I was best man at your wedding. Gee,

I almost hung up, thinking it was a wrong number. You sound suspicious."

"Hello, good friend."

"Gee, that's better. Sorry to hear about Sylvia but she gave me the number. Ran into her in, of all places, the lobby of the Waldorf-Astoria. You know, where a guest can still arrive in his private railway car. Hey, and I guess you heard all about me and Ertha."

I had heard. But not the whole story. Old Max divorced by his first wife because he was broke without prospects, she then didn't waste time trying to take him for all he was worth, which Max pleaded was nothing at the time except for a vintage Bentley. And then he became instantly more considerably rich as he immediately had married Sylvia's pal Ertha after a whirlwind romance. The newlyweds then moved southwest to enjoy a dalliance in a severely affluent suburban clime located in Houston, Texas, where Ertha's father was an oil magnate who readily assisted his very affably charming new son-in-law in making his way around in the corporate jungle of petroleum. And buying them a wedding present of a spacious house with coffered cathedral ceilings in a fancy district with two acres, four-car garage, five and half bathrooms, swimming pool and a cook and maid in attendance.

"Gee pal and old buddy boy, all went fine and swell for a while out on the old cocktail terrace until a comedy of unpremeditated imbroglios ensued, the unbelievable happenstance of which you could not ever in your wildest fears conceive."

It transpired that old Max who, it had to be admitted, couldn't control his sexual appetite and would, as the opportunity presented, jump in the nicest possible way on anything that moved and even a few that didn't, had screwed someone else's wife after a football game in a kiosk adjoining someone's tennis court. The event of this alleged intercourse hit the local headlines when a robber, trying to rob the house next door with the owners away, got ripped apart and killed by two Doberman pinschers. Old Max and the beauteous lady, a multimillionaire's spouse, discovered present on the other side of the fence, were called as material witnesses. And Max's quote— "Hey gee, we were playing backgammon when we heard all this barking and then screams. We thought it was someone kibitzing about and having fun." Nobody believed, including the judge, that they were merely playing backgammon. But the judge at least said they weren't on trial. However, Houston society decided they were, and the scandal suddenly found Max out of a job, minus his twenty-four suits and three cars and, after a divorce, out of a marriage and without a roof over his head which literally happened overnight, for, added to his woes, the cuckholded husband put out a contract on his life, effective if he wasn't out of Houston by sundown.

"That's right old pal, pronto I beat it back to New York. But I wasn't the one who first cheated. All that happened old pal after another story. Anyway, I drove the whole way back east in my old Bentley, the top down, the wind blowing through my hair. Later I find out old Ertha is all the time fucking an old flame. A two-hundred-and-fifty-pound linebacker on a professional football team, who gave her a venereal infection she gave to me, is how I first suspected what was going on. But wait till we meet and I tell you the rest of the story."

Old Max, who himself came from Evanston, Illinois, on Lake Michigan and a fairly affluent family and was fond of reminding me in the navy that Evanston had the highest percentage of college graduates of any big town in the United States. He had old-fashioned ideas of behavior and etiquette amounting nearly to prudishness, not surprising, as Evanston was also the national headquarters of the Woman's Christian Temperance Union of which his mother was an important member. He said he was disgusted by the kind of betrayal involving Ertha's past lover. Which embarrassed hell out of him having to go back home to visit his family doctor and milk down his prick just as they did at a short-arm inspection in the navy when some medic was examining suspected cases of a contagious inflammatory disease of the genitourinary tract. Max in his own act of unfaithfulness, maintaining that he was only just yielding to a brief temptation, led on

by a woman in heat, whom it would have been grossly ungentlemanly to rebuff. Sure, he could get his own back on
Ertha, but what the hell, life was too short. He wasn't
going to yield to any low-down retaliatory behavior, no
matter how much he was provoked. And even as he was at
the moment monstrously provoked by the monstrous
amount of alimony he was sentenced to pay. Having now
that he was back east, got himself a slot downtown in a
brokerage house at better than a decent salary, a membership in a fancy athletic club, and had taken over the lease
on Ertha's old rented apartment on Waverly Place in the
Village, from which Ertha was presently trying to evict
him, and which he had now filled with his collection of
seashells and plants.

"Well old buddy boy, I guess I'm truly back in this
town with its ten thousand major attractions. Gee, come
and see me, old pal. I could do with a real friend. After
Ertha and I divorced, I thought, Gee, she's already rich
and doesn't need any money and suddenly now I have
lawyers breathing down my neck for accumulated maintenance, with threats that they will end me up in alimony
jail. I admit I had it kind of good out there in Texas,
and her family was the reason. But now I feel I'm being
taken unfair advantage of. You soon find out what a
woman's really like when they get lawyers and get you
into court. And it takes the poor bastard for everything
he's got. And if you can find any other better way to make

him suffer, do that too. Sort of brings on a paranoia. You begin thinking that no one on this goddamn earth can be trusted. You even find you're looking for an excuse to hate people. That's why it'll be so goddamn good to see you pal. I'm taking the afternoon off. Why don't you on Friday come to afternoon tea. Scones at teatime and all that goes with them. You know these nice old customs they got in old England help to keep you sane in a city like this. And maybe it's a good thing I don't live far from the Women's House of Detention to remind me of the foibles of the female. Gee pal, it will be great to see you."

Meanwhile another naval pal I knew who knew Max said it seemed old Max had in addition to his vintage Bentley, taken to wearing tweeds and become very English in both his accent and attitude, including flying the Atlantic several times to check up on having a pair of shotguns made by a famed London gunsmith. Also he'd headed to Georgia for numerous quail shoots, that is when he wasn't making himself familiar with certain factions of the British landed gentry with whom he took up while indulging brief bouts of foxhunting. And I recalled his fastidiousness and complaints in the navy about the constant vulgar language. And then to find him uncharacteristically wearing nearly skintight tailor-made bellbottoms which he said sent the girls nuts when he went back home on leave. And was just like a West Virginian we both knew aboard ship, who also on leave, was so mobbed by waiting women when he got off the train that they tore off his uniform and left him on the platform in his skivvies, until the strongest girl rescued him and took him home to screw him insane as he said, but left him just sane enough to fuck again.

Friday dawned sunny. With winter over, a mild breeze blowing up grit and dust in the eyes. And taking a bus north and forgetting to get off at the stop for Waverly Place, I had to walk back downtown again. And as would happen, past the Women's House of Detention, a grim edifice seeming to stand like an island of feminine horror at the crossroads of Greenwich and Sixth avenues. There, high up at the windows, were wild jeering faces screaming out between the bars, voices raucous and vulgar shouting down into the street.

"Hey Romeo, let me suck your cock, if you've got one, while my girlfriend in here sticks her tongue up my ass."

One shakes a fist up at these unseemly women, but then in instant retaliation, suffers just some more shockingly vulgar discourtesy and ill behavior, which one has so reluctantly become accustomed to in this town. You hear such vile invective coming out of a woman's mouth, you kind of wonder what normal women are harboring in their brains. But at least in the Villagey atmosphere here, there are a few trees. And unlike nearly all the rest of New

York, convening streets slanting in different directions. Turn left. A vegetable store. Next to it, a Chinese laundry. Mother and father in there around the clock sweating over hot irons while the sons and daughters are at Ivy League colleges, their nose stuck in books. This is it. Right here. At these stone steps. The engraved name above a bell. Press. Wait. Hear a buzzer. Push open the door. Climb up stairs. At the top stands Maximilian Avery Gifford Strutherstone III, grinning in a yellow cashmere sweater. How do I know it's a cashmere sweater. I don't. But on Max it sure looks like one. And on his feet highly polished mahogany loafers and thick fluffy sweat socks. Growing up, we kids had a name for it—"studied casualness in dress."

"Gee pal, old buddy, this is a great treat. How are you doing."

"I'm fine, Max. How are you doing."

"Well, today I'm doing fine. Fine. Come in. It's so damn good to see you."

With a sweep of his arm, Max ushering one in. Under the leaves of palm plants to sit drinking Lapsang souchong and biting into the warmth of scones fresh from the oven and deliciously slathered with clotted cream and black cherry jam. All everywhere neat and clean. His shell collection in a display cabinet. A blue parrot in a cage. The floors polished. College pennants on the walls. Harvard, Yale, Princeton, and Colgate, the latter located mid–New

York State where, Max after the war, came back east to go to college.

"Well Max, looking around here you sure pass inspection. And I am both relieved and impressed that your return to bachelorhood could possibly have demonstrated such endearingly soothing aspects."

"Yeah, old pal. Old bachelorhood ain't half-bad. No nagging. No goddamn bossing around. No whining, no bitching, no sulking. No immense surprise sprung on you every time you turn around. Just deliciously soothing tea like now and wonderful conversation. But hey, Steve old boy, my good pal, I'm sorry to hear about you and Sylvia, I really am."

"What have you heard."

"That she took off. But at least you know in the crunch, you don't have any worries."

"What crunch."

"You know, like a divorce."

"Why don't I have any worries."

"Well, I mean like alimony. A vise clamping closed on your short hairs, you complain, you squeal, you shout, but which holds you in pain for the rest of your natural life. But you know that can't happen to you. Just look at who your in-laws are. Imagine, if it ever comes to that, information like that getting out in a divorce court and blaring all over in newspaper headlines."

"What information."

"Don't be naïve, Steve. The amount of old moola of course. That kind of publicity gets a real play and goes everywhere. In fact, who do you know thinks of anything else except how much money somebody else has got."

"Well, I'd like to know what kind of publicity you're talking about and where everywhere is, because I don't know who has ever heard of the Witherspoon Triumphington's for anyone to care. And if they did, what difference is that going to make that my adoptive father-in-law is a tightwad. He cut off Sylvia's allowance as soon as we got married."

"Steve, I don't mean him, I mean her. I mean, look when that comes out, at who she is."

"Well, I already know who she is. She's a very fine and a very beautiful lady."

"Hey come on Steve, you don't have to hide anything from me."

"I'm not hiding anything."

"Well, for God's sake, you must know from Sylvia."

"What should I know from Sylvia."

"That her adoptive mother is known, at least among New York's best society, as being one of the richest women in America. And probably in the world. Compared to her, the tightwad husband, who maybe has some sort of past celebrated lineage plus a few horses and polo ponies, and plays court tennis at the Racquet and Tennis

Club, and goes salmon fishing on the Spey and fly-fishing in Finland and quail shooting in Georgia, he hasn't got a penny. Never had. In fact, it's probably all her fishing tackle and they're probably her horses and polo ponies."

"How do you know all this."

"From Ertha, for a start. I know. Practically everything about the family. I mean she practically lived with Sylvia for a while in their place upstate. I'm amazed you don't know. Sylvia had a little doll's house in the woods where they would stay together. Sure, the two of them were sleeping together. I mean, they're only part-time lesbians. If it's really true you don't know who's got the money."

"Hey, what are you trying to say, that Sylvia is a lesbian."

"Hey, Steve, old pal. I'm just relating facts. No need to get hot under the collar, ole pal."

"Well, if I don't happen to know any of these so-called facts, and even if I did, I don't see why it should be anybody else's business."

"Hey, come on Steve, who wouldn't know these things in a world where that's what people live and breathe on such information. I mean, shit, boy, Sylvia was raised as if, and thinking she was their natural daughter. You can bet you were checked out sixteen different ways from Sunday. I mean, I don't know exactly what Sylvia inherits, but it's enough anyway that they thought they had a slick fortune hunter on their hands when they found

there were traces of bootlegging in your family background."

"I categorically deny and resent deeply that aspersion."

"It's only what I was told, Steve, for God's sake. But I
mean, if you make enough at bootlegging it nearly becomes respectable. But then when you tried shaking
down old Triumphington in one of his clubs for a handout, the alarm bells started to ring."

"Hey, what the hell are you trying to say."

"Hey Steve, old pal, don't go white as a sheet. Sorry,
that's the news I got. Not that you were blackmailing or
anything. What the hell, bootlegging could have meant
that your family were goddamn rich. I mean, look at the
big recent rubouts in this city by the guys who were once
bootleggers. There must have been enormous profits
somewhere once for the guys to be behaving so seriously.
Here, have more tea. Gee pal, last thing I want to do is
hurt your feelings. That's what I'm saying. There's so
much money involved. Just from the inner workings of
Wall Street and from my own brokerage house you'd
know how much. All very confidential, but a senior partner buys and sells on Sylvia's mother's behalf. And boy, if
that ole gal doesn't know how to trade. Some of this stuff
involves trust funds so massive, you wouldn't believe.
Then there's a banking guy who manages a petty-cash ac-
count for her in one of their banks. Where the petty cash
is in seven figures. A little munificence in a creative cause

would be nothing. You see what I mean. Take it from a former second class yeoman."

"Well, I know for a fact she's terrified of even spending a dollar, but I think it's all an outrageous invasion of someone's privacy, including my own."

"You know, old buddy boy, how some people, especially an Episcopalian like myself, feel about the general Irish. Goddamn famine and all that. Eating the green grass by the side of the road when they were tossed out of their hovels. Dying like flies. And ever since, that terrible stuff has been engraved, so to speak, on their behavior. And going after the main financial chance is the Irish ethic. They'd do anything to get their hands on money."

"I resent that aspersion also. My parents honestly sweated and slaved so that they could give their children a decent, honest upbringing."

"Okay. Okay. Steve, I don't mean you. You're the lace-curtain variety. I'm just giving a whole bunch of hypotheticals. But I always assumed you were on easy street."

"Well, I'm not."

"Hey, we're still good old friends, ole pal, aren't we. And are going to stay that way and not let somebody else's unbelievable riches come between us. Gosh almighty, meeting someone like you in the navy, out of about three thousand men aboard ship with whom I had no mutual cultural interests or who even knew who Shakespeare was, nearly saved my life. I would have gone nuts, which, I don't mind admitting I nearly did pretend I was for a while, hoping for a medical discharge. And remember, you did save my life. I could have been beaten to death after that big crap game when that son of a big bitch lost that fortune, thinking I was using loaded dice, when all it was was that I was just lucky, like I usually am. Here, old pal, let's top up the old tea and have another scone."

"I'll have another scone. I may need money, and have a desire to have funds, but I'm not a fortune hunter nor am I ever going to sue anyone for their money."

"Of course you're not, friend. Who knows better about something like that than me. Who said anything like that, anyway. It's not your fault that with your mother-in-law there's big money, with millions and millions around. And I apologize if I sometimes sound cynical. But you just name where it's warm and culturally pleasant and boy, you find out they got a place there."

"Well from my it seems limited informed knowledge, I only know of two."

"Pal, well then you don't know. There's an estate in Palm Beach. Apartments in Paris and Rome. I know for sure there's a house on the Riviera. Ranches out west, Utah, Oklahoma. Even a big section of Montana. They got something going even in Alaska."

Unless old Maximilian Avery Gifford is acting in a deranged manner, with dreams of another's untold grandeur, a brand-new bombshell exploding. The suffocating smell of cordite. Holy cow. Old Dru from being rich to now being unbelievably rich. How rich is unbelievable. Bigger than the largest mountain. The gold hidden deep in a secret cavern underneath. Fall helpless into the soft-cushioned abyss of another's affluence. As lethal as it could be luxuriously sweet. In which one could suffocate in the sickly fumes of the most fragrant perfume. To get my moral, if not physical ass broken and my dignity mangled. But I suppose could also make fainter the echoing sound of Sylvia's jeers. I should have realized the vast dimensions of her contempt when she would say things like "Hey, you're going to be wiped out with an obscurity so great and complete, you simply didn't exist." Well, that may be so, except now I'm at least in good company, along with maybe the richest woman in America.

"Hey, old pal, I can see I'm subjecting you to discomfort. What do you say we change the subject."

"I already thought I had indicated to change the subject."

"Sure. So let me ask. You're still at the old composing, Steve."

"Yes. It so happens."

"What are you working on now, maestro."

"Do I assume you're really interested to know."

"Of course I am, old buddy boy, Steve."

"Well, I am composing a minuet."

"Hey that's great. Really great. I don't know what the

hell a minuet is. But I mean, it must be tough on the old mental process."

"Well, I suppose it contains passages which in experimenting with a jazz cadence and blues motif, might be thought daringly modernistic. I'm also considering working on an operetta. Putting together music with overtones of the Civil War, songs like 'Loreno' and tunes reminiscent of that awful conflict."

"What about 'Marching Through Georgia,' pal."

"Although I am against the concept of slavery, I've got to say I am on the cultural side of the gentlemen of the Confederacy and all their descendants and that particular piece of music."

"Well, pal, that march was sure admired by the North."

"As were many people who were scoundrels and despots during the Civil War."

"You said it, pal. But in your chosen profession, don't musical matters take precedence over things like geographic patriotic partiality."

"Yes they should, but not cause anyone pain or aggrievement. Such as the spiritual wonderment which can be obtained from hearing a thousand voices thundering out, singing from the very bottom of their gladdening hearts."

"Jesus, pal. You really do don't you, feel strongly and take your work seriously."

"Yes, I apologize for my showing sentiment like this."

"Pal, only a true man has courage to show his tears. Here, a handkerchief clean-laundered. That's what I always admire about you guys who create. And gee pal, let me say it sincerely. No one can say you ain't got virtuosity. And I know one day when your name is up there with the greats, I'll be bragging saying I knew you. But hey. Just coming down to earth for a second, I mean, are you going to make any goddamn money out of tinkling the old ivories. I mean real money."

"There is an answer to that. Short and not so sweet. The answer is no."

"Well, that's honest. But hey, gee pal, that could be tough. I guess you could if there's no crunch and there comes a sort of reconciliation, lean a little bit financially on Sylvia."

"I'm not going to lean financially upon anybody."

"Well from my recent point of view, old pal, that's goddamn sensible. And you know old friend, in the matter of being honest, as much as I love this great country of ours, I'll be damned if I approve of the kind of women it's producing these days. Maybe it's just as well two good-looking, personable guys like us didn't get mixed up in marriage forever with two old lesbian witches skulking around us for the rest of our lives. God forbid we should have also ended up having children. What's the matter, pal. Did I say something wrong."

"No. But I have feelings. My marriage was important. Sylvia's life is her own to do with what she will, and I'm not going to judge her. Even though she thumbed her nose at me and my music."

"Well sure, okay friend, having got that off your chest. And I guess we've had a real heart-to-heart talk here, which in a small way indicates what we do in mapping out a little bit of the future of our lives. I mean, we can't go repeat what stupid stuff we did in the past. I got a couple of good little old clubs up there on Central Park. In one of them you can play squash and chess and swim in the same building and while you sleep, get your suit pressed, shirt laundered, missing buttons sewn on, then drink and eat, play billiards and then go bowling. Wait, that's not all. You repair to the sportsman's bar. You order a beer, sign a chit. About just before six o'clock, two chefs appear in the bar and on a couple of big tables they've got a baron of beef and a massive ham and bowls of gravy and slices of various breads. At your request, they carve off slabs to your delectation. Gratis and entirely on the house. And you come back for more if you want. I mean goddamn well free of charge. So if you're short of a couple of bucks, you don't have to go out to a Horn and Hardart, and you're fed for nothing. What about the sound of two big slabs of the best roast beef gracing a plate. Rare and swimming in great gravy and on rye bread. How about that I propose you for membership, old buddy."

"It doesn't sound like I could afford it."

"Hey, you can afford to keep in good physical shape while everybody else is falling apart in this town. Hey friend, I can advance you the initiation fee. Then when you're squared away why not the two of us look up some of these charity benefit affairs where they have cotillion dances. I mean, hell boy, get out there. Meet some new women. Anticipation is the spice of life, old fella. I joined one of those smaller clubs they got over there on the Fifth Avenue side of the park. We got to live for ourselves for a change and get something more than we've been getting out of life. Let's not kid ourselves. We've been ditched. At least I have, by the richer, the higher and mightier. Even so, and even if we go half nuts in this town, what's stopping us still wearing the mast of sanity. I mean, God, did you see the whole front page of the goddamn paper, some guy waving a knife, looking to kill someone he said was inside a house on Fifth Avenue, right by the club I joined."

"Yes, I saw that. It's an outrageous disgrace."

"Well old buddy boy, we've been really having a philosophical talk. Just like we used to do those off-duty times half-going Asiatic out there in the Pacific. And you know pal, just between you and me, I sometimes think what a damn fool I've been. I had a good ole heiress girl-friend from childhood in Chicago I could have tied the knot with. They had an estate right on the lake shore, her family had a big engineering business. Straight away I could have slotted in somewhere near the top. Isn't that the problem being a damn fool. And the solution. It's simple. Stop being a damn fool. Right."

"Max, I think you're right."

"I know I'm right. I still got some good connections from out Chicago way and my club out there. But leave your options open and be ready is my motto. Here. I'm going to go right now and break out a bottle of the pretty decent champagne I got waiting right in there in the refrigerator. A little bit of the old Charlie Heidsieck. You'll take a glass of the good old bubbly."

"Yes, I should enjoy and very much like to."

"Attaboy. Only thing wrong in this apartment is, with no room in the kitchen, the decent-size refrigerator I need, I've got to keep out here in the living room. Tomorrow's Saturday. No goddamn office in the morning. Hell, why don't we just go out and celebrate in this city where they keep bragging that they got the world's tallest building. That Chicago is one day, I promise you, going to end up building. Let's go uptown over there to the old Waldorf or even better the old Biltmore, where they keep the women out of the gentlemen-only bar, and knock back a few. All on me, pal. Find a couple of bimbos for ourselves. I feel better already. Boy, it's sure nice to see you again, pal. Untwist the old wire on the champers. Pop the old cork. Take these two tulip glasses I got polished ready and waiting and fill them up. Put the bottle in an ice bucket. Here we go. Your good health."

"Thank you. Thank you very much. And to your good health, friend."

"Steve, get yourself a couple of good shotguns made, old buddy boy. Some tweeds. Plus twos. Plus threes. I'll tell you the name of a good tailor over there in London on Savile Row. British quality is what you want these days old bean. Like my Bentley four-and-a-half-liter Tourer, vintage 1930, I got sitting over there on Eleventh Street in a garage. Drove it, the top down, the breeze blowing through my hair, all the way from River Oaks Houston to New York. Nicest two weeks ever had in my life. Have me a big steak and few beers every night. Talk with the townsfolk. Always be the volunteer fire department guys sitting around bullshitting outside their fire station. Went via New Orleans—what a town, boy, for some pretty pleasant evil, if that's what you're looking for. Then north through Vicksburg, Memphis, Nashville, then detoured a little south again to Chattanooga. Now there's a decent little old town. Had a couple of names and addresses with me. And, without repercussions, holed up with a nice little ole gal from Knoxville. What a gal. From a damn good family. She wanted to tag along. But I was traveling light. Now that I think of it I should have let her. But sent her back home on a train before heading across those Appalachian Mountains to Lynchburg, then on to Baltimore, Philadelphia, New York. Now how do you like that, isn't that champagne really something."

"Hey Max, the champagne is really wonderful."

"Well old bean, I also got me laid down some good old port with a London wine merchant over there."

"Max, as much as I should like to adapt to this quality-first manner of living, I think I got to wait a brief while with these kind of plans. I can't even afford to buy new underwear or socks."

"Steve. Come on. I already told you. The way I used to wangle things for you in the navy. What's mine is yours."

"I don't believe in fact, you did say that."

"Well, close enough to it. Jesus, three years we were chess- and bridge-playing pals out there in the Pacific where death could always be in the next second. Lobbed at you from the other side of the horizon. But boy, when we lobbed back with our little ole sixteen-inchers, they went off, *wham, wham, wham.* Nothing was as beautiful as that bright orange cloud of pure fulmination coming out of the muzzles of those guns. We have all that in common. I want you to feel you've got a true friend."

"Well Max, putting aside the gunnery, chess and bridge a moment, let me attest to your always having been a steadfast ally."

"Okay. Before it knocks us, let's between us knock this city for a loop. It's the weekend, pal. Know what I mean.

A loop. A goddamn loop. I don't mean overexert ourselves pleasure seeking. Just flow with the more felicitous tide. Come on. Down the old champers. Here, have a couple more pretzels and let me refill your glass. Gee it's good to see you and bring back a few ole memories. Let's you and me drive up Madison Avenue in my old Bentley."

Excusing myself to take a piss, I passed through Max's bedroom. Hung along the wall on a clothesline were at least fifty silk ties. And on the floor at least twenty pairs of shoes in shoe trees.

Now dressed to leave, Max beneath his dark blue blazer, buttoned closed with large silver buttons, sported a crimson silk cravat adorned with black dots and stuck with a gold pin. Max surely was a picture to behold in his racing green Bentley. Yellow plaid cap on his head, goggles shielding his eyes as he smiled over the motorcar's great long bonnet, as he called it. The chromework polished, gleaming. Headlights like two large bulging eyes. The massive engine throbbed into life. And open to the balmy breezes, we drove past Washington Square. This motor vehicle so perfectly fitting the setting of this terrace of redbrick and limestone-trim houses.

"Hey pal, isn't this beautiful. All in wonderful harmony. Where people must have once lived in dignity and must have peacefully gone about their business out their doors with cane and spats to take constitutionals in the park, without some-goddamn bastard conducting a hold-up, poking a goddamn gun or knife in their ribs."

Max was right. It reminded one of more peaceful times and of the costumes and musical glory of opera. But such visions of grandeur were shattered on reaching Union Square as we motored north on Broadway. Stopping for a red light. A barefoot black man sitting on the step of a bank, brushing the demons away, his other hand searching in his pocket. Legless beggars on roller-skate platforms. Political literature for sale suggesting agitation and protest. Racks of cheap garments in the emporiums for the poor and dispossessed. A shopping mart with six pairs of socks for fifty cents. But Max impervious to the downtrodden. Racing the great engine, hooting his horn as we turn up Broadway to Madison Square and head up Madison Avenue. Max singing out to the street the "Whiffenpoof Song."

"We are poor little lambs who have lost our way. Bah, bah, bah."

Pulling up in front of the Biltmore Hotel. Depositing ourselves out of the Bentley. Max peeling off a couple of dollars from his thick bankroll to give the doorman. "Park right here, sir." A blind man kneeling nearby upon a rug on the sidewalk and playing the saxophone. A passage from Haydn's Horn Concerto No. 1 in D Major. Executed with a degree of distinction. Shudders the heart to come upon such accomplishment and such impoverishment.

Old Max seemed neither to see the poor gentleman nor to hear me drop a quarter coin *clank* into his tin cup as the musician murmured, "Thank you."

"Hey come on pal. Don't dawdle."

Max behaving as if it were his own private hotel announcing as he led me in a tour of its grandiose lobby that it was the Democratic party headquarters, pointing out the drugstore, the barbershop, beauty salon, travel bureau, florist, ticket agency, Turkish bath, cocktail bar, and, with a bow, inviting me to survey the splendor of the Palm Court. He seemed specially to be taken with an elegant brass clock. Two semiclothed figures stretching upward to support the round white dial. Max breaking out a couple of cigars.

"Here pal, have a Bolivar. Now pal, right here, right under this clock, is where people for better or worse, meet and make their assignations."

Max guiding me back to the door to the "Men Only" bar. The wood-paneled room hung with oil paintings. Its comfortable red leather chairs. We sit up at the bar on stools, elbows on the shining mahogany. Tinkle of ice. Three other drinkers in the dim light. Two with their newspapers. The other in silent attendance, staring out over his drink into empty space. It's said it's a place where some men come to be in solitude to delay catching the train back to their wives and children. Or decide not to go at all.

"What can I do for you, gentlemen."

Crew-cut bartender in his white jacket and bow tie attending and smiling upon this customer Maximilian Avery Gifford, who was puffing his cigar and who could pass, if this were a Saturday evening, for a rah-rah boy just arrived back at Grand Central after a college football game. At first nonplussed to be asked for a war-vintage bottle of Pol Roger champagne.

"Well sir, I don't believe I know of that brand or if we have that available."

"Well we're just a couple of old buddies celebrating a bit of a reunion and it sure would be nice if we had the appropriate grape to do it with."

The bartender gently humored by Max, and adjusting his bow tie, warming to his task, instituted a search down in the cellars of the hotel. Old Max ready to award those who give cheerful service, smiling his appreciation and putting his foot up on the bar rail, waiting with perfect patience over his vintage soda water and relighting his cigar which had gone out while reciting the minutiae of our surroundings.

"Hey, old pal, didn't I tell you it was really something. Known to its customers as 'the sanctum.' Oyster stew, roast beef, sirloin steak, and apple pie. Four dollars at lunchtime, seven dollars and fifty cents at night. You see, old pal, this is where a guy could get away somewhere in peace on his workdays. Boy, I could have used a refuge like this back in ole Houston. To take a breather from the thoughtless, monumental, selfish meanness of that ole gal when she wanted to be mean. And over such goddamn trivial things. Impulsive irrationality was her middle name. Spoiled rotten by her father especially. Lavished every goddamn thing she ever wanted on her. I don't think there was, but there were times you could almost think something funny had been going on there. She cleaned out everything she could, even the least little trinket or piece of crap of mine. Then poured gasoline on two of my best English suits and burned them up in the barbecue. Even mangled my tie pins. Gee, she sure wasn't like the same girl you met back in my little ole apartment on West Thirty-fourth Street."

"Here we go, gentlemen. As ordered. Pol Roger, vintage 1947, which I am told was a superlative year."

The bartender deadly serious with his success, producing the bottle of Pol Roger champagne just beginning to gather dust. From the second year of peace after the war. Of three the hotel had left. Ten minutes to wait to chill. Glasses filled. Max ordering another bottle to be on the way and chilling and raising his present glass in a toast.

"Old pal, down the hatch. And to the future. And why don't I now do a little organizing of your life for you. I sort of got a real goddamn beauty on the go right at this moment. A hatcheck girl in a good restaurant. But that's only temporary work for her while she's between modeling jobs. Used to be an air hostess. I know she's got a couple of good-looking friends. What do you say I take us all on a double date. Come on, next Saturday. Motor uptown in the old chariot. We'll have a workout together at the Athletic Club, play some squash and then dine in one of the most beautiful dining rooms in all of New York. From the eleventh floor looks right out and over the whole of Central Park."

"Max, I don't know right now. I might have enough on my plate for the moment as it is."

"Pal, don't miss opportunities. All you got to do is date the right girls and go to the right places."

"Well I sure don't mind knowing who the right girls are and what are the right places."

"Well, it's obvious. We'll smell around a little in the *Social Register*. I know a few names and that little old volume got the telephone numbers listed. And even where some of these little old gals, the daughters, are matriculating at college."

"Are you sure, Max, these matriculating girls at college are the best people."

"Hey come on pal, don't be obstructionist and a killjoy. And hey, and I don't want to overcome you with flattery, old buddy boy, but you got what it takes. Charm. Talent. And let's face it, how many people take you for a lighter shade of old Rudolph Valentino. Look where his looks got him. There's a chance for everybody. I've seen the girls turn around to look when you go by. Hey, what about you take up a modeling career. Get your picture in the magazines."

"Max, I'm a composer."

"Sure, I know that. But the real facts are that this is a rough, tough city for artistically dedicated people. Unless you're one of the lucky. Those who can fall back on big money and coast along on their enormous private incomes from inherited wealth. But nothing is stopping you, old buddy boy, from keeping your music composing going on the side. But now like me, you're a free agent. Or at least I'll remain one till they clamp me in alimony jail. Which if they do, that's where I'll stay. No kidding. You can be treated pretty well in there. I don't see why I should have to support a previous poor wife and now on top of it a rich divorced wife. And buddy boy, I haven't told you the whole story yet. But I will after another bottle of ole Pol Roger champagne from down in this good hotel's cellars. Pal, this is the champagne old Winston Churchill drank winning the goddamn war when the sirens of the air raids were wailing over London and the goddamn bombs were falling. When the spirit of the British people was being severely tested. Ah, and here we go with this next bottle. Hold up your glass. Attaboy. Drink a toast. Hey bartender. Have a glass. Hey, we're having a goddamn reunion. It must be getting to be at least five goddamn years after the end of the war. A toast to the U.S. Navy. Anchors now, goddamn away. You see, pal, someone in this city cares. To your good health, sir."

Max sending a second drink down to the gentleman at the other end of the long oval bar, who was staring out into space but who now smiled, raised his glass, and said, "Skol" back up at Max, who toasted him in return. Max was getting gently merry. And as he did so, attempting as one remembered from the navy, to become a comedian and insisting with a sudden English accent that the barman join us in yet another toast.

"I say there, my good chap. It's time off from hard work. This time a toast to my good buddies and my buddy here next to me, who served on the old *Missouri*. That's right, fifty-seven thousand five hundred tons slicing through the waves at thirty-five knots. Go through a hurricane like a knife through butter. And those nine sixteen-inch guns, *bam, bam*, with my pal here in the turret, could hit a floating orange crate the other side of the horizon at a range of twenty-two nautical miles. Ain't that right, ole pal."

"That's right, Max, you've got the range perfectly."

"You know pal, old buddy, boozing and even the pain of a hangover floats one's spiritual ship away from the real shit's creek for a while. Remember that ole liberty we had ashore with that couple of great ole gals from Goucher, big old nights in that big ole mansion in Baltimore. Roast duck dinners. Champagne flowing. And the night we went with those gorgeous gals to see the play *Christmas Season* with Ethel Barrymore."

"Yeah, I remember, Max. It was New Year's. And I kissed the girl I was with while we sat on the stairs."

"Boy, Steve. Yeah and you were giving her a big line you were a poet and she asked you if you were going to keep up your bantering of clichés indefinitely. But the music was playing, streamers, mistletoe. That was a good old couple of nights. Boy, I guess as for women, one man's meat is another man's poison and one man's poison is another man's meat. And like the guy announced at the neighborhood jamboree, 'Welcome, folks. Everyone gets a feel at the community chest, provided, ha ha, you don't keep your hands to yourself.' Now before we pull up our own little anchor, let's sing a song. A good old naval song."

"Tell your troubles to Jesus
The Chaplain has gone over the stern
And is floating away
On the waves"

Max's eyes were glistening with tears. It was hard to imagine how someone could have become so fond of the navy and the smell of vomit from seasickness that could pervade the ship in heavy seas. And the bells and tannoy. "Now hear this." And general quarters in the middle of one's sleep, jumping down out of a bunk and into one's battle gear. And reminding as could happen ashore in a barracks bunk, that if your testicles were dangling, you could leave them caught behind in the wire springs as you jumped. Of course, Max as a yeoman shifting papers, could and did wield a shipboard power that could help or hinder. And he did indeed smooth one's life more than somewhat. And here he was, the same old pleasant friend, optimistic, smiling and peeling off bills from his wad to give the attentive bartender a tip and reminding me of my ineptitude with this girl, accusing me of practicing social small talk and sophistry.

"Now there you go, my good man."

"Thank you sir. Hope we will see you again soon. Pleasure to serve you. The Biltmore 'Men Only' is open from eleven A.M. till midnight Monday through Friday."

Max peeling off further notes to pile on the astronomical check, and leaving the bartender an astronomical tip, on which I could have survived a month. Out in the lobby, Max pausing to make a general announcement to the evening clientele checking in.

"Welcome folks, to this famed good ole hotel. And a damn good hotel it is too. They got bottles of Pol Roger in the cellar. But we drank it all. Sorry about that."

Max waving good-bye and clicking heels and bowing to an amused arriving lady, sweeping her way up the steps as a figure at the check-in desk turns, smiling.

"Damn good champagne, sir."

"And you sir, know your champagne just as ole Winnie did."

Max taking up again his so-oft-sung old naval tune, his attempt at dulcet tones and phrasing fading through the somber carpeted peace of the Palm Court. His voice wasn't that bad, but nothing like old Enrico Caruso who once upon a time at the Met was a star attraction in this town.

"So nice to see you again, sir."

"Well me and my pal here are having a jolly good time in your jolly good hotel."

"Well sir, if I can be of any assistance at any time, may I then give you my jolly good card."

"Jolly good."

The assistant manager giving Max his card, we were now in the nicest possible way being gently encouraged out of the Biltmore. But there was no doubt that his slight affectation of being English smoothed Max's way. Bows and scrapes to Max joyously asmile at the door as he stopped to lift up the flap of his blazer and dig into the trouser pocket of his gray flannels to pull out his ever-ready roll of bills. Steps aside to hover over the saxophone player, now rendering a work of Charles Gounod's later years, a passage from the *Petite Symphonie* in B-flat Major.

"Here we go, old maestro, ole buddy. Better I stick this for you in your breast coat pocket in case someone tries to steal it out of your little ole cup and dish you got there. Five dollars for the good music, my friend. And for your dedication shown to your chosen profession. Because along with me here is my old composer pal, who says you play that charming work with verve and distinction, rendering it in a witty manner and although I don't know what in God's name the hell he's talking about, it is truly soothingly good for the spirit to hear."

Despite his "ole pal, buddy" behavior, one felt a strange degree of comfort to be again in Max's company. That somehow could dignify and add aplomb to one's life as he chose what had to be stylish, if discreet, public places to visit in this city. And far from the atmosphere sometimes felt in the Automat, where more than a few of the customers, who trying to make a cup of coffee out of the dregs of everybody else's cups, sat huddled over their desperate hopes to stop them fading into dying dreams. Not all in one's life had to be doom, deprivation, and damnation. And Max encouraged one to think that despite the ending of our marriages, there still remained a purpose in our lives. To get the hell up and back out of the doldrums caused by women. And it was much rewarding to my own spirit to witness Max helping out a fellow musician. Plus, I was admitting to feeling a not-unpleasant little bit merry myself.

"Max, I would like to say that you truly are a gentleman."

"Well pal, why not be kind to the wandering minstrel. We're on our way pal, old buddy. Come on. Let's go stop in at the old Plaza. In the Oak Room there resides some of the best elegant dignity this city's still got to offer. And you know, despite the early inroads women have made on us, we're going to grow up into a pair of very rich and successful guys. Hey, what am I talking about. You're already hobnobbing with old Drusilla, ain't yuh, boy."

"Max, I'm not hobnobbing with anyone."

"Hey boy, believe me, you could have it made. Money to burn. Get yourself some good guns over there in Mayfair. Holland and Holland, to be precise. What's more important than shooting and fishing. Serious gentleman's work. The two most essential pursuits in a man's life. And you know, this composing of yours, now that I understand it a little bit, I'm all for it. I have kind of got to like in you that quality the general public refers to as an 'artistic temperament.' Now you take that ole guy Ludwig Beethoven's life. Wasn't pain, debilitation and deafness, providing the background for his best work. Like tonight good ole champagne is providing the background for our reunion evening. And we're on our way to contribute a little something more to it. And look at this guy the saxophone player over there, down on his luck. Can't see the notes he's playing or a goddamn thing. Faces goddamn blackness in his life. But yet produces beautiful music."

The doorman opening the Bentley door and with a

whisk brushing the floor and with a cloth wiping the seats. Max climbing on the running board, smiling about him as people pass, admiring this machine. And ready to start the engine, turning to bow his head back to the hotel with suddenly a look of consternation overcoming his face.

"Hey, wait a second, Steve, did you see that. God-damn. Holy good goddamn. Hey look. That son of a bitch the saxophone player. I have a good mind to take the goddamn five dollars back. Took it out of his goddamn pocket and was looking at it. Son of a bitch can see as good as you or I. Boy, if that don't half-take the cake and make you lose your faith in people."

Max putting on his driving goggles and helmet, slam-ming his foot down on the accelerator and the four and a half liters of engine pulling away with a gnashing of gears and explosive exhaust. Horn honking out into and up Madison Avenue and past men's emporiums of fashion. And already doing fifty miles an hour before we reached a red light several blocks north at Forty-seventh Street. Max's conversation turning back as it did these days, to the war days as we sailed forth farther north to Fifty-ninth Street.

"You know pal, an incident like that phony blind musician would remind you of that old motto you heard recited on board ship in the navy. When you find a friend who is good and true, fuck him before he fucks you."

People's heads turning to look as the great machine

155

throbs by and with a squeal of tires and one bumping up over the cub, turns into Sixty-fifth Street.

"Remember that old apartment pal I had in the Garment District. I was kind of goddamn glad to get out of there. And glad too, I took over the lease at Waverly Place from Ertha when we went to Houston. I said 'Let's keep it, nice to have a bolt-hole in New York.' Boy, prophetic words. And you know pal, the truth of the matter is coming out. I would have liked to have a good marriage and children like my own parents. Guess you must feel the same. But I'll be goddamned if I'm going to throw away my life again on some goddamn woman who has no personal principles. Christ, you remember that sinking when all the guys were clinging to rafts out in the Pacific and just waiting to be eaten by sharks one by one. Jaws tearing off a leg and coming back to tear off another, some guys torn in half."

"Gee Max, the war's over. What do you say we kind of get on another subject."

"Sure, pal, no problem. But it's just how I feel sometimes. But there, right there, we're passing the external architecture of my other club. There it is, pal. In that nice Georgian mansion building. That's where you go where you can sit with a good old bourbon and branch water. Absent yourself from the world and all the stress and strain and be at peace with yourself in the collectively discriminating atmosphere you can enjoy with the kind of good ole boys they got as members. Take you to dinner there sometime. You'd like it. Now we'll give this little old four and a half liters something to make noise about right down Fifth Avenue."

The big motor turning down Fifth. Past the steps down to the zoo. And slowing outside another redbrick mansion on the corner where a policeman stands on guard. Max swerving and horns honking as he drives, ushering the Bentley to a halt at the Plaza Hotel under the elegant ornateness of its porch. Max taking off his goggles and helmet and along with a five-dollar bill, enough to rescue me from penury, handing them to the doorman. Climbing the steps, stopping at the top and with his sense of occasion, bowing to the fountain across the street. Following him into the lobby and past the Palm Court's marble pillars and potted plants, a piano tinkling a Strauss waltz. More marble along a corridor of jewels. Display cases of diamonds, pearls, emeralds and rubies gleaming behind the glass. And into this somber paneled interior. A romantic mural of Central Park behind the bar. By a window, Max inviting me to take a seat at a table and stretching out his legs and proferring and then lighting a cigar. Puffing out the smoke as he adjusts his purple silk handkerchief in the breast pocket of his blazer. A waiter hovering near.

"Krug, my good man. Krug. Vintage 1947 would be appreciated. A bottle."

"Coming right up, sir."

"Now Steve, did you hear that. No ifs ands and buts. But 'Coming right up.' Well pal. Here we are. And I particularly like the Umbra. And you see, old bean, a first-class place, a first-class waiter and exactly what we want on its way."

"Max there is little doubt that this is ambience of the highest order but this is going to be three bottles of champagne."

"It's four in fact, pal. But who's counting or cares if you're just that little bit inaccurate. And goddamn. Here we are back at the old Plaza. Where we're going to go get something to eat soon in the subfuscus somberness of the old Oak Room. But bloody hell, whenever I think of that goddamn phony blind musician, it gets my goat."

"And I don't mind telling you Max this is really a totally wonderful way to spend an evening, never before having set foot in this most attractively sumptuous place. Nor I suspect shall I ever afford to be able to do so again. And especially to be able to get tipsy on champagne."

"All my pleasure, pal. That's why I was a little miffed about that girl with real smart brains called Joy. And she wasn't giving you much Joy in return for all that bullshit you were giving her. But old buddy, for all your ole highfalutin flowery bullshit of the past, it really is good to see you. And be encouraged by a remark you just made about music. And you know the one thing I always have admired you for was your goddamn downright honesty. Remember aboard ship that's how we met. You found my wallet in the head. Dropped out of my pants while I was taking a crap and left it behind on the deck. You wouldn't even take a reward. Or tell me your name. Took a dickens of a time checking all over the ship to find you again to really thank you."

"Well Max, at least for the time being, I appreciate your turning me into a saint."

"No problem, friend. No problem, believe me."

Delighted waiter smiling, lifting bottle from its ice bucket, displaying the label, dark crimson and gold: KRUG & CO, REIMS, PRIVATE CUVÉE EXTRA SEC. Slowly filling glasses with this saffron-hued effervescing liquid as Max holds his goblet up to the streetlight out the window and toasts the waiter.

"Here's to you, good gentleman. Your swift expertise and to the year 1947. And to my composer pal Stephen O'Kelly'O, right there across the table, popping a peanut in his mouth. And you know pal, how you can get pressed down into the deepest dumps and depression, and talking or nobody or nothing can get you out of it, and then you make a break for it. Get in touch with an old pal. Get the old Bentley out. And like the little bubbles do from the bottom of this glass, the gloom

159

lifts from the spirit. And while it does old buddy, just let me give you a little more idea of the whole story, pal. The sons of bitches down there in Houston are trying to get a case together to charge and sue me for embezzlement."

"Gee Max, embezzlement."

"Yeah. Imagine."

"That's pretty serious."

"Yeah, it is, old pal. No one likes to be accused of cooking the books in old spaghetti sauce. Said I married Ertha for her money. I mean, all right, it was an incentive if other negative things were strongly taken into consideration. But you'd admit pal, that she stood out fairly well in the competition and I might have married her for herself. A damn attractive girl. Wouldn't you admit it."

"Yes I would, Max."

"But then they said I was planning to forge Ertha's signature on checks. And friend, the trouble is, it's true, I did practice writing her autograph. I collect the goddamn things. Even the old captain's of the ole *Missouri*. I mean, handwriting has long been my well-known goddamn hobby to study for Christ's sake. She caught me—her words, not mine—as I sat there in my monogrammed silk pajamas at dawn one morning in the library, and looking over my shoulder, when I thought she was still upstairs asleep in bed. That's the kind of subterfuge I had to contend with, tiptoeing downstairs in her bare feet and sneaking up behind me as I nearly had a whole page covered with autographs. I was comparing copies I had of President Roosevelt's and Harry Truman's. But about ten times, I had written hers. All right, I knew it was an ill-advised crazy thing to do. But it wasn't because I was in any way desperate and trying to do anything underhanded. It was because she had such crazy illegible handwriting. Which I thought would be impossible to imitate. It ended up I could write her signature better than she could. And who knows, she could have become incapacitated or something, broken her wrist or gone gaga in her old age. I mean, if she couldn't speak, who was going to translate her handwriting. I mean, Christ, how many times in the navy did I have to end up doing that, executing a favor for the deserving."

"Gee, Max, have you got a lawyer."

"Sure. But even to get falsely accused of such a thing in the kind of confidential trusted work I do in a prestigious brokerage house. It's like they're blackmailing me."

"Max, stand fast."

"Pal, I sure am. But I got to stay loose, too. Options open, keep on the move. Motto is, don't dawdle, don't delay. If I had, not that long time back, I could have been killed. Or maybe the better word is *murdered*. Right at the front gates of the old house in Houston, which in fact had only just been built. We're driving out to a black-tie dinner party in the sky blue convertible Cadillac her father bought us as a wedding present. Or correct that. Bought *her* as a wedding present. The gates are closed when usually they're always kept open. She didn't want to spoil her finery so I had to get out of the car to open them. And then as I was loosening the latch I happened for some reason to turn around. You could hear the car's back tires sending pebbles up into the sky and Ertha behind the wheel, in the driver's seat and the goddamn car less than twenty feet away seemed like it was already doing fifty miles an hour as it came at me. I jumped, and *wham,* she hit those gates not only open but flattened them right off their hinges of solid steel and the car shot right out into and across the road and ended up on the front lawn of the big mansion across the street. And gave the poor old ornery bastard who lives there a permanent fibrillation, he claims, of the heart."

"Gee Max. I mean couldn't it all have been accidental."

"Yeah, that's what she said—her high heels slipped off the clutch or something. Except that an heiress's butler with whom she was having an affair and who was supposed to be trying to embezzle and blackmail her, was killed like that just a few months before. Plus, the goddamn Austrian cook we had and who I didn't trust, was watching out the window. A whole conspiracy could have been going on. Nearly fell over, I got so sick to my stomach."

"Holy cow, Max."

"Yeah. The cook, sort of a family retainer they had, was on her side. And yeah, holy cow, I started to watch my food. Powdered glass or arsenic or something like that in the soup to flavor it."

"But hey, come on Max. What wife from a good family and reputable ladies college, would want to do to a good-guy husband like you something as seriously heinous as that."

"Who said the family was any good, pal."

"Well, their lives must have been fully financially satisfied out of the petroleum industry. Didn't you tell me her father had an oil find that was so big that when it gushed, they thought it was an earthquake."

"Oil wells can fast go dry too, pal. Happens all the time. So does murder. Because for a start, I carried three-quarters of a million dollars of life insurance with Ertha as the sole beneficiary."

"Holy cow, gee Max, that's an awful lot of insurance."

"Yeah pal, makes you kind of careful of making sure none of your beneficiaries is close behind you as you look down over a cliff into the Grand Canyon. You think you team up in marriage for the greater good. March up an aisle. Bouquets of flowers on the altar. Big grand reception. That's why you didn't get an invitation to the wedding. Made a big fuss. Said you married Sylvia for her money. And I guess it was in honor of my being in the navy that we ended up sailing out of Galveston on a chartered yacht, for the honeymoon. Glamour and glory. But boy, both can be here one second and gone the next. Replaced by an ole starved diamondback someone's put in your car, with its rattles muffled."

"Holy cow Max, do you mean a rattlesnake."

"Yeah pal. Zoologically *Croatlus adamanteus*. It's a little goddamn different to an ordinary rattler, with its massive head and fangs. Big goddamn thing. And what it does when it bites you is give you a hell of a lot less time to live before you die."

"Holy cow, Max."

"You bet. Here, let's replenish our goddamn glasses with the old Krug. Right. But here's what's worse, pal. I learn what's all behind it. I used to go off on the weekends to do a little duck shooting. And I suspected something was going on. One coming weekend, she asked if I was going and how long I'd be away. I said yeah, the usual. I packed up my kit, including a little ole baseball bat and got into the ole Bentley. Now I know this sounds a little like plotting. But I had surveillance sound equipment already laid out in the cellar, where I had it rigged up to the bedroom so I could hear every goddamn thing going on in there. Then conspicuously driving away with a wave and a few beeps of the horn, outside town, I park the old Bentley to be minded by a garage I got friendly with, and I hang around a bit, waiting to head back in a taxi at what

I calculated would be the crucial time after nightfall. I get out down the road a little on foot and reach the house. Then watch through the window. And I'll be goddamned if the son of a bitch wasn't smoking my cigars and the both of them playing my records, dancing for Christ's sake cheek-to-cheek, and goddamn well drinking my port which I had shipped over and laid down from London. Well, I wait till our bedroom light goes on and sneak in and go down into the cellar. There, I'm waiting for the strategic time to arrive while I'm listening on my equipment. Boy, you don't want to hear people talking about you. But at least I knew when the time was right for going upstairs. Sorry to laugh, pal. But goddamn, as I slowly opened the bedroom door, if you could have seen the look on her face, it should have been framed in gold leaf. I had the goddamn baseball bat raised. I was smiling as I tiptoed in. The two of them are naked on the bed and there he is on top of her, humping away and she's struck dumb, looking over his shoulder as I'm approaching with the baseball bat. The timing was perfection. She's more than struck dumb. She can't believe it. He's groaning on the verge while I was on the verge of an inconsolable paroxysm of laughter. His bare ass faster, up and down, up and down as I get closer, bat up higher in the air. Louisville Slugger. I thought, when the hell is she going to scream, 'watch out, Buster.' But she knew that if she didn't give me the opportunity to land the bat across his bare ass, I'd have to cream him one with it right on the skull. Whamo, old friend. Buster was the bastard's real name. But then I'm thinking, maybe she really is struck dumb. Women are unbelievable, aren't they, pal. I think it was kind of turning into a frisson for her. I don't mind telling you old buddy boy, that baseball was my sport. I was sort of a Lou Gehrig in high school. This was my favorite bat. I had held the record for single home runs with it. Gee, it was great. I brought it down on the bastard's ass so hard it must have seemed like a three-thousand-year-old sequoia fell on him. Or that he was having the greatest orgasm in history. Anyway, he was a big son of a bitch and I wanted to be sure both hip joints would be fairly well out of action. Plus, I had brought up my shotgun and had it leaning by the door and had on my cartridge belt full of number-six shells. And just so everyone understood my mood, I took up my ole Holland and Holland and let off one barrel to demolish her dressing table mirror. Ertha let out a sizable ole yelp at that. I marched him out stark naked into the night, under the trees and still with a goddamn erection. But he lost that by the time we got down the drive and out into the street. I had already blown out his car windshield and his four tires to pieces. Told him to walk home. And walked behind him a way. And you could hear me singing the national anthem of Texas loud enough for the neighbors to hear. 'The eyes of Texas are upon you. All the live long day. The eyes of Texas are upon you, you can not get away.' Boy, he sure was one ole poor scared hombre."

"Gee, Max, isn't trying to get you for alimony and embezzlement a little bit anticlimatic, but understandable. I'm beginning to think that my life with Sylvia has really been blissful. Do you think there is anything positive peeking up out of the grim horizon."

"Well pal, I guess instead of life being lifelong all lovely, it can be all hatred. But just to be humanely treated is all one wants from a woman. Who after they dig what they want out of you, leaving you a husk, then desert to go back to being masters of their own fate to maybe go dig something of further benefit to them out of some other poor guy's life. Like in the spider kingdom. But pal, let's let Krug get rid of the present concentration on my insoluble old problems. Here's looking at you, old bean."

Glasses tinkling in yet another toast. And the waiter delivering the remainder of the champagne to the wood-paneled vastness of the Oak Room. The evening clientele collected at the array of white tables gleaming with porcelain and glassware and polished knives, forks and spoons. And where a cheered-up Max and I dined within the somber splendor of its walls. Oysters with the remainder of the Krug and filet mignon, creamed spinach and salad with a booming Burgundy, as Max termed it. To then, as the hour before midnight approached, sacredly address, as Max also termed it, wild strawberries flown in from France and with a fine native whipped American cream to further glorify the tarnished gold glory of Château d'Yquem. My ass even felt a shiver of sympathetic pain that must have been felt by Max's wife's boyfriend as the baseball bat landed. And now on all sides the reassuring voices and faces and the swiveling eyes of those saved from poverty. Even a famed movie actor and actress basking in the furtive attention of all the other diners. And across this vast high-ceilinged room, all were neither sad nor glad knowing they could pay their check for dinner. And like Max, be able to retire to clean sheets to wake up on yet another day to do the same again. But the emotion of the evening taking all the turns and twists of a Tchaikovsky overture. And all I wanted to know was why it was that movie actors and actresses achieved such public idolatry when such should be reserved for the great composers.

"Well pal, I guess none of them get anywhere till they're dead."

"Well Max, guess you're right. Anyway, this is a real fine evening I won't soon or ever forget."

"Pal, that makes me glad. Plus, in this smashingly splendid room is where you belong. Anyway it's an appropriate place from which to contemplate my ending up in alimony jail."

Max raising the golden liquid, a blissful smile across his lips, closing his eyes and placing his nose over the rim of his glass and inhaling.

"Pal, just put your ole proboscis to this pure nectar."

"It sure is, Max. And I'm sure costing a fortune."

"That's what money's for, pal, to aggrandize the spirit by elevating the perception of the senses to pleasure. But not to ignore all the other most important things in life of sentimental value."

"Well Max, while I'm contemplating buying a baseball bat I'm also enjoying this wine and turning over the wisdom of your remarks in my mind."

The first real meal since the evening out with Dru, and famished as I was, I could feel the champagne and wines and now the food bringing back energy flowing through my veins, my body suddenly reviving in a most miraculous way from what seemed a long term of tiredness. And one realized these wisdoms which were of a culinary nature, were profound. And tonight there could be no more triumphant host. But poor Max, even as a high school home-run king, could go down as an embezzler. And through my mind went a flash of dread and then I could hear choral voices singing and a bugle blowing taps at dusk and the Stars and Stripes flowing in the wind as it was being lowered in the breeze and the sad words of "Now the Day Is Over" being rendered. And I felt that Max needed some encouragement and maybe even a suggestion as to where he could run to ground, to use one of his own expressions.

"Max, maybe you need somewhere to be for awhile out of the limelight, so to speak. Maybe back to Chicago where Benny Goodman, the great clarinetist was born."

"Yeah, pal. The feel of being somewhere home would kind of keep the ghost of disquiet at bay. I always remember that while we were still in the navy my greatest fear was not sharks or torpedoes or bombs or Jap kamikaze pilots, but going ashore on liberty with all the pent-up frustration accumulated incarcerated for interminable days belowdecks, behind steel bulkheads at sea and then, for what you think is going to be relief, ending up in some same godforsaken sailor-saturated port where the streets were black in winter with swabbies and suddenly overnight going white when summer uniform was the order of the day. It sure demonstrated a spectacle of regimentation that could end you up getting drunk. And then—and this was my real nightmare—ending up going to a tattoo artist to have a girlfriend's name tattooed with a heart conspicuously on your shoulder or arm, with an arrow stuck through it. Or worse, to be overcome by the drunken temptation to do what old Chief Bosun Mate Lomax did, long before he ever became a chief, who had a tattoo of a fox chased by hounds running to ground right up his anus. I suppose my sense of dignity kept the more undignified seafaring temptations at bay. And you know, old buddy, in a like-minded way, after tonight I don't ever want to see you having to frequent Horn and Hardart or in straitened circumstances having to go sit at the counter of that Nedick's food stand place down in the subway on the middle level at Fifty-ninth Street and Lexington Avenue where I used to incognito go. And where on the bottom level just below, if you wanted to be even more incognito, you could take the BMT to Queens."

"Gee Max, I in fact did occasionally go there and sit."

"Well pal, at least they had the best baked hot dogs, if sometimes a little overcooked for one's liking, but then you could apply plenty of relish and mustard if you wanted to overcome the taste. Boy, in the first few days I got back to New York before I got my job and I was so damn homesick to get back west to Chicago and the Loop, I used to wind up there on the station platform with the feeling I was hiding away from the whole city, hunched at the counter over a coffee bought with next to my last dime. Here, old buddy, a little more of this old Château d'Yquem."

"Max, as much as New York is an unforgiving place, it is heartening to know that this most wonderful wine is here to be found. And I suppose one must presume that even in a harsh urban reality, sometimes humanity and understanding are encountered where you least expect."

"Well, so far, outside of my good ole city Chicago, pal,

I haven't found much understanding and I don't expect to find too much humanity. But I'll fight the good fight against all those who assail me."

An almighty sadness overcame me as Max's muted words of defiance to this city were uttered, that perhaps things were even worse than he had described. And it was strange how the comraderie one had in the navy where you would trust your life, and had to, to a buddy, once back out in the civilian world it was erased. Every man for himself. Disheartening despair appearing on old Max's face, his chin falling forward on his chest. Sudden look of fear flashing across his eyes. My own fears, deeper sown. And always lurking. In the navy, it was the terrible loneliness going ashore on ole liberty and getting drunk in some god-awful place like Norfolk, Virginia, with nothing, as Max said, but sailors everywhere. And with no ship heaving under your feet and feeling homesick and thirsty and just looking for a meaningful way to waste one's time, you could end up getting so desperate that you'd go to the local library, pretending you were literary, to try and proposition the librarian behind a stack of books.

As we left the Plaza there was a little group of admirers around the Bentley as Max made a sidewalk ceremony of donning his helmet and goggles and the heavily tipped doorman opened the Bentley door and saluted. There were more than a couple of cheers as we circled around the Pulitzer Fountain and drove off down Fifth Avenue. Past the great glass display windows of women's jewels, gowns, leathers, and fashion goods. Farther downtown came darker buildings. A man stretched prostrate asleep on the steps of the New York Public Library, its massive elevation looming into the sky. Then the Empire State Building from which a suicide had jumped the day before. Max signaling with a jerk of his thumb.

"Always look upward here, pal, in case someone is coming down."

Back in the Village we went into a basement where they were playing jazz. Sloshing back unidentifiable brandy and dancing with two girls, one of them trying to get Max to take her to Bermuda. The other one accusing us of sounding ritzy and that we were there slumming, until I explained we were two deep-sea divers ashore recovering from the bends. And that Max had dived much deeper than me.

"Hey gee, is it dark down there under the ocean."

"You betcha."

Although the quality of brandy was poor, the music was of a quality of serious musicians. And while the girl danced off with someone else, telling me with her first captivating words that if I wouldn't buy her another drink, she couldn't see any long-term future in my company, I passed my alcoholically influenced compliments to the musicians and was invited to sit at the piano to knock out a few jitterbug beats of my own. Perceiving I had an appreciative clientele, I played a passage accelerando from my minuet and could sense the cascading notes reaching deep into my listeners' guts. My fingers producing fifty lightning notes a second, I knew I might turn the entire nightclub audience into jibbering emotional wrecks as I did once drunkenly sitting at the piano in a previous nightclub while in an animated alcoholic state. And now came a voice over my shoulder.

"Holy Christ, fella, where did you learn to play like that. It sounds like it's a full orchestra."

On the spot I was offered a job by the management playing jazz piano five nights a week at twenty dollars a night and thirty dollars on Saturdays. Nobody wastes time in this city hiring you at a low salary if you're really good at something. But I was turned down when I offered a Saturday evening of Scarlatti.

"Well fella, thank you very much. We don't know this guy Scarlatti, but you think about it, twenty bucks, and call us tomorrow."

But Max was both shouting and clapping, euphoric and unstinting in his applause, his cravat now wound around his head to make him look like a pirate. And it was balm to my ears to hear the previous voice over my shoulder again.

"Hey maestro, I'd sure like to hear the two Scarlatti slow F Minor sonatas, but boy, what was that before you were playing. Beautiful, but wasted on the people frequenting this joint."

It was reassuring to be reminded yet once again that there was always someone somewhere in this city who out of its vast sea of chosen ignorance, would emerge with fine sensibilities to let his intelligent, appreciative voice be heard. And I tinkled the ivories up and down the octaves a couple of more times till the joint closed up at four and it wouldn't be too long before the coming dawn would have the sun blazing up out of the Atlantic Ocean. Max with one of the two girls in tow, at last depositing me on the nonritzy foot pavement in Pell Street. And I somehow had a strange premonition that something terrible could happen to Max in his generous and friendly pursuit of pleasure in this town. The girl's arms hanging around his neck as he shouted, "Hey, here's the scuttlebutt, pal. Next weekend, Sagaponack, out on Long Island. Nude-bathing party in this cute girl's swimming pool. I know her parents who have this kind of nice estate on the ocean. On the way maybe we'll stop off again at the old Oak Room for another bottle or two of Krug."

"Well Max, thanks. I'd like to respond affirmatively to such a distinctive stimulus and high spirits but I may attend upon the prophet and preacher Father Devine's memorial parade up in Harlem."

"There you go pal, eccentric exotic, as always."

"Well, people of an African origin are naturally pos-

175

sessed with a beautiful sense of music sadly missing in the white man."

"Well, we'll talk more about that later, old pal. And hey old pal, hasn't it been some great night. And you were great. And hey what about the naturally possessed sense of philosophy the Chinese have. Hear any good proverbs lately. You're practically living right in Chinatown."

A smell of rancid cheese in the hall increasing as I climbed the stairs. The lock broken on the door. Papers and music sheets strewn on the floor. Chairs knocked over and crockery smashed. Someone in the apartment while I was out. Fear and sadness. Depending upon who it was. Too tired to stay awake to find out or to clean up the mess. Chain the door. Take the carving knife and go fall asleep in the broken bed. Close eyes to the despicable of the world and another vision of discontentment awakes somewhere else in the brain. That Sylvia was having a nightmare next to me as she usually did. Her teeth grinding as they would in her sleep every night. Asking her, Annie, "get me out of hell." Her voice mumbling in the darkness, "Annie," the name of the mother she craved to find. And I woke in a sweat, wiping tears from my eyes, having dreamt the words she said when once, packing to leave on one of her searches and wanting to know when she would be back, she suddenly screamed, "How the hell should I know when. When I want to find my fucking mother. To know what her face is like when she's crying. To know what her face is like when she's smiling. I want to be able to thank someone for telling me where my mother is. So that I can know that I had a mother. And it's none of your fucking business when I'm coming back. Especially to this dump, when you know more people are bitten by other people than they are by rats in this city. Good-bye."

That was one of the doors Sylvia slammed closed between us. Resenting that I knew my mother and had watched her work peeling potatoes in our kitchen for her large family. And in my dream, Dru came. She seemed to be approaching me down the center aisle of St. Bartholomew's Church which suddenly changed to a great lawned vista where now we walked hand in hand toward a glowing marble temple in the distance, choral voices humming to the tune of the taps one had so often gone to sleep by in the navy. Her slender figure swathed in flowing white veils. Small beads of diamonds in bracelets she wore around her wrists and in a many-stranded necklace crisscrossed upon her throat. She said, "Let us two lie down." Her blond shining hair coifed back from her brow. And in my dream, rolling, groaning and grasping at her body. It was a rude awakening from such a dream. For she had just huskily whispered in my ear words that sounded like some hackneyed song. But worthy enough to hear for those extremely hard up.

Lover boy. O lover boy.
Strength of my desire.
Fire of my fire.
Love me some more, lover boy.

But what more could one ask for but to have a reverie of ecstasy about someone whom Max described as one of the richest women in the world. And who, if that a dilemma be, can be accused of no crime but who, in being rid of the struggle to financially survive, might be found far richer in her soul. Yet who, on that evening when the East River was flowing by below us and Brooklyn's lights twinkled in the distance and I played my minuet for her, said she felt haunted by what seemed a curse growing up, which made her, through tragedy and by trusts and wills, richer and richer. Her closest little cousin girlfriend with whom she played, died of scarlet fever. Her father when she was thirteen, got electrocuted by lightning on their private golf course while he was throwing the switch for the sprinkler system. Two years later, her mother was killed in a head-on collision coming around a bend on a coastal road at Cap d'Antibes on the Riviera and her favorite uncle one day later went out on his estate in Virginia and blew his head off with a shotgun. And a more distant relative hearing of the shocking news, then went and stood on railway tracks in front of a train along the Hudson, near a train stop named Camelot. And none of this did Sylvia ever reveal. As if she expected something worse to happen to her.

I couldn't tell Dru my own deeper devastations but I told her my most haunted story of having, as a small boy, to kiss a dead aunt at an Irish wake. And then related about the clairvoyance of one of my closest boyhood friends who lived in an area called Irishtown in a big spooky gray house surrounded by verandas, in the shadow of which we used to sit on rainy days singing songs inside their big chauffeured limousine parked permanently in the drive. And my friend was haunted by his mother who could by telepathy scare the shit out of him wherever he was. Even off somewhere miles away and usually spending money his mother gave him to pay off some urgent bill like his school tuition and which he was spending on our underage drinking pleasure of Tom Collinses in the Astor Hotel downtown, pretending that instead of being delinquents out on a spree we were bigtime playboys. He would, after our first couple of Tom Collinses, always panic and interrupt our philosophical speculation and say he could hear his mother calling him. "Hey," I'd say, "how can you, more than twenty miles away, hear her." "Because," he said, "she knows I've spent the money for my school tuition getting drunk— that's how I know she is calling. And she's going to beat the hell out of me when I get home. Box my ears. That's how I know she's calling." And finally I believed him, because he would disappear into the big gray house with all its verandas shrouded in the trees and I wouldn't see him again for weeks until he would finally appear, thinner, having emerged from incarceration locked somewhere in an attic or cellar, his food passed into him through a flap in the door. And although he never said so, I was certain it was bread and water.

Despite the long night out with Max I felt strangely full of energy this next day, my head slowly clearing. Propping a chair against the broken front door I made a feeble attempt to clean up the apartment but the goddamn cockroaches rushing for cover every time I lifted something up sent me instead with a desperate urge to sit at the piano and compose. My fingers itching to race across the keys and to mark new notes in the manuscript of my minuet. And placing the score in front of me on the piano, I sat in the manner of Rubenstein, fingers poised to lower them on the keys. Then as my fingertips touched, there was a strange silent sensation. No note sounded. I propped open the piano top. And drew in my breath in horror. There inside, except for a few of the heaviest bass chords, were all my piano strings, curled and wound upon themselves and cut and chopped to pieces. And the phone rang.

"Hey, hi. God, I at last got you. I phoned several times yesterday. It's Dru."

"Hello ma'am."

"Stephen, what's the matter. You sound awful."

"Well, I am presently digesting a matter presently assailing my spirits."

"Oh dear. We're not, are we, like two ships passing in the night."

"No ma'am, I hope not."

"Well, my ship's signaling, sending you some semaphore."

"What's it saying, ma'am."

"It's saying, Stephen, you're my sunshine. And I need some badly right at this time."

"Well gee, ma'am, I could do with a little ray or two myself at this time."

"Well in that regard, perhaps you can in two hours meet me."

"Yes ma'am. You bet I can."

"Wait outside the Yiddish Theatre at Seventh and Fifty-eighth Street."

"Sure thing ma'am."

Upon the prospect of seeing Dru, my sense of crushing defeat and abysmal futurelessness wasn't yet totally absolute. But with the unpredictability in one's life rampant, even ole Dru might be getting ready to bust me one right on the kisser. Take that, you inferior impostor. How dare you ill-treat my beloved adopted daughter, and blatantly marry her for her money. Now find a shirt. Something silk and refined. Dress for the occasion. Search amid Sylvia's dozens of discarded brassieres and leotards. Get out my gray flannels. Wear a carefully striped tie of quiet distinction. Select a light green plain sports jacket that I might have last worn on the prep school boat ride. But avoid one that annoyed the school prefect of discipline who said, "Do not. Ever again. Wear that. In this school." And in these garments I will look out of uniform in this part of town. Jam the apartment door closed. Walk out and down this Oriental street to Mulberry and cross over to the West Side. Try to do as I often have tried. Walk away the burden of sadness mile by mile. Step by step. Head up Hudson to Ninth Avenue. Eardrums assaulted by the modern symphony of the flow of backfiring, horn-blowing, gear-grinding trucks and cars. Pass the lunch-rooms, saloons and pushcart vendors. Hoping that as one gets farther away from the cut piano strings, it will ease the pain and drive it out of the soul. And yet, there, just sounded, is a most beautiful bass, base reverberation. The deep throb of a ship's whistle blasting on the river, pulling out of dock. Slow, stern-first to midstream. Faintly hear the echo of the throbbing sound coming back across the Hudson from the sheer rock cliffs of the Palisades. Bound to be one of the great liners off to Europe. Upon which I would so much like to sail. To that older world where the musician and composer can so much better avail of their dignity. Even in Vienna, where the whole audience is waiting to hold you up to ridicule. Ready for even some poor little bastard violinist in the back of the strings to miss a single note or play a wrong one. In order to boo and hiss the whole orchestra. But as things are now I shall never be able to get to that distant but civilized shore. And am instead reminded of the only trips I can afford to take, by the hoots of ferries back and forth to Hoboken, Jersey City, and Weehawken. And in this city, obscurity perpetuates on great men. As they, their fierce fury spent, recluse themselves from the eternal indifference of this city. Somewhere not far from here, Herman Melville was a customs inspector. And no one gave a hoot or cared. In that side street, there is the Straubenmüller Textile High School. And maybe plenty give a hoot and care that it's there. And here I am now in Hell's Kitchen. Where you can never tell if they have, in the back of liquor stores, a policeman crouched behind boxes, a gun in his hand. He waits for a stickup. A cross marked on the bullet so that when fired and hits, he doesn't have to shoot twice. Bang. And the holdup man, a big hole blown in him somewhere, drops dead. Kids roaming the streets with zip guns, firing bullets out of pieces of pipe. Hypodermic needles shooting stuff they buy on the street corner into their limbs to get a few hours of mindless reverie. In this world where the hoodlums abound and where I've been caught frequenting my family's bar, of which no one is allowed to know about or to go to because of the disgustingly undignified things that have happened there. A girl giving a blow job to a drunk customer in a back hall-way leading to the men's room. But where, still under drinking age, I ventured on a few dawn occasions to meet this same girl with a pockmarked face who had to support her out-of-work father and younger brother by giving blow jobs for two dollars. Holy cow, she was like a mil-lionairess on a busy day. And to whom I enjoyed to talk and who told me that she, once on her knees giving a guy a blow job, got socked in the face because he said she was doing such a dirty, disgusting thing, and didn't pay her. And that's how she got her broken nose and spoke so sonorously and told me not to wear a striped tie with a striped shirt. I was for awhile unrecognized till this son of a bitch who didn't pay for his blow job picked a fight and started to call me "pretty boy," and before he could draw his gun, I kicked him in the balls and busted him one in the chops. Bullets later, or knife, or whatever he had, fly-ing, the bartender spirited me out the back door. Soaked to the skin in the pouring rain, I hid in an empty garbage can before I finally got a chance to run away. But nothing now, and no knowledge I have of this city, is lessening the pain. Even here in the Garment District. And only words come to mind that could be construed as pedantic speak, which I repeat over and over. That I utterly utterly con-demn the cruel inhumanity wrought upon me by persons of grievous intent. And I swear I will with every ounce of my one hundred and seventy-six and a half pounds bust into the next century the next rude, inhumane son of a bitch I come across.

Stephen O'Kelly'O climbing shadowy steps up into the bus station. The roar of diesels as these great land cruisers come and go, seeking and returning from destinations. And my own destination only a little more than half an hour left to go. Already suddenly three o'clock in the afternoon. Detour these last minutes away through the bus station. In this endless stream of people. Over the tannoy announcements for distant places. Rochester, Albany, Princeton, Mount Kisco. This man approaches with a sad mystifying look on his face as if all the world's conundrums were all at once being dumped on him, and talks to me as if I were to blame.

"Hey, pass the word. Wrong information is being given out at Princeton."

"Thank you sir, for telling me."

One does not want to expostulate to a perfect stranger and in reply say, as I was tempted to in the good old-fashioned New York vernacular, hey bud, why should I pass the word when I don't give a good goddamn flying fuck that wrong information is goddamn fucking well being given out at Princeton. So shove it up your ass, will yuh. And hey, what's Princeton, some kind of bologna sandwich. But the seemingly crazy individual was much in earnest and said the same thing to the guy walking behind me. Who as it happened, was extremely grateful to

185

hear the information. As I stopped to listen to a brief en-
suing conversation I at least had the pleasant distraction
of focusing my eyes on a girl who was looking at me and
whose quite marvelous face I had just previously caught
as she was passing me by. She was an inspiration of wom-
anhood. And now following her slowly walking in front of
me, her leather coat sweeping about her beautiful legs,
and her long flowing brown hair halfway down her back.
Her calves just as were Sylvia's, splendidly athletic in her
flat-soled shoes. She slowed and suddenly stopped and
turned to me, as if knowing I was behind her. Except for a
sadness in her eyes, her face had an inspiringly healthy
look of an autumn apple just plucked shining at dawn's
early light from a tree in New Hampshire.

"Excuse me, sir. Could you please tell me, sir. Do you
know when the next bus is to Suffern."

"Sorry, I don't know. Only wish I did, to tell you. But
I did hear that wrong information is being given out at
Princeton."

With the vaguely familiar beauty of her face and a
strange pleading in her lovely big pale blue eyes she
seemed to wait for me to say more. Somehow I realized
my facetiousness was inappropriate and I apologized
again. She stood there in my way, her lips seeming to
struggle to speak, moving but silent of words, as if she
wanted me to stay and talk with her and didn't know how
to fully convey the invitation. She must have been aware,

even as I was out of sight walking behind her, and picking up the scent in the air, that I was admiring her. Her eyes searching my face as if for some recognition and somehow asking for companionship which she must have sensed would have been forthcoming. And it would have been. But as it was now getting late to meet Dru, what could I do but apologize.

"I am sorry."

"So am I. And that I'm not going to Princeton."

And I found myself tempted to say I had to rush to meet somebody but to tell me how I could contact her again, an address, a telephone number. But so discouraged she seemed, and before I could ask anymore, her face cast down, she turned away, walking back in the direction from which we had come. Watching her go I was hoping she would come back. For she stopped just as she was about to disappear in the crowd. She turned and looked back at me. With the most shattering look I have ever seen. Her lost-looking eyes, that made you want to run to her. Throw your arms around her. Squeeze comfort, calm, and peace into her soul. And whisper to her that everything was going to be all right.

I was in a dilemma as whether to stay or go. She was, as she turned away, vanishing into the crowd, pausing to reach into her large cloth gypsy bag. And then moved on. The moment gone for all eternity. As I, too, go. Count my steps again. On parade, marching. A cadence forever branded on the mind. Your left, your left, your left, right, left. My mother kept a picture of all her three sons who were in the war at her bedside. Just as she would wait through the night, sitting in the dark on the front sunporch, until all the children who had gone out had come home. The sound of a gunshot. Just behind me. A shiver down the spine. Duck. Hurry another couple of steps out of the line of fire. Waiting to smell the suffocating smoke and cordite, sweat and stench, as if I were back in my ship's turret instead of a bus station. Look around. People gathered. Voices raised.

"Call an ambulance."

"You mean a hearse, fella."

At the edge of the crowd of onlookers, a claw ripping across one's heart. On this concrete floor, amid the filth of gray blots of chewing gum and crushed cigarette butts, there she was. Through the legs of the crowd. The girl with the look of an autumn apple. Fallen to the floor, a pistol in her hand. White bloody bits of brain showing through her long flowing brown hair and blown out all over the little space she lies in. In her wonderful simple clothes. As if she were going to walk the autumnal hills of Vermont as the leaves were turning in their color that she so resembled alive in life. Nothing now but her wholesome beauty prostrate on the ground. Blood spattered everywhere. One outstretched hand. Fingers reaching lifeless at her possessions. A small notebook, a pen, tiny

mirror and ring fallen from her bag. Voices. And my own loudest of all.

"Hey you son of a bitch, put that right back, it belongs to the girl. Or I'll wrap your goddamn guts around your backbone."

Immediate upon death in this city is theft. And her hand reaching as if to cling to that she most cherished, and not till my last-uttered violent words did this bastard put the ring back. Belonging to this girl who in her wandering of this world carried within her little cloth bag of pretty colors all her tiny treasures. Said "Excuse me, sir. Could you please tell me, sir." And she must have been asking how she could ever go from sadness and despair to joy again. And all I could tell her was that wrong information is being given out at Princeton. Which maybe she didn't know was also the other side of the deeply flowing Hudson River, in the same direction as Suffern. Turn away now with my own sigh and heave of sorrow. Filled with tears. More broken strings. There was music in her voice. Magic in her brief words. Their sweet apple sound. As if I had known her all my life. Childhood sweethearts. And we loved each other. Born and grown up in the same valley. By a river. Near the same hill. Or on the next street in the same town. "Excuse me, sir. Could you please tell me, sir. Do you know when the next bus is to Suffern." And not needing anymore to know. And perhaps had I known, she wouldn't now lie so still, pale blue eyes staring nowhere. Surrounded by this swarm of loveless strangers. With only their curiosity. And now police come. One with his gun drawn, pushing back the insistent crowd. His partner picking up the shell and taking her pistol. Asking questions. Who saw this. And pressed as I had been to get to the Yiddish Theatre, I couldn't, couldn't leave her. Not like this, all dead and all alone. She was someone I'd met and knew, even if only for seconds. Wait the minutes away until the stretcher bearers come. And they came. Gently lifting her form. Placing her lifeless arms across her chest. A shoe off. Her couple of trinkets and cloth bag beside her. Her face half-covered with strands of her long brown hair. And carry her out of sight, leaving only a darkened red stain over which feet pass now. At just after three o'clock in the afternoon, this terrible occurence. Samuel Barber's *Adagio for Strings* in all its somberness flooding through my mind. The high screams of the violins ringing in the ears, announcing this tragedy. And I went to see. The bus she wanted had already left before she spoke to me. And I could have saved her life.

Stephen O'Kelly'O standing in the crowded front of the bus station. The figures moving around him. Amid the arriving and departing in this shouting and screaming city. Where it seems I've walked this day the longest of miles. Taxis pulling up. People with their luggage getting out. People with their luggage piling in. Destinations.

Take me to the Taft Hotel. To the Dixie. To the Edison. Park Central. Algonquin. To the St. Moritz, where old Max stayed overlooking Central Park when briefly in from Chicago. And take me, too. To escape from death and hell.

"Where to, buddy."

"Seventh and Fifty-eighth, please."

Sit stopping, starting, speeding and honking through all this tawdriness as tears fall from my eyes. Slow to a halt for a red light. Taxi driver glancing in his mirror. Turns to speak over his shoulder.

"Hey, are you all right, buddy."

"Yes I am, thank you."

"Well you ask when you know in a city as big as Brooklyn, the Bronx and Manhattan tragedy is happening every second around the clock. And things are happening out on Staten Island, too. You kind of keep your eye out for somebody who might be in trouble. I was four years in the war. Eighth Army. You ain't wearing a Ruptured Duck, but I know by just looking, guys who've been in the war."

Stephen O'Kelly'O alighting from the taxi in front of the Yiddish Theatre. Taxi driver, the side of his face covered in a scar, handing back the change one told him to keep.

"It's okay, buddy. My policy. I don't take a tip from veterans or when I carry what I think is sorrow in my cab.

Had a guy yesterday, no hands, just hooks like the ends of wire coat hangers coming out of his sleeves. Iwo Jima. Sorry about the little accident. I'll say something else, too. Not many of my passengers ever say please, or thank you."

Stephen O'Kelly'O under the canopy of the Yiddish Theatre. Late. Twenty minutes. In this city never predictable. While my good friend the taxi driver from the Eighth Army was turning around to tell me of his considerateness, he nearly killed us driving up on the back of another taxi stopping for a red light. The driver in front, getting out to view the damage, dismissed it and forgave him with a disdainful wave of the hand. A rakishly stylish-looking gentleman on the sidewalk pausing to watch. And, in Max's brokerish way, announcing to the two taxi drivers, "I say there, you two. Assert your mannish instincts. Find fault and fight. Go ahead, hit him. Ask him if he wants to be an advert for a casket company. And I agree to referee."

As always in this city, the next moment is invariably an unexpected surprise, never giving you a chance to learn about the metropolis. Just when tragedy submerges the spirit and the harshness one encounters seems to overwhelm, a thoughtful kindness erupting seems to beget another. Or a savant joker to intervene. And benevolence emerges. As might, in the midst of mournful cello chords, come the cheer of grand orchestral blasts. Just as, after all

193

the violence and death of the war, camaraderie is still to be found. Together with maybe an eternal world-weary sadness left in the eyes. Such a young girl couldn't have been in the war. And yet what whirlpool of despair could have sucked her spirit down enough to make her want to die. To be swept up and taken away with the human debris of this city as are the pieces of bodies taken up piece by piece out of the subway tracks. Glittery-eyed thousands come aspiring from the corn-growing plains, from Kentucky gulches and gullies, and out of the potato fields of Idaho and westward all the way to the California shore of the Pacific Ocean. To dare their lives here on this deep stone emplacement of Manhattan Island where the drills and dynamite dig to send the tall spires up into the sky. Where stardom awaits in so many dreams. To then be crushed by the endless friendless indifference. Smothered under the doom of loneliness. And here I have rushed and wait outside a venue for the language of an ancient world to be heard. For a Dru who may have already been. Found me not here, and now is gone and will never come back because I am late. Stare up at the soaring gray edifice of Max's athletic club across the street. Three giant windows where inside Max said they had a swimming pool. A palace dedicated to the manly sports. Frequented by many prominent social and political figures who could afford the membership fees. How ya doin'. I'm doin' fine. In this city where I was born. Grew up. Was early indoctrinated. Knowing girls like the pock-marked girl, and the desperate effort she made giving the potbellied blow jobs so that it enabled her to take groceries back to her hungry father and brother. She finally admitted she had her nose busted when she spat the sperm of the Irish Roman Catholic man who wouldn't pay her right back into his face.

And here I am, Stephen O'Kelly'O outside the Yiddish Art Theatre and across from Max's athletic club, whose gray elevations go soaring into the sky and only with a quarter left in change that the taxi driver wouldn't take as a tip. Asked the pocked-marked girl what would happen if she raised her price to two dollars and fifty cents. She said she thought business would suffer. When she first started out, she took what anyone would give her which she was glad to get. And the demand grew so she named a price. Took her customers up to the roofs of buildings. And blew them too in elevators before they reached the top. Where she held out her hand ready to say thanks. And here I wait for someone who can buy and pay for anything she wants. And knowing she's not going to come makes the minutes passing terrible. But wait just in case she does come. Walk to the corner and back. And take one last look at the Yiddish Theatre program. At least these are a people by whom music is seriously regarded and from whose race great composers and instrumentalists come.

A long and opaque-windowed gleaming black chauffeured limousine pulling up to the curb. A black-uniformed, peak-capped chauffeur getting out. Crossing the pavement and tapping Stephen O'Kelly'O on the shoulder. Who swings around, making the chauffeur jump back in shock.

"Excuse me sir, but Mrs. Wilmington is waiting for you in the car."

Stephen O'Kelly'O crossing the pavement. Bumping into a pedestrian. "Excuse me. I am most heartily sorry." But she has come. Under an assumed name. Climb in. The soft-upholstered, glass-enclosed interior. The dim light. The city shut out. A chinchilla rug across her knees. God she can be stunning and even more beautiful than ever. Her hair swept back tight on her head as it was in my dream. A smile on her face. The very tiny division between her front teeth. Patting the seat beside her with a wink of her eye. A big glass arises to cut us off from the chauffeur. Her welcoming affection so eases the pain that I come to her with. And one hears "The Great Gate of Kiev" in Mussorgsky's *Pictures at an Exhibition.*

"Hi ya, Stephen kiddo. Glad to have you aboard. If that's what they say in the navy."

"Gee, how you doing Dru."

"I'm doing much better, thank you, upon seeing you. This is the fifth time we've driven around the block and through the park and nearly ending up in Harlem. But heavens, you do look pale as a ghost."

"Yes, ma'am."

"I'll forgive that 'ma'am' just this hundredth time more. What's wrong."

"Well, I'm a little better for seeing you, Mrs. Wilmington."

"Well, I'll take you at your pleasant word. And do forgive my little precautionary disguise. I'm afraid necessary. Which is, as you may have noticed, the vehicle we ride in. If I do not have a particular person always scrutinizing my movements, then I have those whom I don't know about. At least when the former is around, which happily he isn't at the moment, I can ignore those snoopers I don't know about. And I've had the very wildest idea. Remember when you played Rachmaninoff. Well I thought that we could make a pilgrimage to Valhalla and visit his grave. Then perhaps later we could have dinner. Is that all right."

"Gee ma'am. I mean Dru. That would be nice."

"I can see we're going to have to be tolerant. Perhaps very tolerant. I think, in fact, I might quite like it if you do call me ma'am. But I would prefer if it didn't make me feel a little staid and stuffy and perhaps just even a little bit illicit, considering our relative positions."

Dru speaking into a small microphone. Chauffeur nodding his head as we travel west on Central Park

197

South. Slow down. Stop for a red light at Columbus Circle. Spacious enough for this open-air forum dotted with a few speakers attended with even fewer listeners. One on a soapbox wielding his fist to an empty street. Another patrolling with a sandwich board.

DOWN WITH

WRONGDOING

UP WITH RIGHTEOUSNESS

SAYS THE TRUE

AND ONLY ZORRO

Nearby, a shoving and pushing fight in progress. An old lady beating the protagonists with her umbrella. Nobody looking like they are going to change the world in this little oasis of discontentment. The gray stone ancient hotel there. And a warehouse. And we speed through the traffic to the elevated highway along this great noble river of the Hudson. Dru smiling, pointing through the thick glass of the windows.

"Up there atop that building, a newspaper magnet lived. Had an apartment with a swimming pool in it. He built himself a palace in California with a much bigger pool."

Under the soaring silver sweep of the George Washington Bridge, the highway weaving its route along the shore of this solemnly deep river. Staring out the window and holding this hand giving a reassuring squeeze that I was told growing up, transmitted a message of true love to come. Listening to this voice as it tells me more. That beyond all this solid rock is Fort Tryon Park. The Cloisters. Lawns, terraces, and where they have the most secret of wonderful rock gardens. The remains of a Romanesque twelfth-century church. And dissolved over this voice telling me of these rocky cliff sides, the prostrate girl, her leather coat spread each side of her like the broken wings of a bird. Her face turned aside, twisted upon her neck. A hole blown through her skull. The blood on her hair. White specks of her brain. As if now strewn dotted across the beautiful passing wooded green contours of countryside.

"Stephen, you're awfully silent. I won't of course pry, but you must tell me if something is wrong."

"Nothing is wrong, ma'am, and you sure do know New York."

"Well of course one shouldn't speak of it as being anything important but one's family have over the years done various things in various parts of the city which I suppose, out of curiosity, one would sometimes investigate, making it familiar."

Farther north, the highway curving past the hillsides with their strange distant amalgam of buildings, each isolated like the beginnings of abandoned empires. Then just as Dru knows what she does about the island of Manhattan, all growing familiar as places where I walked and knew were passing by. Where my best friend had a trapping line in the swamp in the valley of the Saw Mill River. Catching muskrats to sell to the Hudson Bay Company. And right in this, the area of a borough insisting to be known euphemistically as Riverdale but in reality the Bronx. That word, just like Brooklyn, conjuring up boorish accents and behavior. That makes one in unambiguous affirmation want to brag about where one comes from. As we pass another hillside. Over which the ghosts of childhood hover. Race through my memories. Of what happened beyond in those suburban streets. The artfully chastising, if not horrendous things we did to the neighbors. Especially at night, and most of whom were highly deserving real grumpy bastards with similar wives. Point now upward and toward houses in the trees.

"Dru, that's where I grew up."

"And someday it will be immortalized."

Words such as Dru's were glowingly pleasant to hear. Even as untrue and impossible as my humility made me feel them to be. But at least such sentiments could get you through another couple of hours of life believing there was reason to live. And not die brain destructed, facedown in a bus station. As go by now the little conurbations from Heather Dell to Hartsdale. My soul quieted a little from the turmoil of the spirit and my accumulated restless nights, I nodded off to sleep. Dreaming I was a salesman in a jewelery store and just having failed to make a sale, I woke. My head resting on Dru's shoulder, her fur rug up over my knees and the limousine parked on a cemetery road. A chill in the air as I got out to follow Dru in her flat walking shoes. And just like the dead girl's, her wonderful legs. Her calf muscles flexing in front of me to where we stood in front of the Russian cross on Sergey Rachmaninoff's grave. Standing there in silent reverence on the grass, paying our respects. And I could hear the fervent poetic eloquence and intensity and the melodious sweeps of the strings in his Symphony No. 2 in E Minor. Then walking and wandering not that far away, there was the final resting place of a baseball player. The same one Max said he emulated.

"Stephen, didn't that baseball player hit a lot of home runs."

"Yes he certainly did, ma'am."

"I suppose more people know who he is than know of Rachmaninoff."

"Yes ma'am. But he hit forty-nine home runs in a single season. And had a batting average of three seventy-nine over his best ten years. And he lived in my neighborhood, Riverdale. I guess you might say he was a hero, knocking balls instead of musical notes, out into the ether. Folks called him Lou."

"Ah, at last you're talking a little. Stephen, you don't

mind if I comment that you've been so quiet, as I know you usually are, but then even quieter than that."

"Well ma'am, it is a rewarding feeling to stand like this out here in the fresh good air of the countryside and to find these two gentlemen, both outstanding in their professions and achieving so much in their lives, now both resting here in peace."

"You're staring at that stone there."

"Yes, ma'am."

"What are you thinking about."

"Epitaphs."

"Such as."

"Men are slow to gain their wisdom and faster to become fools."

"You know Stephen, sometimes when you say something, I feel I am meeting you for the first time. Do you believe in God."

"Well ma'am, I guess there's got to be somebody like that somewhere. A guy comes into Horn and Hardart on Fifty-seventh Street saying he is. Do you believe in God."

"Having been self-sufficient unto myself I have never felt I had any need of a God but often wonder if with no one to turn to in terrible trouble, I would become religious. But you do, don't you, in so loving your music, have a religion. But recently you have you know, rather made me feel that one has been listening to Tchaikovsky's *Sérénade Mélancolique.* Ah, that at last has put a smile on your face. You see, I am boning up on my musicology. Tchaikovsky, he did didn't he, write so much."

"He did ma'am, and by the way, Tchaikovsky's *Sérénade Mélancolique* does have some very forcefully exuberant passages."

"Well, I suppose my accumulating musical knowledge is bound to leave me occasionally feeling like I'm plunging over Niagara Falls in a barrel, hoping my ignorance is not to be revealed with the barrel breaking up in the turmoil of water below."

"I should be glad, ma'am, to save you from drowning and swim with you to shore."

"And if I were like a bottle full of fizz with the stopper jammed in, would you pull it out."

"I should be most glad to, ma'am."

"Come on. We're going back to New York."

Her smile radiating from her face as one eye winked and the other stayed brightly sparkling under her wonderful eyebrows, as if they sheltered the gleam that came glowing warm out of this woman's soul. As her hand grabs mine and leads me now out of glumness down this little grassy incline. To the long black shining sleekness of this limousine. The door clunking closed with its heavy thud. As we go bulletproof back to the silvery towering skyscrapers. People say they like New York because there are people there. And here we sit side by side, at opposite economic poles of the universe, our minds married by the faintly heard music of all these wheels humming along on the highway. Everywhere and everyone in New York, it seems, are grabbing and stabbing at immortality. Scratching names in cement as we did as kids on the street-corner sidewalks. Carve John, Jerry, Joe in brass. Or Alan, Dick, Ken, or Tommy drawn on a wall. It could last a day, week, or a whole month before, worn by footsteps, washed by rain, or faded by sunshine, another name or a new building comes to wipe it away. But ole Dru's name, out of the sunshine, away from the rain, is writ in brass on a pew in the cloistered elegance of St. Bartholomew's Church. Which still adorns there so peacefully on Park Avenue. Attesting to religion, wealth, and power. And permitting pure beauty and sentiment to pervade the spirit. The pocked-marked-faced girl who tried not to ridicule her fat-bellied clients said once to me to always tell everyone how great and wonderful they are, in case they ever get that way. And then you'd be telling the truth. And better late than never.

The massively heavy limousine with its clunking doors pulled up again at the Yiddish Theatre. Under the lights of the marquee, we step out. Dru handing the chauffeur an envelope. And judging by his friendly voice, it could contain a lot of money and he could be a hick hayseed in search of his fortune and blown in from the West. Or maybe one of the more pleasantly pastoral people you'd find up a gulch in West Virginia, where rougher cousins might, if you trespassed on their land, or looked at them sideways, stick a shotgun up your ass and blow your bowels out.

"Thank you kindly, Mrs. Wilmington."

Diamond bracelets sliding back on Dru's wrist as she waved down a taxi. To take me speeding along Central Park South. And this part of town makes me wonder how is old Max, who could always make one quietly chuckle at his dilemmas and the meticulous ways in which he oriented his life. And to recall his description, for which I must write a musical score to dramatize marching a naked football player out of his Houston house and down the elegant rich suburban public street and to which the national anthem of Texas can be sung.

> *Son of a bitch*
> *I'm going to make you pay*
> *The eyes of Texas are upon you*
> *All the live long day.*

As now we turn into the winding roadway north through the park. Evening light descends through the tree branches and over the stone outcroppings. Dru lowers a window. A faint roar of a lion comes out of the zoo. A horse and rider cantering along a bridle path. And into this sylvan peace at night come marauders who will stalk the honest citizen who now hurries heading for peaceful safety outside the park. While we go uptown on Fifth and crosstown on Eighty-sixth Street.

"Stephen, you must know Yorkville. Plenty of Germans, beer, plenty bratwurst, plenty sauerkraut."

"Yes ma'am. Plenty Czechs, plenty Slovaks, and plenty Hungarians."

Near the East River and the peace and quiet of another park, taxi stops. A large town house behind tall railings. Gray stone facings. Gargoyles. A gleaming black anonymous door. The shaming embarrassment of waiting for Dru to pay. Whose terror is to spend a dollar. Tips the driver. Might have given him a quarter. And I haven't got much more than that left in the world. Watch her legs. Which go curvaciously every year to Colorado or even to Europe to ski down some Swiss mountain. With the wonderful sure movements of her finely boned hands takes a key from her purse and unlocks the heavy barred gate. Her easy steps up to the door. Another key opens it into a spacious black-and-white marble-tiled entrance hall, across which we could waltz together. Stone busts on plinths and in niches. Commemorating guys bound to be big-time but not one single composer or face familiar enough that I can recognize. As I follow this lady up this sweep of curving staircase. Who speaks back over her shoulder.

"Stephen, when you fell asleep in the car on the way to Valhalla, I wanted to wake you up to see the quite beautiful sweeping massiveness of the Kensico Dam but you were so deeply, somnambulantly talking in your slumber."

"Was I."

"And I did think I had better not interrupt you. That's how considerate I can be."

"What was I saying."

"Of what little I could understand, nothing incriminating. You were saying, 'Wrong, wrong. Wrong information is being given out at Princeton.'"

"Was I saying that."

"Yes you were. Not something the college authorities would like said."

"Well, I think it could refer to a bus timetable."

"Ah, but at last some color seems to be coming back into your face. You were so pale. And I know everything is going to be all right with your work. And also your whole future."

"I hope so. So many would wish me ill and would stand in my way and let me down. Things seem to insist to happen that seem to hinder me in my aspirations and effort to achieve my goal which is to create and conduct."

"Dearest—I may, mayn't I, call you that. Especially as you can't seem to always remember to call me Dru. It's all these old fogies sitting on their laurels and coasting on their reputations who should perhaps with the kindliness of time be swept away into the luxury of their retirement homes, there to comfortably await their secure niches in the history books."

"And give ciphers like me a chance."

"How can you say that when your work is so beautiful. At least I think so."

"And ma'am, I am entirely charmed that you do."

"You do you know, sometimes sound as if you're not entirely from the Bronx. And apropos of your exerting a certain Gallic savoir faire, would you be open to an invitation if I were to ask you to come with me racing. October, that wonderful month in Paris where the chestnuts are dropping from the trees in the Jardin des Tuileries and also the time the Prix de l'Arc de Triomphe is at Longchamp, where I have a dear mare running."

"Do I, ma'am, take my not sounding as not being from the Bronx as a compliment or possibly a mild rebuke."

"Take it merely as an observation my dearest. From someone whose thoughts are entirely in your interest."

"I shall, Mrs. Wilmington."

"Touché. We do, don't we, dig for ourselves entrenchments of deviousness out of which extrication becomes difficult, if not ultimately impossible. But that is reserved for others. With you, I never feel that I am in tainted company in which future betrayal portends and when you sense someone is lying to you."

"And I should be delighted to head to Paris. And we might together while there pop into the church of St. Sulpice and if lucky, hear Gounod's *St. Cecilia Mass*."

"Done, my dear."

On the staircase landing, gilded bronze jardinieres. Reminders of one's lace-curtain origins of an onyx sort, when one enjoyed in childhood to push these over to marvel with pleasure as they smashed upon a tiled sunroom floor. My refined Irish parents' efforts to maintain elegance in the face of their progeny, who treated all such things as junk. And this residence festooned with riches. Past which Dru leads me by the hand along a corridor. Crystal chandeliers everywhere. Furniture shapes unseen under white sheets. Where a key hangs hidden on the back of a chair and opens up a door. Dru turning the gilt handle, diamonds aglimmer on her wrist. While I don't have a thing to wear to Longchamp. And follow into this darkened shadowy chamber this woman who can go anywhere in the world and do what she wants. Dru striking a match. The flame illuminating a golden coronet atop a massive canopy bed.

"This candle to burn while we make love."

"Holy cow, Dru. Holy cow."

"Next, dear boy, you'll be saying gee jiminy winikers, or is it winkus or something vaguely akin."

"This is all so sumptuously beautiful that it's made me become what I believe is usually referred to as being nervous."

"Well, this is my closest girlfriend's house. Or rather, 'cottage in the city,' as she calls it, which at the moment is entirely empty. In any event, servants do play havoc with the privacy of one's life. And I hope that you're not going to suddenly go shy on me."

"No ma'am. I'm trying to stay as brave as possible. But we could be committing adultery."

"I assume you're kidding."

"Yes I am, ma'am."

"I see we're quite firmly back to 'ma'am' again. And you're behaving like a virgin. But of course adultery and worse is exactly the kind of illicit sin we are, or rather at least I am, committing."

"Well ma'am, maybe I didn't mean for our association to go this far so fast."

"Well, in exactly another second it can pretty quickly disappear into a taxi and head down First Avenue. I shall call one."

"Gee, please don't. I don't know what to say."

"Well, whatever it is that you don't know what to say, you'd better say it. And if I may suggest further, without undue delay. For putting it in the parlance of the outspoken, I do not intend to aimlessly fuck about. In platitudes, clichés, or otherwise."

"Well, I guess if it's not a platitude, I want to be with you. And I guess I think about you."

"Well, how nicely halfhearted of you."

"I think you're wonderful."

"Well, that at least might be considered as a mild improvement. And perhaps it's better that you know that my involuntary winking can at times be voluntary, as it was at Sutton Place that evening when we all went out for dinner. And also, if I may put it so bluntly, when your hard-on grew so enticingly large. When we first met up, you were blushing and indeed as I believe you described yourself to someone who shan't now be named that it had you crouched over like a cripple in a hopeless effort to disguise the predicament that your engorgement presented. And now need I say, my dear boy, that that shown to me then was the biggest green light in the world. Or am I deluding myself and am now to hear you deny that such tumescence was inspired by me."

"No ma'am. I don't deny it. I openly admit it."

"Good. At last we seem to be getting somewhere. Now show me where it hurts. Because from what I can see of your posture, you again seem crouched over in such pain."

"I guess I'm also nervous with the lack of scruples. Gee, I think I feel a little bit guilty. Sorry, I mean chilly."

"Of course the words *guilty* and *scruples* do rather go together, but I am absolutely sure you meant to say chilly. It is, after all, somewhat unseasonably cool in this house. Now dear boy, as we are prolonged standing here, do I keep the candlelight alive. Or do I blow it out and immediately turn on my flat heel and saunter straight out of here."

"I guess I am traumatized by some recent events."

"I'm assuming I'm not one of them."

"No, ma'am, you're surely not."

"Well, am I to blow out the candle or not. Blow, I presume."

"No, no, don't."

"Well then, as I am not quite yet old enough to be your mother, please forgive me if I don't speak in pedantic euphemisms in order to request to see that cock of yours already bursting the seams of your trousers."

"Ma'am, you don't mince your words, do you."

"No. I don't. Why should I."

"I agree, ma'am. Why should you."

"We all, don't we, seek to reach a plateau of pleasure upon which we think we can glide indefinitely. And I suppose some of us accept the risk of doing so dangerously."

"Dru, I guess I've had a couple of things happen today that have dismayed me. But please. Don't blow out the candle."

On the gray marble chimneypiece amid a collection of Islamic looking pots, one candle out of a dozen in their tall tulip glasses glowing in the mirror. Softly flooding its single flame of light across the room and spreading shadows within the shelter of the great canopied bed and beyond.

"Holy Christ, Dru. Get back."

"What is it."

"Behind you."

"Oh that. It's dead and stuffed. I meant to warn you."

"Holy cow. It's a rattler. Diamondback."

"Oh dear boy you are, aren't you, a nervous wreck, but at least you remembered my name. Next perhaps, you'll call me sweetie pie. But that's an eastern diamondback. I suppose, alive, our most deadly of snakes."

"That looks at least seven feet long and in the dark it looks alive with its fangs ready to strike. Hey what kind of a place is this. Could be black widow spiders everywhere you put your hand."

"I suppose the Irish, not having snakes in Ireland, have an exaggerated dread of them."

"You betcha, ma'am."

"Better not bring you into the next room where my friend has two stuffed black mambas that extend as high as you or I up off the floor and which are wrapped around objets d'art. The world's most feared snake alive, but I assure you my friend preserves them harmlessly dead."

"Oh boy, this is getting to be some day."

"To make it better, may I presume as I'm doing that I undress for you with the intention that it may distract you from your troubles and, as it seems, your fear of snakes. And perhaps then allow me to become stuffed or at least penetrated. And please do keep calling me 'ma'am.' Do you like what you see."

"Oh boy, you bet, ma'am. My God, surely ma'am, you're a Venus."

"Well at least a protectoress of gardens which I believe Venus symbolizes. But perhaps I am a little taller and perhaps slightly thinner than the statue. I swim half a mile every day at that Georgian redbrick rendezvous for women on Park Avenue. And now good sir, I should like to be at your mercy. Does that not, in anticipation, give you just a trace of smug satisfaction."

"You betcha. Holy cow."

"So, why not take off your clothes."

"Oh boy."

"And don't forget to say gee winikers."

"No, ma'am. Gee winikers. Forgive the state of my undergarments."

"And, my good chap darling, don't leave on your socks. And you do don't you, need darns in the toes. And my, you are aren't you, well endowed. And to cut a continued description short, you're an Adonis. Please. Don't move. Just stand there as you are while I lick my chops."

"Well ma'am, truth be known, I'm merely a reasonably healthy light heavyweight twenty-six-year-old male, nearly twenty-seven, and past my prime, plunging inexorably on my way to the infirmities that surely shall soon devolve upon me upon hitting thirty. Or at least by thirty-one."

"Oh my God. You must think then that I am well and truly over the hill."

"No, never, ma'am. For certainty never. A body such as yours is a dream."

"Such flattery of course, will get you somewhere. Ah, but you are, aren't you, really extremely well endowed. Indeed to the degree that one might more likely expect to encounter along some of the coasts of Africa, where one goes to play sometimes. But don't you ever tell anyone that."

"No ma'am. For sure. Mum's the word."

"This is so wonderful. Just so good to look at you and contemplate without touching what will happen when we touch. Such gorgeous delight. I love the way a belt goes around a man's trousers. Take yours off. You have no idea how long I've waited for this. Like being brought as I was as a little girl when we'd return from Europe, to be taken to see the phenomenon of the big face up on the billboard blow gigantic smoke rings out over Broadway and to have demonstrated to me how great America was."

"Holy cow. I'm no smoke ring. I don't smoke."

"Well, come on lover boy. I'm hot enough to smoke. Don't be shy. I'm giving you a target as I bend over. Belt me with that belt."

"Gee Dru, I'm not shy; I'm just amazed at what we're getting up to here."

"We're getting up to good things. Ouch. That was nice. And just a little harder. Ouch. Ouch. Now, lover boy.

I adore to be submissive. For a few seconds. And then to be dominant. *Grrr.* Do you like that sound."

"Boy, you bet."

"Now lie down and let me talk to you and tell you more. You are my prodigy. Groomed for stardom. Heralded as the great young hope. Hailed as the most exciting young conductor composer since last week. Sorry, I meant to say in all America. Stunning even the most critical audiences with your repertoire. On the podium, his baton swaying so marvelously. Let me talk to it. Hello there, you. Yum yum. What is it they call syncopation."

"It is when a tone is started on an unaccented beat and continued through the following accented beat. Ragtime is an example."

"Stephen my darling, although I don't know what the fuck you're talking about, can we syncopate. We do then, both have beautiful bodies, don't we. We will, won't we, while we're here like serpents, enmesh in a sinewy embrace."

"Yes ma'am. But let's keep well away from that snake. Stuffed or not. I don't trust that goddamn thing."

"Now please, don't panic again, dear boy. Truth of the matter is, I adore to be in the presence of danger and of those doing unspeakable things."

"Holy cow. Like what."

"Can't tell you. Even though I would love to. I said it

217

was unspeakable. So I won't tell you now. Maybe soon. Maybe sometime. Did you know this was going to happen to us."

"Yes ma'am. No. Or let me correct that. The truth is, I didn't. I didn't dare."

"You're so sweet. But just stay there as you are. Don't move. And you actually like me. Don't you."

"Yes ma'am."

"You gave me the only unmistakable signal. And you do at times exhibit a galantry far beyond your years. And you're not like everyone else. Who all over this world are always after something."

"Well, I'm not too sure ma'am, that I'm not after a few things."

"Well, if that ever gets to include me, I don't mind. And can only hope I've got what you're after. At least while I'm alive. Or who knows, perhaps even after death. Think of enough things to do with it. Even think of the possibilities of cryogenics. One does ask one's psychic questions, such as, will there be a resurrection of the dead. And as we shake off our icicles, does that mean, then, that we all stop dying. She doesn't seem to really know, so meanwhile I rely on the wisdom of life being always to pursue something. Or at least hope to find something to pursue. And I never fully can. Even with a whole litany of deserving good causes which for distraction ends me up buying so much antique junk at auctions

218

that it has to end up stuffed in warehouses I've never been to. Stopped buying when I found you to seduce. No. I'm only kidding. But anyway, here you are. With me. And having this little naked talk like this. Now closer. Touch me."

Drusilla, her tall, white slender body stretched in the candlelight on this large canopied bed. Oil portraits on the walls. Out of someone's American past. Early settlers putting on airs. Their eyes staring at us. As well as the malevolent, deadly, glinting eyes of the rattler, mouth agape, head as big as a hand, fangs as long as a finger, coiled to strike. And in these seconds swiftly passing, touch her, feel her lips on my skin. What is unspeakable. Of which she speaks. Tied to a post and beaten. Fucked while laid out in a coffin or hanging from a tree.

"You have such a worried look, darling, my dear. You're wondering, aren't you. Have you ever done anything as quaint as made love to anyone in a coffin."

"Gee Dru, that, believe it or not, just went through my mind."

"Ah, now that the cat's half out of the bag. It's a black cat. With nine lives. And my precious one, at least one life is left to live."

"Holy cow. I feel as if I'm dreaming."

"You are darling. And relax. I ask only that you call me sweetie pie. Lie back on your back. I shall kneel beside you, let my hair hang long and loose, loose and long. The lovely silkiness of your hair does make one envious, angel."

"Sweetie pie."

"O God, call me, call me that again please."

"Sweetie pie."

"You know I always always wanted, instead of being chaperoned by some governess down some big gloomy hall of some big gloomy old house, to imagine I lived in some cozy little place down some shady street of maples in a small town and would be called sweetie pie by someone nice. As if someone like you were the boy next door and walked every day past our little lawn and white picket fence maybe on your newspaper route. And flicked the latest local town news up on our porch and stood a second or two to look at my house where I lived with my mother and father and our dog named Esme or Putsie or something and our cat named Snooky Wooky. And when you went past, you wondered what I was doing inside. And I'd be washing my hair in beer because it would make it shine. Then on Friday night, you'd have your hair brushed, pants pressed and maybe, with even a bow tie, you would come up the little paved path to the front door. And when you pressed the bell, chimes would ring 'God Bless America.'"

"Holy cow, Dru. You're kidding."

"No. No, I'm not. And don't you laugh."

"I'm not, and I sympathize with an enlightened form of socialism where perhaps life could be like that. But maybe we could have a little Stravinsky in the chimes."

"Well, I'm not kidding."

"Okay. Sweetie pie."

"And let me finish. You'd arrive for our date at seven o'clock. And then sitting with my dad, telling him you made first-string quarterback on the high school football team, while I, upstairs, brushed my hair for the final umpteenth time. Then as I came slowly down the stairs into the drawing room, you saw me and smiled."

"Dru, I think it might be called the living room."

"Okay, living room. So who cares about architecture at such a beautifully romantic point. And then we go out under the maple trees down the street, holding hands on our second date because you got to like me so much on the first, when we went together to the movies, that this night we maybe would even have our first kiss. And I'd give you my sorority pin to wear. And you'd give me your fraternity pin. Isn't that what they do in high school."

"Gee, Dru, I ain't never been in a fraternity."

"Oh, who cares. I've never been in a sorority. But we'd then be having strawberry sodas at the local candy store on Main Street. Or should that be pineapple. And you'd suck on your straw and make noise at the bottom of the glass and I'd suck on mine and wouldn't make noise because I was a little lady well brought up and then you'd look at me, a pretty ribbon in my hair and say, 'Sweetie pie.' Oh God, that gets me so horny and I do have, don't I, such simple wants. To want only you to call me that. Now I shall blow you. Know you. Taste you who tastes so good. And know you will always, when I want you to, always call me sweetie pie."

"Yes ma'am."

"Slowly touch me softly. Touch me gently, sweetly. Touch my skin with yours."

"Surely I will, ma'am. Sweetie pie."

"Now sink your magnificent Irish cock into me, dear boy. And fire your big gun."

Under the great canopy of this bed. Stare up into an infinity of darkness as one does into the infinity of the rest of one's life. Lying embraced with these strong long slender limbs. Her lips pressed lusciously on my neck. Her teeth closed on my skin. In the amazingly exciting wonderful world of music as it has been down through the ages, sexual deviations have always been the norm, if not the rage but Dru has presented something new. Provided one hadn't already jumped into a coffin with her, one would walk by her picket fence. Saunter up her front path. Hold hands and maybe even kiss in the movies. Scoff back my favorite pineapple soda. But I'd be the rude one making noise at the bottom of my glass. She did say once her childhood was painfully lonely. Incarcerated. Always with a governess. Her mother away traveling, so she became a sad little creature. Such a rich little girl upon whom few could look with any fond pity. Led by the hand along long corridors of big houses. Taken everywhere couched in the soft upholstery of big cars. In Paris, the chauffeur would briefly stop along the Chemin de Ceinture du Lac so that she could watch other children play in the park and sail their little sailboats and she could try to pat their little dogs. And warned not to because they might bite and have rabies. Then going back to Avenue Foch, she would count the dandruff flakes fallen on the chauffeur's back. And now I feel the tips of the diamonds of her bracelet pressed on my back, enough gems to support me for the rest of my life. Aided and abetted by the twenty-five cents I still have left. This the sweet depth into which one sinks. Seeing her again as I first ever saw her. Smiling. Her lips just parted. That I kiss. One eye opened just that little bit more than the other. Candlelight gleam on the soft waves of her hair fallen to her shoulders. A twist of her soft, pliant body. Huskily she whispers, "I madly desire you dear boy. Can you feel my hardened nipples now against your chest." Yes. As I commit this betrayal of a mother to her adopted daughter. And my own betrayal to a wife. This woman, who now it seems can with just a flicker of an eye, send me running out to my own death. Vulnerable to anything. Threatening my integrity. Maybe making it possible to conduct my own symphony. Have my own orchestra. Plenty of violins, oboes and percussion. Forty for a start in the brass. Fifty in the wind. Seventy-five in the strings. Five on drums. Two on xylophone, or maybe three. There are not enough xylophones these days. Two concert grand Steinways. A whole chorus of great contraltos.

"Jesus Christ, Dru, did you hear that rattle. I just thought the goddamn rattler moved."

"An electric button in the bed we must have just touched. Just a little joke my friend has to scare the shit out of boyfriends who she feels need the stimulus."

"Thanks a bunch for telling me after my heart failure."

"Nothing honeybunch is failing. Nothing. Aim. Fire."

"Dru. Holy cow. Dru."

"Squeeze your cock tight in my cunt. So you can't get away. My honeybun sailor boy in his turret. Boom, boom."

An echoing hoot of a boat out passing on the river. And the lives that make not a sound in this city anymore. The world assaults you with tragedy and anguish when least you have anger to fight back. "Excuse me, sir. Do you know when the next bus is to Suffern." Still see her stopping, turning to look her last look. One so handsomely healthy beautiful, desiring death. "Excuse me, sir. Do you know when the next bus is to Suffern." Thought she said I'm suffering until I found Suffern on the map. Across the Hudson River. Through it the Erie Railroad runs. North to Sloatsburg and Tuxedo Park. The adagio from Dvořák's Symphony No. 9 in E Minor sounds slow, like all freight trains that go by lumbering click clack on the rails of the tracks, whistles blowing in D Major.

"Oh honeybunch, Stephen, fuck me, fuck me into the beyonds of the eons."

"Doing my best, ma'am."

"And you are dearest, even doing better than that. As I take, if I do say myself, a singularly selfish interest in screwing."

The rattler rattles again. Sending a shiver of the sharp fear of death up the old roosel. The black mambas coming alive in the other room. Said to be a snake that with its head held as high as a man's face, attacks without provocation. Maybe just what this lady who lives here entertains in her imagination and enjoys for a frisson. But that other death. That destroyed face. Her eyes still open, staring as she lay on the bus station floor. Left there nameless and lost in the passing swarm. To whom does one go to get the right information from Princeton. Or to find her grave. To put a flower there. Will my music ever be heard before I die. Brahms with his second piano concerto, was hissed at by the Viennese people. Who so shabbily treated so many of the great composers who lived there struggling in their midst. Shake my fist at them. When Brahms died in Vienna, at least all the ships in the harbor of Hamburg where he was born, lowered their flags to half-mast. Oh my God, Dru. You're surely the cat's pajamas. I'm standing on your front porch, my hair washed and combed, my fraternity pin shined, to take you for a Saturday-night soda. I must play for you Brahms's heroic orchestral sounds. The piano erupting forth to intercede in passages such as does a brook babbling through the silence of a forest. Then the piano notes thundering. Oh fuck me lover boy, Stephen. Kiss my tits. Kiss yours. Give me all that you've got. I'll give you everything that I've got to give you. That Max suggested came from the profit of oil, tobacco, soap-suds, coffee, chocolate, soda pop, and renting out elec-tricity. Do I dream her voice can be heard singing. Darling, your music is going to be heard. It's wonderful. I love it. I'll buy the goddamn orchestra for you. They'll be glad to have a job. Get a whole warehouse and fill it up with instruments. And you can conduct. And the dirty bastards who have kept you down will shrink sneak-ily back into their feeble shells. No one is ever going to be able to ignore you again. Not in this town, they ain't. And I know you're wondering. Of what I said was unspeakable. It's other's carnal knowledge of corpses. Watch the living fuck the dead. A form of necromancy as you might say which puts one into erotic turmoil. And to hell with all the hubris, zeitgeist and the ditsy eponymous. Sorry about those nutty words. They make as much sense as saying that it is good to be rich. And your own goddamn parents' fault if you're poor. But boy, if you think it over, can anything be more true than that. And that only women with money can afford not to be whores. But can be whores anyway if they want. Call me ma'am again. You gorgeous man. And let me call you angel.

Listening to her whispering voice. Calling me angel. Sweet bliss on this wistfully sad day of unfavorable omen. Like snakes that strike. Demons come from nowhere. And are by the symphonic strains of Boccherini driven away by a rhythm I do believe may be entirely too fast to fuck to. Invited to France to go top-hatted racing. Whereas I am too broke even to go to a hot dog stand for a mustard-encrusted and sauerkraut-smothered frank-furter. But without a bean I am at least crowned with the joy of this woman's beauty and body, whose husband like ole Max is away shooting and fishing. And then she said as I listened.

"Dear boy angel, there will be one day in your life when you need not worry about the mundane anymore. Even if great wealth from commissions doesn't devolve upon you or appointments materialize to conduct the great orchestras of the world. And, oh God, I am sated."

In the candlelight, Stephen O'Kelly'O by the bed, bending to kiss Dru on the brow as she lies, arms outstretched, staring up into the ornate folds of the canopy. Strains of Boccherini's Cello Concerto in G. Allegro, adagio, allegro. As one navigates around the rattler. And steps into the splendor of this bathroom. Toiletries abound. Bath salts. Emollients for the skin. Caswell-Massey sandalwood lotion. The oldest chemist's and perfumers in America since 1752, it says on the bottle. But not a sign of any soothing balm for the brain or I'd help myself to some. Glass-enclosed shower. A sunken marble tub. A whole afternoon disappeared into evening and sudden disillusion. A plaything for someone who can afford to play. Dru said she had to rush.

"Oh darling. Would you take a rain check on dinner. I've got to get ready to go to Montana. I'll telephone. Will you be there. Jonathan's back in the morning. And Sylvia's gone, as she usually is, God knows where."

Dru suggesting we leave the house one at a time and send me first. Warning of newspaper columnists who hang about the Stork Club to witness café society idling away their nights and that their prying absence could never be assured. Even though she'd only once gone to the Stork Club. She links her arm in mine as we go down the stairs, kissing me on the forehead as we stand in the middle of the black-and-white-tiled vestibule.

"Lover boy angel, illicit liaisons require meticulous planning, total discretion, and unwavering nerve, *cela est selon circonstances.*"

"As for me, *sûrement va qui n'a rien.*"

And I wanted to fuck her again where we stood. But where, backing away to the door I nearly knocked over a bust of Archimedes, whom I at least finally recognized and could remember had once run through the street naked screaming "Eureka" upon his discovery of something to do with the weights of a metal and the volume displacement of water. And plenty about precious metals was on my mind as I was abjectly broke and had no money for a taxi and would walk instead of taking the subway back downtown.

"Lover boy, still waters flow deep."

"Well, Mrs. Wilmington when can I open the floodgates again."

"Now that I look, I have rather a lot of appointments to keep tomorrow. Up early, nine-thirty A.M. pedicure, ten-thirty A.M. hypnotherapy, then my swim at the Colony Club and lunch with the lady who loves her stuffed snakes. After lunch, my current psychic. Then four P.M. to five P.M. the osteopath and massage. After that, I must catch up with some business correspondence. Then I must shower and get ready for a dinner party. Then home to pack to fly to Montana first thing in the morning. But let me telephone you."

"Ma'am, I believe my telephone has been disconnected."

"Oh dear. Not, I hope, for nonpayment of a bill. Well

229

I'll send you a telegram. But you know you have given me an awful lot to think about. And while I'm gone, I'll think."

A squeeze together of bodies. Kiss on the lips. Tip of her tongue darting to touch mine. Opening the gleaming black door on its shiny brass hinges. Walk down the four steps outside into the night, aglow in the gonads. The mayor doesn't live far away. Knock on his door. Inquire if he'd like to commission a special mayorial New York City anthem to be sung at all official happenings. A celebratory cantata for the rich. And a special march with plenty of syncopated drumming to be played for the poor as he goes in the parade up Fifth Avenue on St. Patrick's Day. But on the mayor's doorstep, I'd be arrested as a nut. Better to turn left on East End Avenue. Start my long journey along the East River as rain begins to fall. Pass the Welfare Island Ferry Slip. Walk under the roaring traffic over the Queensborough Bridge to Queens. A panhandler ahead.

"Excuse me, sir. Would you have fifteen cents to have a cup of coffee and to get to Queens. To visit my dying mother in the hospital."

"Here you are, friend."

"Sir, you are a real gentleman."

"At least a coin for a beer."

Farther on now, cut west on Fifty-seventh Street. Get a look at least at all the windows of luxury along this stretch down Fifth Avenue where Dru pops in and out, shopping in these buildings whenever she has time between appointments. And she could give fifteen cents to several million panhandlers. Be called a gentlelady. But at this moment she's somewhere warm and fed and not on the point of starvation. Arriving wet, sneezing and coughing and cold at a dump of an apartment in Pell Street.

In desperation, I paid a late-night visit to the forbidden family saloon in Hell's Kitchen for a free roast beef sandwich two inches thick and then traveling north to meet her in the distant northern Bronx, borrowed money from my second-favorite sister in order to buy groceries. And on a depressingly gray grim rainy Monday early afternoon, returned to Pell Street laden with lamb's kidneys, fruit, two cans of beans, bottle of sauerkraut, an eggplant and a small can of olive oil along with a pound of cod from the Fulton Fish Market. And now after days of desperation, learned that Dru had just returned from Montana. Which news came as I was opening the door to the apartment, to hear Fauré's Requiem. For there seated inside in the living room, attired in her most sedate of finery, a suit of black raw silk, was Sylvia. And it was as if a flash of pain shot across my chest. Seeing her there, sitting back in the broken armchair, listening, with her marvelous legs crossed, black patent-leather low-heeled shoes on her feet. A black cloak lined in purple satin folded across the piano stool. Reminding that her elegance could vie with even the most chic of women in New York. And I waited for the words. Hey, you no good dirty Irish bastard, you went and fucked my adoptive mother behind my back. But her words came matter-of-factly and nearly cheerful.

"Hi, I got the landlord to let me in. You have a new lock."

"That's right, someone busted in."

"Well, you've often enough heard me say I want to find my real mother."

"Yes, I have heard you say that."

"To know what her face is like when she's smiling and when her face is sad."

"Yes. I've heard you say that."

"Well, I found her. I have her address. And I'm really truly sorry for what I did to the piano."

"Well, someone repaired it. Only needs more tuning now."

"I know. And it's all paid for. I don't know what over-came me. But I shouldn't have done it. And I do owe you an apology. Which goes beyond the cut piano strings. Your minuet, maybe not brilliant, but I think it's pretty good. I took a copy of the score and was going to tear it up but instead had it played. But now I'm here to ask you to do me a large favor, which you don't have to even con-sider if you don't want to."

"What is it."

"I want you to come with me to see my mother. I don't

want to go alone. She lives in Syracuse. There's a train to-day at two o'clock out of Penn Station."

"How did you know I'd be here."

"Dru seems to know where you are all the time. At least I can take my dream now, and if it gets finally ripped to shreds, bury it. As for a father, and after what has been vaguely hinted of my mother, once a beauty queen, how can I ever dream that my father was anything much."

"What does 'much' mean."

"It means more, I guess. More than my mother. And I suppose if you come right down to it and dispose of all the bullshit in most people's minds, it mostly means money. And since I don't have much of that at the moment, I don't guess I'm anything much myself. I exhausted all my girlfriends' largesse, which wasn't much, either. And leading them on, I compromised myself with a few ex-boyfriends. But I don't suppose it's occurred to you with your Irish Catholic morality, that making a living is no problem for a girl with my figure and looks in this town. But I don't want you to strain your imagination or jump to conclusions. Dru of course, is back from Montana."

Ominous news. Thought once when she was supposed to be in Montana that I caught her face looking up at the windows from across the street. Amazing what women will do to you and then present themselves again to apologize if they want you to do something for them.

As she says she'll pay the fare, I try to think of an excuse not to go. To have to sit a few hours on the train. Could fall asleep and say things like I did about wrong information at Princeton and instead say, hey, Dru, what a fantastic delicious fuck you are. But had already vowed that after the girl in the bus station, if it were in my province to do so, I would avoid if ever I could, to disappoint anyone. Even to giving the panhandler lurking under the Queensborough Bridge nearly my last dime which I knew would disappear down his throat in beer. But found another quarter and an Indian head and buffalo nickel in the corner of my dressing table drawer. I always find myself making sure the coin says "Liberty" on it. And on a quarter dollar, that it says "E Pluribus Unum." An eagle in flight over three stars. And added up, it was thirty cents. And fifty cents was the biggest amount I ever got as a child to go visit the Museum of the American Indian. And now, to forgive this distraught girl her trespass against me. And find her alone in her vulnerable helplessness. My prick suddenly gone rigid. My face flushed with embarrassment. To suddenly have the most appallingly overwhelming desire to fuck Sylvia on the spot.

"Okay, I will go with you."

"You don't mind, do you, Stephen, changing your clothes."

"What's wrong with my clothes."

"Nothing, except perhaps not entirely suitable for

meeting my mother, whom I've never met and who doesn't even know I'm coming. Would you mind wearing a white shirt and if you have some kind of old sort of striped school tie. That is, if your school ever had one."

"Holy Christ."

"Well just in case we were invited to stay to dinner or something. How do I know she doesn't have someone like Gilbert looking down his nose as he has occasionally dared to do to me wearing something he considers too casual for the room he refers to as the drawing room."

"What about the holes in the toes of my socks."

"Well, you're not taking off your shoes, I hope."

It was as if all was *en fête*. Two smartly dressed people getting resentful looks heading around the corner of Pell Street into Mulberry where Sylvia had one of the family's Pierce Arrows parked, with its special arms that adjusted downwards for elbows and footrests that adjusted upwards for your feet. The Triumphington chauffeur in tow, called Jimmy, and terrified, eyeing the passing pedestrian traffic in case someone tried to open up his locked car door and jump on him. But he was as safe as any of the big Mafia dons, who weren't that far away, also with their big black limousines parked with their chauffeurs.

"Stephen, I'm scared."

"Sylvia, it's all going to be all right."

Up past Union Square, Madison Square and all the hotels, where in each I wonder who it is who lonely lurks.

The Flatiron Building like the prow of a ship sailing north on Broadway. Turn west on Thirty-first Street. St. Francis of Assisi Monastery right in the middle of the block. And arriving safely. The Travelers Aid Society, whose office is in this massive station housing the Pennsylvania, the Long Island, Lehigh Valley, the New York, New Haven, and Hartford railroad lines.

With her cloak aflow and a slender bouquet of red roses and a white-beribboned aqua box from Tiffany's tucked in her arm, Sylvia bought and paid for parlor-car tickets. The train moving slowly off through the darkness of the tunnel under the Hudson. Stare out into the passing bulbs of light and the snaking wires, pipes, and conduits. Sylvia pulling off her black kidskin gloves. Leafing through her pile of magazines and newspapers. Quickly reading as she turned the pages with her manicured fingernails. A faint trace of lipstick on her lips and a white silk scarf held at her throat with the long gold pin that she wore in her stock while foxhunting. Any second I thought she might turn to me and say, You're fucking my adoptive mother. Or, That son of a bitch Max friend of yours, who married my best friend for her money and ruined her life. But she leafed again and again through the fashion magazines and even fell asleep for a while between the towns of Poughkeepsie and Albany.

Outside the station at Syracuse, I got increasingly nervous as I somehow sensed that Sylvia's mother did not have a long driveway up to her mansion and a Gilbert administering her household. And Sylvia's hand trembled showing the taxi driver an address on a piece of paper, as if she didn't want to say it out loud. And I could see why by the questionable first reaction of the taxi driver and his further suspiciousness as we progressed through Main Street to what was clearly the wrong side and shabby part of town. Stopping on a potholed unpaved road of warehouses, shacks and an engineering works parallel to the railway tracks. Sylvia anxiously leaning forward in her seat, glancing at the slip of paper in her hand.

"Driver, this couldn't be the place."

"Ma'am, this is the road you showed me on the paper. And there's the number forty-eight right there plain as can be seen."

"Jesus Christ. Well then, wait."

"You betcha, ma'am. It sure looks like rain."

Sylvia leaving her cloak behind her, climbing out of the taxi and standing on the roadway in front of the closed garage doors of a car-repair shop. And hesitating at the foot of a flight of ramshackle stairs up the side of a dirty paint-peeling brown clapboard frame building backing onto the railroad tracks. Shades drawn on two windows on the floor above the garage door. A sign. DRINK MISSION BELL SODA. Behind the building, a great monster of puffing steam passing, pulling a freight train. The taxi driver turning to speak over his shoulder.

"That old freight could take its own good time going by on its good way to Chicago via Buffalo and Cleveland."

The grinding squealing wheels as a pair of hoboes lope alongside the open doors of a big boxcar, hopping on board. One missing and stumbling, the other grabbing him up by the coat and hand. At least loyalty somewhere, friend to friend. Sylvia still waiting on the roadway, her bag on a strap over her shoulder, her white-beribboned aqua box from Tiffany's couched in the crook of her arm. The wail of the train's whistle in D Major. Then the elegance of this black figure suddenly climbing up the worn and broken wooden stairs to a landing at the top, and pausing at a rusting screen door. Move to where I can see in case some unknown hostile hand drags Sylvia in. Get out of the car and step up on the broken sidewalk. A passing vagrant stopping. Seems to be one wherever I go, always asking for the same dime. And got to give him something. Who knows, he might have been in the war.

"Hey, mister, got a dime. For a cup of coffee. Or maybe you could spare a quarter for something to eat."

Reach into my pocket and flip what will soon be my last quarter toward this wanderer who, missing the catch, picks the coin up out of a small puddle of water. Wipes it on his sleeve, puts it in his pocket. But for the solemn sadness in the man's face, you could envy him his freedom, with no one taking the trouble to denigrate him. Some-

one's father, brother, could even have been in a gun turret on the old *Missouri*.

Sylvia standing still as a statue. The last cars of the train passing. The caboose with it's rear red lights disappearing with another faraway lonesome wail of the train's whistle. Sylvia maneuvering her Tiffany box and bouquet of red roses to peel off one of her black kidskin gloves. Pulling open the outside rusted screen door and pressing a bell. A dog barking. The faint tune of chimes ringing. The first bars of "Home on the Range." The shadow of a figure inside the screen door as it opens, slightly ajar. Sylvia stepping back. A woman, wisps of dyed blond hair in curlers, one hand holding closed her pink dressing gown at her throat. A growling, gruff woman's voice.

"What do you want."

"Annie, I'm Sylvia, your daughter. And I know you are my mother."

The sound of the waiting silence. This slattern and slovenly coarse woman in her soiled pink dressing gown suddenly lunging out the half-open rusting screen door and spitting into Sylvia's face.

"I know who you are. Get the hell out of here, you bitch, all dressed up to the nines, and leave me alone and don't come back."

First drops of rain beginning to fall out of blackening skies. A tight constriction in the throat. A shudder in the breast. How could the sorrow ever be greater that you can feel for someone so distressed in a grief so deep. To offer to take their hand and lead them away from hurt. As once was offered me as a little boy when big tears welled and rolled out of my eyes and down my cheeks when someone said I was bad.

Sylvia descending the wooden steps, a purple silk handkerchief wiping the sprinkle of moisture from her face. Her bag slung askew across a shoulder, tears bulging in her reddening eyes. Her gloved hand holding the glove from the other hand and her shiny aqua box from Tiffany's and the bouquet of red roses under her arm. On the last step, her ankle twisting as she slips. A wounded animal cry. As she turns. Raises an arm. Throwing away the red roses on top of a pile of old tires stacked underneath the stairs. And dropping the Tiffany box to the ground, kicking it away with the toe of her black patent-leather shoe to join the grimy debris of the gutter.

"My mother. Jesus, that was my mother."

The next train back down to New York was in another hour. Sylvia, in a defiant gesture of extravagance on top of the modest fare tipped the taxi driver ten dollars.

"I sure thank you kindly, ma'am. Hope to see you again sometime."

"You won't. But thanks."

In the station Sylvia sat on a bench as I walked back and forth on the platform. A guy trying to pick her up soon retreated away from her absolute silence. As she stared up at him, through him. And away from him. On the train, as I sat on the aisle Sylvia looked out the window. I tried to comfort her with a gentle pat on the arm.

"You, you've had a family. You know what it's like to have a father and mother. You knew real sisters and brothers. Well I found my real mother through the Red Cross tracing service. And exactly as I used to think she was. In a shack by the railway tracks. And I won't ever know now what her face is like when it's smiling. Or when it's sad. But I sure as hell know what it's like when it's mad."

Sylvia putting her black-gloved hands up to her face. The towns going by. The conductor punching tickets, reciting off their names. Rome, Utica, Schenectady. This was America. A vast land of the brave and the free. Free country to be rich in. Free for a goddamn sight of a whole lot more to be poor. Free for anybody to tell you to go to hell. And sometimes, like a few of the Mafia kids I played with growing up, they were friendly till you told them to go to hell, and you always knew they'd wait patiently till it was a good time to try to kill you for it. And that's why if you were Irish you would always try to wade in swinging and kill them first on the spot. And Sylvia was told to go to hell. And had already to stand as she did, waiting till that train went by. And then stood for just those few seconds, for someone to spit in her face. A door slamming, to leave her so utterly forlorn on the landing of her mother's slatternly abode. A child who sought the loins she came

242

from. To be with that flesh again. To touch it. To take her hand. Be held close. Be comforted in her skirts. And all dressed up to be desecrated. Told to go away. Never to come back. Another soul shot down in cold blood. Wrong and terrible information is being given out at Syracuse.

"Albany next. Albany next. All get off for Albany."

The conductor singing out up and down the carriages. Till we stop and wait in the station. In the hiss and throb and steam of the trains. Then head out of this capital of New York State and towards the majestically flowing river. As the rain streaks by across the window. So much beautiful passing countryside passing. Then through the towns and the grim industrialization, the factories and the rail sidings. That road in Syracuse. Potholed. Strewn with debris. Will now have a surprise to be found in a Tiffany box. A loving cup. Maybe the taxi driver who saw it, will go back to see. And read engraved on the silver:

To my dearest mother
Annie
From her loving daughter
Sylvia

And where in the same city of Syracuse there's a university where my closest childhood friend, who hunted

243

and trapped and explored the lore of wildernesses and who was killed in the war, had planned to go to study forestry. He taught me Indian games of swinging down to the ground from the tops of sapling trees. He knew how to tie knots and make and follow trails through the woods. He'd give me a ten minutes head start and track me to anywhere I would try to hide. Another life ended that promised so much. To inspire another generation. And his memory kept me alive to the wonderful principles he practiced. In all matters but girls. All of whom sought his company and loved him. And not till we reached Poughkeepsie did Sylvia again speak.

"I'm so exhausted. And feel so alone. And I am so, so shamed."

To reach now to take her hand to comfort her. Wrap my fingers around her fingers just tightening for a moment until she gently drew her hand away. Her indifference to me confirmed and supreme. And my consolation proffered rejected. But when I insisted that I go back with her to the apartment at Sutton Place, she didn't demur. Said she wanted to collect something. Something that was all that was left of her life. She disappeared to her bedroom, while Gilbert, as if for my benefit alone, announced that Mrs. Triumphington was out. When Sylvia returned, she sat and smoked a cigarette and asked Gilbert to make her a daiquiri. And I asked for a beer. More than anything I wanted to go into the music room and strum out some Beethoven. Feel and listen to the notes tumble soft and tenderly upon each other. But sat there where we'd all sat before. Noticing now the same tulip glasses for candlesticks that were on Dru's friend's chimneypiece. Christ, a diamondback rattler could come squirming out right now from under this sofa. Where sits so near the body which once presented so many agonizing jealousies. She who through all those years of childhood suffered a desperate nagging mystery in her rich life. Searching everywhere for a mother to rid herself of the emptiness she felt inside her.

"Stephen. Thank you for coming with me. I suppose I've discarded guys like you all my life and I guess I should have discarded you a month or two sooner than a month or two later. But I didn't. I guess only because at least you're an artist doing something that has value. Anyway. I'm going to give you a divorce. Of practically the cheapest kind it is possible to get. And forgive me if I now drink my daiquiri in one gulp. I'm going. I presume you're staying. You don't have to pretend. I know all about it."

"About what."

"I said you don't have to pretend. I'm going if you're staying."

"I'm not staying."

"Okay then, let's save electricity on the elevator and both go. But don't you ever say anything to anybody ever about what happened today. And don't watch me as if I were going to fall in front of a truck or jump out of a window."

Back on the street, it was still raining. The doorman running out under an umbrella to get a taxi. Sylvia with a much-worn gladstone bag, put out her hand for me to shake.

"So long, Stephen."

"Sylvia. I'd like to at least know where you're going."

"What the hell do you care. If someone doesn't love you, it doesn't matter where you're going. But I'm going somewhere. Where to have no one who loves you, it doesn't matter. This bag belonged to my real father and I don't even know who he is. Good-bye. Anyway, free of me, nothing should stop you now maestro from fucking my pretend mother all you want."

Most of all, I didn't want her to go anywhere it could be cold and winds make her shiver. Or loneliness make her silent and more alone. Her silhouette through the rain-spattered back window of the taxi, telling the driver where to go. Wait in case she turns around to wave and I can wave back. But the cab pulling away, the shadow of her head hunched forward. The leather of the gladstone bag with the initials J.C.H.D., was creased and cracked with wear. Whoever owned it at least had some pretensions to elegance. And it is a cruel thought, but I hope that, Holy Christ Almighty, she doesn't go off now searching for her father.

Next morning at eight o'clock in Pell Street waking to the eccentric alarm clock. Which at first seemed to be an insistent ring of the downstairs doorbell. But couldn't be, because the buzzer in the apartment didn't work. But it was a dream and a nightmare so real that I woke in a sweat. Having dreamt of Sylvia's death and burial and that I had gone down to the front door where a policeman standing there asked if I were Stephen O'Kelly'O. And informing me that Sylvia fell from a Biltmore Hotel window, and her remains were removed to Bellevue Hospital morgue where if I could make a positive identification, I could collect my wife's effects. I kept asking the policeman at the door did it really happen. And it seemed that he said all the guys from the "Men Only" bar rushed out to see her broken body on the sidewalk where she landed in front of the phony blind musician who so outraged Max. And then in the morgue I was asking was that really her body on the slab looking astonishingly beautiful and uninjured. And I found myself thinking that although she bitched at me and had her own independent agenda which meant, Go fuck yourself if you want me to do anything for you, that perhaps she wasn't such a bad old skin.

Not much lifted in spirits, Stephen O'Kelly'O sitting this day watching out the window the traffic of Pell Street. Where the motor vehicles slowly cruise past looking for space to park. Old habitués go by with whom no word is spoken but whose faces have become familiar to know.

This is now my lonely home. A percolator bubbling. A hot cup of coffee in my hand and munching on crumb cake and a Danish pastry. Wearing a dressing robe, a birthday present from Sylvia, that once jeering sneering voice which finally took on a kindly sound and now is vanished. And a day unfolds when everything looks so solemn that a deep deep gloom hovers into Pell Street. Despite all the kindnesses, forgiveness, friendship, and consideration that is felt and shown to others, still you wonder what bad things there are that the world will do to you next. There goes by down in the street a familiar Oriental gentleman of noble mien, pushing his barrow loaded with boxes and a Caucasian son of a bitch in an automobile behind him blowing his horn. The story of America told in one simple message. Get the fuck out of my way I am in a goddamn hurry. Just like the guy in the bus station who was telling everyone wrong information is being given out at Princeton.

The morning fading away. Noontime coming. The afternoon descending. Premonitions looming of never seeing Dru again. Such different worlds we live in. Yet I was in hers as close as you can get. Her words wonderfully astonishing being conferred upon me as I sank my cock into her for the third time. And she screamed like a wounded animal and the rattler rattled. And my world seemed all in radiant glory as a great cascade of chorus came from Gounod's *St. Cecilia Mass* as I cried out with my own scream of joy. We lay there enraptured, legs and arms enveloped, the moisture of our bodies she said had become one.

Stephen O'Kelly'O turning to look out at the sound of a beeping horn down in the street. And there suddenly below as I open the window for a breath of differently polluted air is Maximilian Avery Gifford Strutherstone III, waving his bright cap held in a hand wearing a lemon yellow driving glove. And dressed in a hacking jacket, cavalry twill riding britches, and grinning up from his open Bentley, beckoning me down. And of course leaning out I knocked a carton of milk off the windowsill and it went plop in front of the landlord, the splash turning his shoes white just as Max shouted.

"Hey pal, old buddy boy. I'm on my way to take a little canter in the park. Why don't you come along and join me for a bit of a spin. And later take you to a meal and swim at my club."

There was considerable gladness to see and hear this friend. The spiritually corrosive element of the city had made itself felt upon me as I attempted to go to sleep last night, when I had a ringside view of a fight erupting down in the street. A drunken man distributing ten-dollar bills and the guy slapping his hand on the back of a passing taxi to distribute his largesse. Taxi stops. Guy gets out. And to the proffered ten-dollar note, instead of taking it and saying, Thanks pal, the taxi driver punches him on the jaw, knocks him down and his head hits the curb. So much for outright giving people money. Like a good and true New Yorker, the taxi driver jumps back in his cab and drives away in a smoking blaze of tires. I was about to venture out to assist the vanquished citizen but a police patrol car happening down the street intervened and soon had an ambulance coming along. Then the junk searchers came patrolling down the street to see what they would take as they examined the best garbage in the world. Which more than half-furnished everything in this room and which was collected off the sidewalks of the surrounding streets. Now I hear Max beeping his horn again as I put on a tie and feel horny for Dru. Where is she in her daily itinerary. At the chiropodist, hairdresser, psychic, or swimming at her club. Her lithe body undulating through the water. The shiver I feel whenever I remember the rattling rattlesnake. Maybe like one used to try and kill ole Max in Texas. And even in its stuffed variety scaring the shit out of me. Dru asked if I were ever scared in the war. I said plenty and especially once or twice manning twenty-millimeter guns, firing at kamakazi that flew straight at you and kept coming through the tracer bullets while you tried, with all the aircraft crisscrossing the sky, to make sure you hit the bandits instead of the angels. My gunner's mate third class nearby, got hit and blown to pieces and his blood and parts of him were splattered and stuck all over me. Now go down these stairs. The dust on the carpeted steps comes up as a fume to asphyxiate you. Like you'd feel loading sixteen-inch guns behind massive armor plate and being driven crazy with claustrophobia. Go out the vestibule. Past bills stuffed in the mailbox. Better there than a worry on my brain. Climb up into the old Bentley.

"Boy pal, it sure is good to see you. How are you."

"I'm okay Max. How are you doing."

"Well ole buddy boy pal, let's answer that by saying we're on our way to take in some riding. Can't really hold your head up socially unless, when the season comes, you aren't already socked in with a good hunt in New Jersey. Isn't that where ole Sylvia hunted before you married. And you objected to the chasing of the fox as a cruel sport. Rumor has it that ole Sylvia has a trace of Iroquois Indian blood."

"Well Max, there are rumors now of so many sorts that all I believe is what I see with my own eyes. The truth is she found her natural mother, and she spat in Sylvia's face."

"Hey, pal, old buddy boy. That's awful. Worst thing I've ever heard."

As we roared off down the street, chill air blowing upon our faces. It was astonishing how Max's appearance could in a second or two transform one's life from verging on an unheralded session of manic depression into at least a milder form verging on a feeble spark of hope in the distance. Even the landlord seemed impressed by Max's car and remained noncomplaining about the milk on his shoes or two months owed rent but I suspected he preferred my not lowering the tone of the building any further if I kept my milk off the windowsill. It was as if moving in such stylish company gave the landlord the notion that affluence the like of Sylvia's clothing and behavior and Max's elegantly flamboyant appearance, largesse was not far away and coming up with the rent was only a matter of a short delay, with family lawyers and trustees ladling out funds from an office near Wall Street which, with Sylvia was in fact the case in receiving her monthly emolument, alas no longer being injected into her bank. And I told Max to say nothing about Sylvia's mother.

"Well old buddy, I won't and at least we're taking you up to a better part of town up there around the park."

It was in itself cheerful to find how in Max's company one's mood could change so fast and a sense of purpose prevail. Even though it be for a superficial pursuit. With every part of this city that you passed still reminding you of something which instantly could become inspiring for one's aspirations. In a metropolis you didn't always realize you lived in as if it were a dream. For unless you did, its lonely sadness could tear you apart.

"Max, my mother used to say, who before she got married worked as a ladies maid for a rich household on Fifth Avenue, that nobody who was anybody lived north of Fifty-seventh Street."

"You don't say. Well pal, things have sure changed. But sorry to hear that about your mother having to do something servile like that. But go back far enough I guess in social lineage in this country we all had to come from the wrong side of the tracks. And rely on the good example of others who made it over to the right side of the tracks. Where one refers to oneself as one."

"Well my mother, as a matter of fact, didn't come from the wrong side. She came from a green field in Ireland and didn't refer to herself as one. But even when she had her own maid and cook in America, she nearly spent all her time in her kitchen anyway, brushing her hands on her apron."

"Hey, that was a pretty kind of menial existence she chose, wasn't it."

"She was domestically dedicated, I suppose. Setting an example for my sisters, who were sometimes helping."

"That must have been nice for your father."

"Well my father stayed downtown a lot minding his bars but I saw him more than once in the dining room, his head in his hands, wracked with worry with his large family to feed, clothe, and educate."

"Hey, tough. Gee, really tough. But I mean, things like

bootlegging must have been profitable in the past for him to have built up a nice little equity. But I guess you had to fight against the moral indignity of it."

There were times when I thought I should give ole Max a severe kick in the ass. There were plenty of families with far more exalted names and reputations than mine who were bootleggers. But there was no question that without ever wanting them to appear any grander than their circumstances, one always attempted to uphold the reputation of one's family. And do as Max suggested refer to oneself as one. But now I also hoped the conversation would slow Max's speed as we roared up Broadway toward Fifty-ninth Street. Max waving back to approving pedestrians who were shouting encouragement at the passing leviathan which was only just miraculously avoiding accidents with screeches of brakes, swerves, and quick acceleration which deaccelerated pronto as a policeman's whistle blew and pulled us over. And Max, with his usual charm, apologized to Patrolman Richard J. Gallagher, ex-Marine Corps, who after a lecture on the exercise of good manners and civil behavior in a big city let us ex-navy types go.

"Gee pal, old bean, how do you like that. Now there's a man who'll advance in the force, unlike some persnickety bastards. Nice to meet a gentleman member of New York's finest. But he couldn't be doing serious police work if he found time to bother to blow his whistle at us."

"Well Max, you were doing fifty miles an hour. He should have arrested you. And I've still got a little something to live for."

"This old baby can do a hundred and fourteen miles an hour, pal. Here we go. Watch."

"Max, please, Don't. I've got to maybe see Sylvia's mother tomorrow and be in one piece."

"Hey old buddy boy, why didn't you say so. You're going to maybe have a séance with the richest woman in the world. Jesus Christ, that can't be bad. I'll slow down for that, pal. We'll slow down to a crawl. Hey old buddy boy, don't be coy. You haven't have you, maybe slipped the old veal to ole Dru. I know mum's the word. But boy, if that news don't beat all."

"Max, I didn't say I had."

"You don't have to say anything, pal."

In the park, Max mounted on his nag riding away under the trees. In his breeches and leathers, a pink carnation in the buttonhole of his cavalry twill hacking jacket and a white silk cravat secured with a gold pin at his throat. One had somehow to laugh that despite his old warrior-style mahogany topping to his gleaming riding boots he had got made for himself in Paris, one felt he wouldn't be getting the kind of warm-up equestrian exercise needed for foxhunting while tiptoeing on an ancient swaybacked hack trotting around Central Park. But in the company of a couple of aristocratic Europeans disposed to horse riding, it was obvious he loved the dressing up in the kit. As I agreed to come back and meet him later, he saluted from the peak of his hunting cap, waved and grinned as he rode off and I waved back and headed towards downtown in the park to spend a peaceful time wandering the zoo.

As the light of the afternoon was fading, I was waiting back at the stables for Max's return on his nag. He seemed in a distracted mood and one sensed his effort to project his usual bubbling geniality. After driving along Central Park South to his club, a dutiful doorman parked his Bentley leviathan and as we passed through the club doors there was a question raised as to his being properly dressed for admittance. Max showing a surprising degree of irritation at a club contingent of officialdom arriving to pronounce upon his attire as possibly contravening the house dress code.

"Look here my good fellows, this is in fact my stock I wear at my neck when pursuing the fox. It was recently being worn as a cravat while cantering in the park. But I earnestly assure you, will in fact, as you now see me retie it, become a tie to be worn when this very evening I change into the suit in my locker to dine with my good friend here. Count Alfonso Stephen O'Kelly'O."

As other club members were now pausing in the lobby to listen to the sartorial difficulty, the spokesman for the contingent ruling on house dress rules finally agreed that Max was dignified enough to be allowed to enter in order to cross the lobby to the elevator in order to rise to change into other clothes kept in his locker. And so booted and accoutred, Max marched clicking his heels, to the elevator where the grinning white-gloved operator welcomed him aboard to ascend. Everywhere we went up and down and through the vast halls of this palace dedicated to great achievement in sport, there came a litany of greeting for Max. "Hi ya there fella, old sport. How ya doin', pal. Play any badminton lately. . . . Yeah pal, had a great game." In the baths, a marble empire of tile and dressing booths housing the swimming pool, it was an oasis from the city where we steamed, showered, and swam. Sun-lamps, hot rooms, spout rooms, and massage chamber. Stacks of sheets to wrap in, and towels to dry on.

"You see pal, ole buddy boy, this is where you can daily escape from your troubles. Find yourself an ole deck chair here. Wrap up in a few sheets and towels. Go out like a light, asleep for a while. I'll get us a couple of cooling drinks to slake the ole thirst while we lie back and luxuriate."

While Max went for a rubdown, I nodded off into sleep in a steamer chair to the sound of splashing water and a couple of nearby club philosophers discussing Nietzsche. When I woke, Max was standing there wrapped in a towel, staring down at me. Then his name paged, Max disappeared for a long time to the telephone as the water-polo team plunged through the waves and then did a strange waving arm dance back and forth in the pool. When Max returned, he seemed wreathed in worry and continued distracted as we descended by marble stairs to an oak-paneled room for beers and had slabs of roast beef as our evening appetizers. A mural of a fox hunt behind the bar to which Max brought notice.

"Well pal, there may not be much of that ole foxhunting anymore for yours truly. This tonight could be the last supper. Judas Iscariot is doing his worst. But come on. Let's go get dinner. Later, I'll take you on a tour."

We took the elevator up to the splendor of the chandeliered dining room with its great windows looking out over the park's trees all the way to Harlem fifty-one city blocks away. Over big rare porterhouse steaks, we quaffed Burgundy along with baked potatoes and the club's homemade bread, apple pie and ice cream. Then Max brought me visiting the endless sporting facilities, from the basement bowling alleys to the rooftop solarium, twenty-four stories up in the sky. Together we stared out into the downtown distance at this city's bright lights illuminating its dark shadows. Come to New York where no one knows you. The mystery within the thousands of anonymous windows. Then descending on the elevator to the hall of athletic fame. Each time the white-gloved elevator operator saluting Max.

"There you go Admiral, second floor."

Max in his gray pinstripe Savile Row suit, silk shirt and dark blue striped tie, saluting back as we step out into this grand hall of athletic honor. Photographs of the legendary in track and field. Oarsmen, boxers, fencers, wrestlers and even badminton players. After viewing the glass cases of medals and trophies, we ascended again to have our brandy and cigars in the billiard room. And it was only when we were parting that I got the first hint of why Max was so deeply preoccupied.

"Well pal, drop you off downtown. You know, sometimes these lawyers get you down. Pal, what does an honorable man do when he is surrounded by those dishonorable. Sons of bitches close in on you with a bunch of goddamn fabrications and falsehoods, trying to traduce one's character and slice up what's left of one's assets. What do you say I leave it that I give you an ole tinkle real soon."

The tinkle from Max never came, as I could not afford to get the phone reconnected. But I learned, calling his Wall Street office that a few days later Max was arrested, arraigned and incarcerated in alimony jail. After a few hours of trying from the nearest local bar, I was finally able to talk to him on the telephone and I felt it were as if I were listening to voices singing the line "O hear us when we cry to thee for those in peril on the sea" from the navy hymn.

"Gee Max, they got you."

"Yeah pal, but I wouldn't quite put it like that, as if I were a fugitive or something. I come from a tough city of graft, corruption and with a fine history of bootlegging and I think I can hold my own in here with television, Ping-Pong and door instead of bars on the rooms where you sleep. Better than being in the navy, pal. Can even play handball on the roof. In fact, I've never met a nicer bunch of human beings in my life. And great to listen to all these guys swearing that not even over their dead bodies would they pay their wives a cent. But as reasonable as this place is where they've got me and these warders treat you pretty good, I do get my down moments. But I tell you this, I am goddamned if I'm going to be sentenced to a lifetime of paying alimony to two goddamn cheating women and be accused of being a fortune-hunting crook by one of them."

"Gee Max, is there anything I can do to help. Maybe see if everything is all right in the apartment."

"Thanks pal, but that Chinese family that does my laundry just down the street—I did them a few favors and they have the key and are taking care of it."

There was something deep and awfully unconditional in Max's words which were like those said to the surrendering nations in the war. Meanwhile I suggested I went to make sure the key was in good hands and that Max's plants were watered and his collection of seashells dusted. But later that day, talking again to Max, he said Ertha's lawyers had got repossession of the apartment. I made arrangements to visit Max in the alimony jail which he said was a four-story redbrick building at 434 West Thirty-seventh Street and stuck between a loft and garage. I also phoned Dru from a Bowery bar and in some concern that I would have the husband, instead of Gilbert, the butler answering. She seemed more than matter-of-fact and cool. Said she was concerned as to where Sylvia was and if I had seen her and I could hardly make sense of what she next said.

"Having learned some manners and honorable behavior while briefly at Miss Hewitt's on Seventy-fifth Street as well as that Manhattan Island is built on jagged gneiss, I fear one finds one must work far too hard to avoid giving the impression of a frivolous, carefree existence. Or, in this case, of an illicit one. Sylvia knows about you and me, and I do hope you haven't, as someone has, been indiscreet."

"No, ma'am, to no one. Can I see you."

"I'm afraid that I'm not so sure you can."

Dru having mentioned honorable behavior and manners, I thought of Syracuse and my long-lost friend of childhood who said it was bad manners to go to someone's house and stay as a guest and blow your nose in their sheets. It was also dishonorable to take away small mementos which could rank as theft. Or to put a final shine on your shoe tips with one of their towels. But Dru's frosty voice held some other message she had decided not yet to tell me. The phone clicked off as all kinds of agonizing jealousies awakened. The memory of that room and her wonderful body. Her ass could smile at you. Her delicate touches of kisses. Her proffered warmth and affection. Even the goddamn snakes and the veiled suggestion I fuck her in a coffin. Which I earnestly assume was not meant to be closed. How many other men have been there with her brought in that black door and across that tiled floor and up that curving staircase. Taking off their clothes, pulling off their belts swatting her on the ass as she enticed with compliments their pricks into her. Rolling over on the buzzer that rattles the rattle of the rattlesnake and sends a shiver of fear through you and maybe even rattles your bones. And thousands of miles away on the coast of Africa there must have been black gentlemen fucking her on the beach. Or who knows, deep in the jungle, writhing around in the undergrowth with black mambas and crocodiles. I looked up *gneiss* in the dictionary and found it was metamorphic rock of coarse grain. And at least it was nice to know what held up all the skyscrapers of New York so that they wouldn't suddenly all keel over on each other or start to lean like the leaning tower of Pisa. Hanging up the phone in this bar with sawdust on the floor and two other customers, I bought a beer. And nearly had a fight with a barfly accusing me of being unfriendly when I didn't speak when spoken to. And in exasperation, I said, "Fella, if I were unfriendly, I would have already knocked you off that fucking stool into next week." The bartender then got unfriendly and ran out from behind the bar. And reaching out to grab me, I grabbed him. And with my thumbs sinking into his biceps, paralyzed his arms. When he agreed that I was strong and could kill him, I let him go and walked out. Max's company gone. Dru frosty and remote. Sylvia vanished. Step over these alcohol-sodden bodies stretched out across the sidewalk. Wondering who might have been a college president or a stockbroker. Return to Pell Street. Through these ancient pathways of this city. Past the oldest pharmacy in America, where, when I can afford to, I buy their toothpaste. Could, when my own days are numbered, be one of those downtrodden. Without a dream nor hope left. Instead of white-haired, standing on a podium into a venerable old age. Adored by the audience. Who, hushed, await my baton raised to signal the orchestra to begin. Let the music of great composers banish away the treacherous gloom. Elevate, cheer and glorify the wonder of sounds that exalt the soul.

Into this familiar doorway of Pell Street. This musty stale smell. Collect the unwelcome mail. Not a single hint of a friend on a single envelope. Push open the door into the staircase hall. A crouched form looming up. The glint of a knife blade. A black visage in the darker dark. The navy taught you to look in the nighttime a few degrees above what you were trying to see.

"You white motherfucking cocksucker, fuck my woman. I'm going to kill you."

A shadow coming into the light. Sidestep a flick knife

jabbed out at my solar plexus. Draw in the stomach. Blazing hatred in the eyes of this black face. Aspasia's boyfriend. Last heard of as a prisoner on Rikers Island. Former dumping ground of refuse and dirt from subway excavations. Subterranean fires smoldering in the rubbish, overrun by rats. Has the city's largest venereal disease clinic. This son of a bitch now released or escaped. Could have, before any shark got him, swum across the bay, knife between his teeth. And on the map when I was looking to see how safe I was from the marauder, if he swam north, he would have landed on a piece of shore, a peninsula of land called Casanova. Get a hold of his goddamn wrist. Twist the knife out of his hand. The fucker's strong. But my piano-playing exercised fingers are stronger. Just like the Gothic arches of masonry of the Brooklyn Bridge which hold its great cables. As I make you, you son of a bitch, drop this goddamn knife. Kick it along the hall as I get hit on the jaw. Heave a left into this bastard's ribs. With all the fluent force practiced in all the amateur nights in which I boxed. Send a straight right into his face for good measure. The soft warm taste of blood. My teeth cut into my jaw. Hit him again. Tough son of a bitch won't go down. Wham, bam. Hit him again. And again. He's down. Got me by the legs. I'm down. Son of a bitch like a snake. Around my back, trying to get an arm across my throat and hold me in a scissors with his legs. Reach my leg over his crossed ankles. Arch my back in the wrestler's grapevine. Make his ankle ligaments stretch and snap as he screams in agony. Tear away the arm around my throat. Get loose. Elbow him in the guts for good measure. Grab the knife off the floor. He's up. Limping and making for the door.

"You white mother fucking cocksucker. I'm going to come back and fix you."

"I'll kill you if you do."

The front door slams. Time to get the hell out of here. And miles away. Before I get a bullet or blade into my guts. Mayham on every side. Escape away into all the anonymity I can muster. Feel for stab wounds and loose teeth. Choking dust in my lungs. Should go after him with the knife. Kill him now, before he comes back, along with a gang. And guns. Plead self-defense so that I don't go to Sing Sing to the electric chair. The electrodes strapped on as you sit staring in the direction of an audience that maybe you can't see but who goddamn well want to see you contort and fry. Smoke come up out of your head. And the smell not be as appetizing as toasted bacon. No one rich has ever gone to the electric chair. Means I'll always be first in line to get my spinal cord melted. And hear them say, Well, bud, you're paying the price of being poor, so we're pulling the switch. Marvelous as Aspasia was as a fuck and singer, I can't feel, without further sampling and verification, that she's worth dying for, except that there's no question this guy thinks she is. The sooner I get to somewhere like Montana with only grizzly bears, wildcats, rattlesnakes and mountain lions to worry about, the better.

Stephen O'Kelly'O slowly climbing back to the apartment. Up the stairs creaking one by one. Pain in odd places. The door splintered and jammed. The bastard must have tried to break in. Push it open with a shoulder. Close, lock, and latch it. After the battle. Sit down and rest. All the symphonies that I might now never write. Instead of soaring passages of musical triumph, nothing now but risks of death and awful despair. Just as I was once, unwanted, turned away from joining the school choir. Because of a lack of serious intent. Which wasn't true. Sat on the steps outside the door where they practiced and rehearsed. Tears falling on the back of my hands as I listened to their voices. The same hands now with a knife cut on the side of my thumb. Blood spattered. As this city now begins to haunt. With Max arrested. Sylvia gone. And she said once when leaving, "One of these times we say good-bye will be the last time we say good-bye. Good-bye."

And I felt a gloomy shudder the way she said her last good-bye. Her presence now could at least give me something to be irritated by. Watch her pull on her stockings on her long beautiful dancer's legs. The muscles that could faintly be seen across her stomach. Her shiny clean hair like the hair of the girl in the bus station. This city without warning. Even with all its red lights, sirens, and signs. Catastrophe comes from anywhere in the flash of a second. Take a walk. Thousands pass you by. Alone with yourself. A world that wants you to show your teeth shining out of your glad face.

Two days staying in the apartment. I lay down to sleep with a tiredness so overwhelming. Between moments of tinkling the keys of the piano, staring out into the Oriental street and reminding myself to call Max but waiting to be cheerful before I did, I washed and cleaned the knife, practised pushing the button that flashes out the five-inch-long blade. Kept it handy through the nights and then tried throwing it, sticking it into the back of the bedroom closet door. Feeling lonely for company but remembering that coming back with Sylvia on the train to the city and passing by so many places that you don't want to be, you realize that nobody in New York has anything to say to each other after all their current jokes are told. And when I did go out on the street to buy something for breakfast, my familiar Chinaman said to me, it is a nice day overhead. And in a desperate lonely disillusion and with the swiftly dwindling money my sister gave me in my pocket, I went back to the Biltmore "Men Only" bar. Same man outside playing his music, pretending he's blind. Missed three notes from Prokofiev's *Overture Russe,* opus seventy-two. Anyway, not one of Prokofiev's greatest works, but an insult to a composer nevertheless. Inside, a new waiter called Angelo. Had cheese and crackers and a beer. Illuminated by lamps, stared at the painting of the nude reclining girls against their green background.

Then, working up the nerve at the telephone in the bar, put my nickel in to dial that Butterfield 8 number, and spoke to her. But before I could utter an endearment, a shock of a frosty voice came crashing into my ear.

"Do you mind if we have for a moment a serious discussion."

"No ma'am, fire ahead."

"When I was a little girl someone said to me, you can afford, can't you, to be of a high moral character. And those others whom you may find throughout your life who are not of high moral character, you may avoid and dispose of."

"Ma'am forgive me, but I don't believe I know what you're talking about."

"I'm talking about having my privacy invaded. It's being deemed entertaining to others to describe me as 'the richest woman in America.'"

"Ma'am, I've never said a thing to anybody about your money or about you ever having any."

"Well, you have a friend who did. And said such a thing to my bankers."

"Ma'am, maybe it was your bankers who said such a thing. And if my friend did, he meant no harm in such a coloration."

"Meaning no harm does not stop the unwelcome attentions of all the lowlife in America."

"Well ma'am, there's no need to worry that it will be repeated, for he's in prison."

"What."

"Sorry, I meant to say he's gone west to Chicago."

The phone line went dead. Cut off at a point when you try to say a word and another word jumps in too soon. Dru will be thinking my friend Max will be consulting with his coconspirators behind bars and is already plotting to embezzle or kidnap her. All I needed now was just one more blow. And I got it. Of rejection. As I then in desperation immediately telephoned back to Sutton Place and Gilbert answered the phone.

"May I please speak to Mrs. Triumphington."

"Who's calling, please."

"Alfonso Stephen O'Kelly'O."

"I'm afraid Mrs. Triumphington is not available."

"I've just been talking to her."

"I'm afraid madam has just left for Montana."

After some prompting and knowing I already had it, Gilbert gave me the number out in Montana. Where if it were to be believed she had gone, I would ring her. But maybe she had really departed there. But with some other guy. Fucking someone else. She did say once, although I pretended not to be one of them, that she liked to have guys available on tap for fucking and just gobble them up. Listen a little to their bullshit and take them on and take them off one after the other. Now on top of it all, a dreadful premonition suddenly seizing me over Max's arrest and incarceration in alimony jail. And I immediately rang to plan to visit him. A voice coming on the phone saying they had terrible information that he had hung himself and his remains were being shipped by train back to Chicago. My fists clenched in a sudden raging anger at the female species. And remembering what Max had said as we lay back on our couches in the hot room of his club.

"How modern can life get, pal. Here we try to keep it a little old-fashioned. Except to come dine and have a cocktail, that's the real wonderful thing about this club, no women. And one should have only conducted one's associations with them on wise Muslim principles. Purdah and all that. Because boy, they have recently sure done me down."

As I felt this numbing news from the "alimony club," as Max now called it, spread to all parts of my body, I had nearly dropped the phone. But the report of hanging was immediately followed by laughter and Max's voice.

"Old pal, I've executed a power of attorney, and deed of sale for a dollar, and all the other things you can do with a flourish of the pen. Go get my ole Bentley quick, soon as you can, out of the garage. I've given them your name and they've got the key. Be a sport and park at fifteen o'clock as near as you can get to Freeman Square. If I don't show up by quarter past fifteen o'clock, you beat it with the Bentley. It's yours, pal, ole buddy. I glow with joy when I think of what I'm going to do. Pure joy. Anyway, no matter what happens, wait for me to be in touch again. This is your lifelong friend, best man at your wedding, signing off."

I couldn't figure out what Max was up to, but I wanted to do him any kindness or favor he might ask. And one thing was for sure. Ole Max aboard ship in the navy was one of the greatest fixers and connivers of all time. I found I was already fully insured and got the Bentley, but trying to figure out how to drive it out of the garage, I almost crashed a couple of times. And when I finally did figure out how to drive it, I found it a nightmare trying to park it. Waited half an hour near where the traffic passed to enter the Holland Tunnel under the Hudson and Max did not show up. Then after a search, I found a friendly garage a couple of blocks away to park the leviathan. The enthusiastic owner of the garage rubbed a spot of soot off a fender.

"Hey, we could charge admission to come look at this car."

Two days later, a telegram was waiting for me back at Pell Street, stating that further news of Max could be had from a funeral home. I chuckled at Max's magnificent ability to create such an elaborate hoax and fakery. I phoned the funeral directors and then was asked to identify myself. And a chill began to creep through me at the sound of this matter-of-fact but solemn voice announcing that Max's body was being shipped that night and put onto the train at Penn Station at about 9:30, and the train leaving at ten minutes past ten, destination Chicago, from platform eleven. I waited as the voice finished to repeat who I was and waited again to hear some denouement of the charade. But when I phoned the alimony jail to talk to Max, I was told no information was available from the Civil Jail of the City of New York except to his next of kin upon identification. There was one thing now that was seeming more and more certain. That this was no fakery. No hoax. Max was dead.

I changed my clothes, got out the ole Bentley, and traveled up to Riverdale. I couldn't believe what I was doing, but it seemed the most important thing I would ever do in my life. As the throbbing leviathan pulled into the drive of this my childhood home, the curtains at the side of the house opened and there were smiles on everyone's faces as I parked and my old dog, who sang out of tune to my piano playing, tail wagging, barked and friendly snapped at the tires. There was one thing for certain that I was finding out fast. It was not who you were in America, but what car you were seen driving in. Even dogs noticed. And mine was adding to his appreciation by lifting a leg and peeing on a wheel. The general admiration for the Bentley at least stifled my gloom and sadness while I feigned to be matter-of-fact and drove my favorite sister around a few local potholed streets, beeping the horn a couple of times passing in front of those houses where I knew the inhabitants flew the American flag and had hated me while growing up.

"Gee, Stephen, what a nice car. Is it really yours."

Explaining my complications as best I could and after taking tea with my mother and sisters, I borrowed some more money and then went up into the attic to get my old navy sailor hat out of a musty steamer trunk. Back downtown I tipped the concierge at the Plaza the way Max did and splurged on a bottle of Krug. Recalling all the better and funnier times we had in the navy. Half-crocked, I parked the precious Bentley back in the garage and then took my time sobering up to walk to Penn Station. Nearly financially broke again after my bottle of Krug at the Plaza, which in my solemnity became easier and easier to drink as I drank it all.

Arriving into this massive cathedral of space, where I had so often come and gone on the train, ditty bag slung over my shoulder and on my way back to Norfolk, Virginia where my ship was moored at the Naval Operating Base. And it became the first time I knew who would win the war. Walking along the docks past the brooding, massive, looming prows of these vessels. One after another. Cruisers, battleships, destroyers, aircraft carriers, as far as the eye could see. And once with Max, as we walked under all the assembled bows to our own gangway, returning from liberty, I heard him chuckle and announce, "Pal, it's America the almighty and boy, don't get in her way."

I got permission to go down on the train station platform. Steel pillars holding up the weight of other steel pillars. The clatter and din. The dimly lit cars. Early passengers arriving to take their seats for the long trip west halfway across America. A girl waiting, standing alone like a statue in the shadows. Her hair blond. And her face, as she turns now hidden by the brim of her cloche hat. Caught sight of her flickering glance. Must be waiting for someone. As I wait. Expecting Max's arrival. Which still has me half-thinking that it will be on a horse clattering down the platform, his shotguns blazing away. Till suddenly a van comes pulling up to the platform and opens up its black doors alongside the train. Two railroad porters and two men from the van maneuvering out a box. I stood aside as they approached, then as the box passed, placed my old sailor hat on top and saw the name and address of a Chicago funeral firm. And now I had to believe he was within. Saluting as the container was gently pushed onto and parked amidst other goods and baggage on the train.

"Go well now, old salt and good friend."

I still thought I would see breathing holes and hear laughter. But all was silent within that box. To be taken west. Out to where Max always maintained the real American gentlemen still existed. The word *gentleman* such an important word in his life. Could see him hesitating to brush back the lock of sandy hair that fell over his left eye

in case it presented him as ungentlemanly. But also the slightly mischievous smile on his face he nearly always wore while rifling through his papers. Super efficient yeoman. He could put some son of a bitch's name on a draft for permanent kitchen duty or a friend to be flown home on compassionate leave to see his recently unfaithful girlfriend. So many plans he made for his own life. Equestrian pursuits. His shoes, ties, and guns. So alive and living only a day or two ago. It is not possible to believe he is here in death. Planned in just the same way he organized and prearranged his existence. Now ten past twenty-two hundred hours. Porter announcing, "All aboard." The sliding door of the baggage car closing. Train beginning to move. At first adagio. And gathering speed. Presto. *Click clack* on these steel wheels on the steel tracks. Good-bye old pal, buddy. Old salt. Bon voyage, anchors aweigh. Go home now. Back to the Loop and the Windy City. That great old town on the lake. Which you used to tell me was the most wonderful on earth. And to which one day you said you would return. Where they would build a building that would be the tallest building in the world, at least for a while.

As it pulled away down the platform into the darkness, the sound growing fainter. The train lights disappearing. To go out under the Hudson deeps, that river that was always flowing not that far away from Riverdale in my years growing up. Where we were children running

277

through the streets, away from other kids trying to give us a charley horse. A bang of a fist on a shoulder or thigh that could leave you laughing as well as temporarily paralyzed. And playing games of squeezing breath out of our lungs so that we would slump into unconsciousness and look dead on other people's lawns. And now I still expected ole Max to come up behind me out of the dark and put a hand on my shoulder. Well pal, ole buddy, I'm out of the alimony jail. Now here's my plan. There's the Riviera, Biarritz, London and Paris to go to in the tradition of the great previous Americans who sought an ancient culture to thrive in. And when life is lived to the full over there, shooting, hunting and fishing, resplendent in the sartorial dignity of sporting Europe, just hope old bean, they won't forget to put a sailor hat on my coffin when my time really comes. And they inter me in one of those artistically embellished sepulchres they've got in the old Cimetière Père Lachaise. But so long for now, good pal and friend.

Looking down into the empty track where another train will soon come to take others away. I knew now that this night would for the rest of my life always possess a simple silence, just as it did when growing up when the midnight approached listening to the music of the great composers on the radio as I did alone in my back room in the house in Riverdale. The leaves of the big cherry tree sometimes rustling against the windowpanes as the gusts of wind of a storm approached. And I would, warm and secure between my walls, wait for the announcer to speak as a preamble a poem by Henry Wadsworth Longfellow. And for him to say, "This is your station, WQXR, ending our broadcasting for the night. And the cares that infest day shall fold their tents like the Arabs and silently steal away." Just as you go Max, old pal, buddy and friend. Flesh cold upon your bones. Who came out east from the west. Now goes west again back home. Trundling past all the one-horse towns. Crossing the plains covered by those cornfields to the horizon. Where there's a sound I can forever hear. Of the distant whistle wail of a train across the night. Turning the woes of life into a haunting memory. By which to rest in peace.

"Excuse me. But you're Max's friend, aren't you."

On the back of his hand, Stephen O'Kelly'O wiping a tear from an eye and turning to this voice behind him. The blond-haired girl in the cloche hat who was standing like a statue. A sallow-faced, beauteous girl. A flash of memory of another voice. Which said, "Excuse me sir."

"I'm Amy from Knoxville. You don't know me but I know all about you. You're Stephen. You were Max's friend in the navy. I'd been speaking to Max every day in jail. Like you, I came to see him off on the train. I just didn't feel he should be alone. And you must have felt about him as I did to have put that sailor hat on his coffin."

Out of courtesy in this dismal dark darkness, I

stepped down a step from the siding and she came closer into the light. And that perhaps I was not expected to speak but to wait until spoken to. I could see from her reddened eyes that she'd been weeping. We shook hands. And together climbed back up the stairs into the vast ticket hall and past the giant stone pillars holding up its ceiling which seemed like a massive brooding sky. The few travelers all looked smaller and lonelier. We walked up the wide stone steps which led out onto Seventh Avenue. Back in the busy world of the city again. Just across and up the street we went into the Hotel Pennsylvania where she was staying. The lights of the lobby too bright, we went into the darker bar. She insisted the drinks we had be put on her bill. Cocktail music from the piano. This wan blond-haired, blue-eyed girl whose skin seemed peach-soft like a child's and whose thin wrists might be too weak to carry her hands. She seemed as if she might freeze or the wind might blow her away. Over her months in New York, she kept in touch with Max. And when we said good-bye, shaking hands, her hand was firm on mine and for a moment I thought she might not let go unless I did.

"Max so many times said that his life was going to be lived the way he would live it or he didn't want to live. When he spoke of you, he always seemed so proud of knowing you and that you composed music."

I had only soda water with a slice of lemon in the bar

of the Hotel Pennsylvania. And apologized to Amy that I could not bring her to Max's favorite place in New York, the "Men Only" bar of the Biltmore. She smiled and said she didn't mind but that she'd be glad to take a ride on the Staten Island Ferry with me instead. I thought of her as I walked back to Pell Street where I had changed the lock and battered a new chain across the apartment door. Next day between efforts to compose, I lay somnambulant. Scavenging for bits of food. Sitting staring at my knees, thinking of the girl from Knoxville. Her kindly strange and so pale blue eyes. I needed courage to be in touch with her. With not even a telephone now to get another voice to come near to your ear and be a sympathetic friend as you sit in your dilemma. Knowing that even the smallest, mildest words voiced of affection, even as distant away as they might have to come, could be a lifesaver. To stop you throwing in the towel. As Max must have done in his final moment of waning defiance. The more you have left of life to live, the more hopeless the vastness of survival ahead becomes. Three square meals a day served on round plates. For which everyone but Dru is looking. When all she needs is exotic oil massages and to be wrapped in seaweed. And then have her privacy to look for pricks. Be in the barrel with her screwing. We could have then been dead together, plunging over Niagara Falls after our last orgasm. Go to heaven together, morals all aglow, with her money and my music.

Resurrecting myself from dejection in the late afternoon I took the radio with me under an arm and unstrapping my watch from my wrist, pawned them both on Ninth Avenue. Collected a total of nine dollars and fifty cents. The watch alone cost sixty-one dollars, bought at a reduction in a naval commissary store. I walked off some of the misery and gloom going uptown and crosstown to the Biltmore. The blind musician who could see was not to be seen. Had a beer in the "Men Only" bar. Angelo the bartender said hello. Every tiny word of greeting comfort is hard earned in this city. Especially when it prevails against the cruel indifference of the infidel hordes. Then went to Grand Central, stood on the balcony looking out over this vast temple of travel. Where I try to distract my mind. And can't. Away from pain. From all that would be death. And listen to life, the sound of voices as a pair of guys go by.

"So Christ, there she is. After all the goddamn hoopla, I finally meet her. Has a face looks like it came out of a truck transmission shop. Only she thinks she's God's gift to mankind."

With just enough money again jingling in my pocket, I telephoned Amy at the Pennsylvania Hotel but she was out. Left a message that I would telephone again. Walking down the slipway to the lower level, I stared into the Oyster Bar. Customers hunched over their martinis and shellfish, scoffing away. And here I am hungry but frightened to go in and spend any money. When the woman whose flesh I last touched could buy the whole world. Or at least a few dozen oyster bars. If only I could hear her sweet voice again. Instead of cold vowels. Her face, that of a goddess. Instead of coming out of a truck transmission shop, could only have come out of the most wonderful heavenly dream. But who in our brief romance had abruptly taken out and put on a pair of glasses I'd never seen her wear before. Changing her face and demeanor like a nightmare into the face and countenance of a schoolmarm staring at me. As if I'd committed every classroom misdemeanor in history. Her voice penetrating my ear as hard as her diamonds around her wrists and neck.

"Although if I ever care to, I'll throw away all the money I want to throw away. But while I have what I have, I want to be charged the same price that everyone else is charged for the same thing."

I thought, Holy cow honey, hell I'm not selling you anything you're paying for. Or charging you. Therefore and wherefore please don't look at me like that through those eyeglasses with those suddenly gimlet eyes. And I remembered leaving the restaurant where we had first dined and she had no money with her and wanted to tip a waiter and hatcheck girl and asked me if I had some change. And my wallet produced, her two fingers came like a flashing white shark in between the black leather folds and expertly tweezed out a searing sheaf of my last dollar bills. Made worse by the wallet being a present from my parents on graduation from prep school, which only my favorite sister attended and could conspicuously be heard clapping for me. Although I can't afford to throw away an old shoelace I feel the same way you do, Dru, about price. Only worse. The vanishing little sheaf of dollars leaving a vast meteorite hole in my spirit as big as the hole rumored to have wiped out the dinosaurs. Right now I worry about what I might be charged in the garage for Max's Bentley. The leviathan sitting there alone, waiting for him alive or his ghost. Its great engine ready to throbbingly burst into life. The brake unleashed and the accelerator slammed down. Would go again like a bat out of purgatory out into the city of New York, endangering lives on the streets. Or even in here in the middle vastness of this great room. Stars painted on the ceiling. Twinkling above. Which as I look up still make me wonder if Max was really in that box. Even attending as I had upon the incontrovertible fact. As was his secret girlfriend from Knoxville. But also remembering words he said of the law that I wondered if he could get around. And he said no. "Because, pal, it states that in all cases a decree awarding alimony is issued to the husband personally and failure constitutes contempt of court." And here I am, possessed of his beloved Bentley. Even his driving gloves so neatly folded in the dashboard compartment. Yet hoping to be able to say, as I was saying it, that Max is still alive. I know where he is. On the high seas. Pulled out of Pier 52 on the Hudson. Dressing for dinner aboard a transatlantic liner. Going to hole up in a London hostelry while he's fitted for suits and shotguns and getting his horse fit to hunt with the Quorn. And ole Max if he did throw a seven, at least did leave a legacy of laughter, which I found myself even enjoying in the bad doom hours of dawn. When the soul is reeling on the ropes. And I could recall his description of the day catching his wife in flagrante delicto and prodding his naked victim down that Houston suburban street where it went past one of the closer houses to the road in which lived a gentleman who sat almost all day drinking beer in the middle of a front room and endlessly reading detective stories out of magazines he kept piled up by his chair while his ex-beauty queen wife shopped for baubles and had facials on the proceeds her husband enjoyed from one of the biggest oil finds in Oklahoma. And as the man heard the singing approaching and the words "The eyes of Texas are upon you. All the live long day," he thought he was somehow being serenaded and that it was his moment in the limelight as a Texas patriot and a devout believer in the biggest and the best. Whereupon he got up from his chair to go to his window and as the procession of the naked man at the business end of a shotgun came into sight and began to pass by his front lawn, he began to laugh until convulsed in mirth, grasping his stomach with both hands and teetering backwards he fell over a cocktail table, cracking his pelvis in a couple of places. Even on the ambulance stretcher as they took him to the hospital he still could not stop laughing. It turned out he knew all about the affair Max's wife was having and had as a result, long ago assigned a detective to follow his own wife while he went on, otherwise undisturbed, reading his detective stories. But now I don't even know why I'm here in Grand Central Station halfway across this vast floor, amid all the traffic of rush-hour people hurrying in all their directions. All seeming to head toward the information booth center floor, with its clock on top, asking about trains to anywhere or somewhere. And suddenly stop in my tracks. Standing rigid. As if an arrow had just plunged between my shoulder blades and deeply into my back. A strange foreboding enveloping. Something dreadful has happened. Making me immediately go into the subway and back to Pell Street. And I found the arrow. Stuck in my mailbox. A telegram. Addressed to Alfonso Stephen O'Kelly'O.

URGENT YOU TELEPHONE THE ADIRONDACKS. DRUSILLA

I went out to the nearest local Bowery bar, where no one was usually wasting nickels on phone calls when it could buy beer instead. And stared at the bleakness of the telegram again. All except for a cheerful label attached, exhorting use of telegrams for distinctive socially correct modern correspondence. I dialed the operator to get long distance who tried as the minutes passed to obtain the number, and the number engaged. And as the call was attempted again and again, new nightmares taking wing. Something somehow more than dreadful had happened. When at last I got through, person-to-person, Dru was unavailable. And Parker, the butler, was on the phone who seemed to be crying but agreed to speak as the operator waited for me to plunge in quarter after quarter, clanking and chiming. To then hear his sobbing voice.

"They both got burned up in the fire, sir."

"Who."

"Our Sylvia and Mr. Triumphington. They're gone. I can't say any more, sir. I can't. Good-bye."

I telephoned Sutton Place. No one answering at that socially acceptable telephone exchange, Butterfield 8, I walked away across this socially unacceptable barroom floor where the toes of my shoes were disturbing the sawdust. Dark figures hunched on their stools, coughing in the stink of smoke and sound of spit landing in a spittoon. And the bird that seems in every bar dipping its beak amid the bottles. Two habitués drunkenly declaring their lifelong friendship with each other. "You take care of me, buddy, and I'll take care of you." And neither by the look of them, could take care of anybody. And do I now wait to go back to the phone and try again. Order a beer. Stand at the bar. Watch once more the little bird dipping its beak. Up and down. Like the words I hear over and over. They both went up in fire. Means flames. Immolation, as women do in India. They're gone. Means both are dead. Only Dru left to speak to. And until I do, there is now no way of knowing if maybe wrong information is being given out in the Adirondacks.

I bought a pizza to bring back to eat in the apartment in Pell Street. Gave one of my quarters for the phone to a vagrant who stepped up from the gutter and silently held out his hand. His tired worn face like the paintings Catholics have on their walls of Jesus Christ. My good mother always said to her children, "Always wait on bad news and hear it in the morning when, if it's bad, it will always be better to cope with after a good night's sleep." But my restless slumber was riddled by a nightmare of rattlesnakes coming from under the seats of the Bentley, beady eyes and forked tongues and rattles rattling, coiled to strike. And Max with his shotgun suddenly appearing out of a coffin alongside the Bentley, shooting their heads off one by one. I then suddenly found myself sitting up in the broken bed, sweat pouring from every pore, listening to the strange silence of Oriental nighttime out on the street and that refrain with a drumbeat marching through my brain, "The eyes of Texas are upon you."

The rest of the night I sat frozen awake, wrapped in a blanket till dawn. Knowing that the bleak light of the sun would first cast upon the tip-top towers of the tallest buildings as they became gleaming spires in the sky. And I would have to further wait until the sun came lower down, glinting on the millions of windows and to finally light up this edge of Chinatown and the world here of our little lives cheek by jowl. The tenant upstairs who burned incense and occasionally played what sounded like an Indian tom-tom, which rhythm I adapted for a passage in my minuet. And the guy who lived beneath who you never saw but who never complained about the piano sounds and drove a taxi by night and studied acting by day. Rip back the covers. Get out of bed. Fight. Fight the world. Fight death. Sit to the piano. Imagine as I always do an audience chattering. Its perfume. The glittering diamonds agleam on women's wrists, necks and ears. And then the conductor steps up on his podium. Bows to applause. Turns to his orchestra. Nods to the performer. His baton raised and brought down. As I play my minuet that took weeks to score for orchestra. In the hope that someday it would be heard. And is here now before me renamed.

Adagio for Sylvia.

Slow the movement. My fingers possessed by sorrow pass over the keys. Each note so touched to softly sound this threnody. Asking her forgiveness. For whatever trespass upon her I might have done. And who was never as cold and hard as could be her adoptive mother. But Sylvia did not as I can remember, ever cook one single meal. Or put her hand to my brow and say, You poor boy, do you suffer. Yet ask her. Still stay with me. Even in death. That our bones can one day lie melded together in the same grave. So that she would not be nor ever be unwanted. For I could remember another story she once told me of when she was a little girl all dressed up for her seventh birthday party. She'd gone to a new school and had brand-new playmates. Dru and her adoptive father away at polo matches in England, her English governess had organized the little "get-together," as she called it, by sending engraved invitations whose printed bumps she said Sylvia could run her thumbnail over and always know when she herself got one that the invitation was top-drawer from top-drawer people. The dining room table festive, set for thirty. Surprise presents for each welcome little guest. A conjurer, circus clown and quartet of musicians. Fire-eaters and a man nine foot high on stilts. And when a handful fewer came than were invited, two little girls who did come said the others stayed away because Sylvia had no real mother or father.

Stephen O'Kelly'O in tattered crimson dressing gown. Of which Sylvia always said, "Why don't you throw that rag away." Horns blowing down in the streets. Day's first traffic jam. Wait till it's over. And it is. Dress and go out.

Get something like a bun and a roll for breakfast and buy the paper. Look now out the window and up and down the street to make sure the coast is clear. Chill-enough day for a sweater. Get my mind to remember to buy a can of tomatoes and pound of onions and be able when I need to, to cook up a spaghetti meal.

Stephen O'Kelly'O in the candy store. Reminders of youth. Of jelly beans, fudge and bubble gum. Reach down to take up a newspaper. An argument in progress as two customers say they were there first to be served. And now I am served. I hand over a coin for a paper. Move outside slowly back into the street. And stare down. And there it is. The bottom of the front page of the newspaper. Under a photograph of the charred remains of Sylvia's doll's house in the woods. Special to the *Herald Tribune* and all the news that *they* think is fit to print in such a conspicuous headline.

PROMINENT SOCIETY FIGURE
IN DOLL'S HOUSE FIRE
WHICH TAKES TWO LIVES

What has been regarded by some as a family jinx has again befallen the socially prominent family of the heiress, the former Drusilla Guenevere Marchantiere, wife of Jonathan Triumphington, who died with their adopted daughter in a fire Thursday that occurred in a small cottage building called the Doll's House located in isolated woods not far from the family mansion on the Triumphington family estate in the Adirondacks. The tragedy occurred when Mrs. Sylvia O'Kelly'O, the twenty-eight-year-old adopted daughter of Mr. and Mrs. Triumphington and married to an out-of-work composer, had noticed a fire that had started in the building where her playthings and dolls were kept from childhood.

According to a witness, an estate workman, Mrs. O'Kelly'O was seen leaving the Doll's House and had already walked some distance on the front drive by which the Doll's House is approached, when, it is believed, in stopping to look back, it was as if Mrs. O'Kelly'O had forgotten something and it was then she must have noticed the fire. In returning and reentering the house, it is thought she did so in an attempt to rescue some very valuable antique dolls kept there. She ignored shouts from the estate gamekeeper not to enter. He described that she seemed oblivious to the fierce flames which had already extensively engulfed the building.

Meanwhile, another workman had gone to raise the alarm and seek help finding Mr. Triumphington, who was at the time at his stables visiting his horses. Mr. Triumphington, upon reaching the Doll's House, now a raging inferno, soaked himself and his jacket in a nearby rain barrel and put the jacket over his head, then, according to the estate gamekeeper, who attempted to stop him, entered the building, in spite of the intense blaze, to rescue his adopted daughter.

Summoned from seven miles away, the local volunteer fire department, having to traverse the winding and hilly rural roads, arrived at the scene, only to find the small cottage-style building, already with its roof collapsed, beyond saving. The victims' remains were identified by Mrs. Triumphington, adding yet another tragedy to the long history of misfortune to haunt the Marchantiere family.

Walk along seeing nothing but my feet stepping one in front of the other. The tears chill in the breeze as they roll down my face. And now all over my body I suffer your pain of burning. Unable to stand your being hurt, driven away as you were by my unfaithfulness. Spat upon by your mother. Haunted now by what drove you most to death. We could have had little children with beautiful limbs like yours who at birthdays played games and had treasure hunts in gardens and gathered around a Christmas tree, opening presents at Christmastime. Amid your dolls. Your elegant limbs charred black. Like those conflagrated aboard ship and roasted alive belowdecks after the blast of an enemy shell. Skin melted. Your hair burned off. Lids of your eyes gone. Left staring out of the bone holes in your head. Lips seared, to stretch in a grin of death over your teeth. Triumphington no phony poseur, as I had christened him. Nor was my wife his adopted daughter without principle and dignity. Who unlike Max's alimony-grasping, greedy helpmates, only said she would give me the cheapest divorce it is possible to get. She intended to die. Walked deliberately into the Doll's House. On her own exquisite long legs. And now so weary and worn, force my own legs to go back into this Bowery saloon where the bartender has got to know me because I've been here twice before. He returned to me quarters in change from my dollar bills, wiping the bar and placing my glass of beer in front of me.

"You must like us in here. And hey, this one is on the house."

Under the roar of the elevated train, step over five prostrate bodies to get here. Crumpled figures in the doorways. Those still sitting up sat with a bottle clutched in the hand, staring out into the shadowy gloom under the elevated train and mumbling to themselves. Either someone's son or someone's father. Then in this bar a brief friendliness comes from out of the bowels of all this dereliction. The long-distance operator's voice sounding familiar, and I finally get through to the Adirondacks and Dru on the other end of the line. Long silences between her words. Her voice less cold than it was with that inference that I was trying to get something out of her. And now she asks if I agree that Sylvia's sealed coffin be brought down to New York with her husband's. A funeral service at St. Bartholomew's prior to the interment and burial in the Green-Wood Cemetery in Brooklyn. And did I agree that Sylvia would be buried beside the Triumphington family mausoleum. Then she said that we shouldn't be seen together but that she was being driven down to the city and we could meet if there was somewhere ultradiscreet, as the newspapers were looking for stories. I suggested the counter selling coffee and hot dogs down in the subway at Lexington and Fifty-ninth Street, as it was unlikely anyone in the *Social Register* would ever be seen congregating there and where she would be safe from recognition or photographers.

In a morning fog settling over the city, the tops of the skyscrapers disappearing. Trying to stop myself plunging into grief as a misty soft rain drizzled down out of the shadowy whiteness. The atmosphere of the world one now lived in, bleak and black. Wore the same dark suit I wore to our first restaurant meal with Sylvia and her adoptive mother. Put on a black tie. If you're in mourning people are not supposed to be rude to you or punch you in the face. Each time I enter or return to the apartment, I look behind and watch the shadows ahead for the glint of a knife or lurking figures. Took the Lexington Avenue subway uptown to the Fifty-ninth Street stop. Hungry, I had two hot dogs smothered in mustard, relish, and sauerkraut while wondering how I was going to afford paying for them. Quickly approaching getting broke again after pawning my watch and radio. And now waiting for what one had to presume was one of the richest widows in America. But who after half an hour was not showing up. And just as I was ready to go and sipping the last of my 7UP and reaching in my pocket for coins to pay, she arrived. Black silk scarf at her throat, her tall slenderness covered in a gray mackintosh of the French Resistance sort that Max wore. A black cloche hat pulled tightly down over her hair. And as she stole up to my elbow, looking like an unlikely spy with her sunglasses, it took more than a moment to recognize her. She leaned over, and I could smell her sweet breath as she kissed me on the cheek and my most private part instantly stiffened.

"Sorry I'm late, Stephen."

"Hi."

"It's a very very sad time. I can't think of anything worse or more dreadful to have happened."

"Yes."

A smell of brandy on her always-beautiful breath. She sat on the stool next to me and ordered a coffee and a Danish pastry. I thought, My God, the cup's not gold and pastry has no diamonds glittering in it. And she's going to eat and drink like any of the people who have nothing better to do than to be here. Her voice softer and quieter than she'd ever spoken before, speaks.

"But now I'm afraid so many practical things have to come first. You can't afford to pay for Sylvia's funeral, can you."

"I can try. And I will."

"Please don't complicate matters, will you. Everything is already being taken care of. Jonathan was an honorable man. And Sylvia a lovely young woman too young to die. And their physical bodies were the most terrible things I have ever had to witness."

Tears rolling from beneath her sunglasses and down her cheeks. A train pulling in would have drowned out any wounded sob. But stoic she sat, opening her crocodile-skin bag and taking out a handkerchief to dab the tears. And here had now come what had to be the cold calculation that was about to involve our lives. Her assumption that I would be glad to be rid of my responsibilities, even though I was relieved and was too ashamed to admit it.

"Sylvia, as you may know, Stephen, was cut off upon her marriage."

Then just as abruptly as this information was offered, she quickly caught herself, nearly dropping her crocodile bag as she reached her hand over and placed it on my knee. Put there perhaps for reassurance as she faltered in assuming her schoolmarm persona.

"Stephen, we can't really talk here. Shall we go. I just want to walk a bit."

I counted out the coins to pay, like tiny steps down the

ladder into impoverishment, pushing them one by one forward on the counter, adding a tip of a little pile of pennies. And we climbed the steps up and out of the subway, away from where the thundering roar of the trains was silencing our conversation. The brim of her cloche hat pulled down, she swayed a couple of times as we walked together along the street. But now in silence passing movie theaters and stores. Maneuvering through the shopping crowd streaming around the big department store entrance on the corner that my own mother, from the redoubt of her kitchen, used to surprisingly say was frequented by people with backgrounds totally without refinement. Then we heard screams and shouts. An elderly lady in a fur coat being robbed. The brigand running zigzag through the pedestrians and then bolting across the street. The squeal of tires of a car trying to stop. A thud. The thief facedown, unconscious in the gutter. A belligerently angry old lady thanking a Good Samaritan handing back her purse. A few seconds of life gone by in this haphazard city. Where the unjust, the corrupt, the criminal and the discourteous can suddenly get their comeuppance from the courteous, the good, the honest and the just. And as we walked on and passed a newsstand, there it was. Publicity rules all. Front page of the *Daily News,* a headline along with Dru's photograph. And next to it a picture of the smoking, charred ruin in the woods.

The gray sky turning dark and glowering. I could feel
Dru stiffen next to me and her walk become hurried. And
in sensing her anguish, it was as if Samuel Barber's *Ada-*
gio for Strings scratched across my brain to express her
soul's terrible pain with violins screaming out their raging
notes. As it had come to me on that earlier day of
tragic occurrence, when another young girl had died
and left a darkened red stain on the bus station floor.
And now on this very day with my own publicity a ci-
pher of conspicuous ignominy. Referred to as an "out-of-
work composer." Yet no one can claim more resolve
to achieve my purpose nor can feel stronger in the
fight I shall fight. With a strength even greater than
that power held by the richest woman on earth. Who
could hire a crane to lift the Empire State Building right
up out of its foundations and put it somewhere else like
Max's Chicago with a live elephant dancing on top. And
garbed as Dru was, people looked at us as we passed in
case she might be the famed reclusive Hollywood actress
rumored to live a bit farther south on this East Side of
town.

"Please, Stephen, tell me. Tell me that everything is
meaningless. That there are no other worlds out beyond
the sky that we will ever be able to take a spaceship to. I

don't want to believe that nothing matters. Even though it doesn't."

And as I watched the random faces pass and for the glint of knives, I was trying to think of an answer to everything not being meaningless. Especially having such recent firsthand information on the meaningful. Something to eat and somewhere to sleep. And if you were extralucky, a concert grand piano or a more portable violin to play. Then you could go on dreaming to thunderous applause with an orchestra having performed Prokofiev's Violin Concerto No. 1 in D Major. Shouts for an encore and flowers flooding the stage. And we pass another newsstand and even a vendor calling out, "Read all about it."

"Oh God Stephen, it's everywhere. Stacked on the newsstands all over New York."

And what could be meaningful to all these people going by. Who can for a nickel read about burning death spelled out in the paper. Because there it was. Shouted out to the world. Happening to the rich and privileged. On the heels of the secret quiet death of Max. And to another lovely girl, in the bus station where wrong information was being given out at Princeton. Then Sylvia's death. To which she calmly walked. Back to her most private little refuge, now to be seen in ruins by everyone including my favorite sister. Then by my whole family which wasn't invited to the wedding and never met her. My mother who prays with her rosary beads every day, said even Protestants deserve a prayer and will say Hail Marys for the repose of Sylvia's soul. And philosophize, saying that children brought with them adversity which could wear out the heart with worry. And now I am as if I were a ship, bow-on crashing through a vast ocean's wild waves. Unleashing broadside salvos over the horizon. Not knowing in my turret if they will sink the enemy. And where you, if it's you they're aiming at, crouch low. It will do you no good at all if a shell direct hits. Just creates the dead to slip into the deep. And the victor on the sea swells rides away.

Walking now two of us in sorrow with her hand in mine. A gust of wind and first drops of rain falling. Waiting for the lights to change to cross west on Lexington Avenue. This widow. Who I was certain was now so sad that despite her gentle inebriation, she would never again be merry. But in just less than a minute I was wrong. As we reached Park Avenue on the corner where the Ritz Tower rose into the sky, her mood and disposition abruptly changed. Just as it did when she became the rigid schoolmarm, removing her sunglasses and gimlet eyed winking unwelcomingly at me. Now suddenly grabbing my arm, she stopped on the sidewalk. Mascara smeared around her reddened eyes.

"Dru, what's the matter."

"The matter is that I suddenly feel so awfully horny and desperately badly in need of a fuck."

"Holy cow, Dru."

"Put your arm around me, please. Give me a squeezing hug. And come on. Let's go. Flag that taxi, sailor."

Grabbing my arm. Her arm linked tighter around mine. Her fingers closed over my wrist, squeezing hard. As I open up the taxi door and shut it closed. Joining the flow of yellow Checker cabs up Park Avenue. As the rain now belts down and the taxi driver waits to ask, "Where do you want to go, folks," and then the quiet reflection on this destination of a side street off Sutton Place. And now I was counseling myself. Not to break down and sink in an awful sea of guilt. That the wonderful word *sailor* sounded comforting to hear. And softened the sound of the words *horny* and *fuck* coming from Dru's lips. Remembering when she said during our first clutching in bed together, "Of course, darling, when you want to be fucked by somebody, then you forget all your worries and all their faults." Jesus Christ Almighty, whatever you expect from a woman, don't believe it. Because it is always going to be something else you didn't expect. And if you were expecting it soon, it would always be later. Or expecting it later, it would always be sooner.

Nearby steps up to a little park overlooking the river, the taxi stopping down this side street off Sutton Place. And some more of what I never expected. Paying the fare, which would now, less two dimes, leave me again flat miserable broke. And the taxi driver scratching his head, delivering two servants to their destination, because that's where they worked.

"Just follow me, Stephen."

Dru producing a key, we entered the black steel door and along to the service elevator. She slumped back against the elevator wall, her head bowed as we went up to her floor. And gently smiled as we stepped out on the landing to her pantry door where the delivery boy had masturbated in front of her. Gilbert taken ill and in the hospital with pneumonia. Other staff in the Adirondacks. The apartment empty. Dru casting her coat and hat aside, locking the door behind her, and taking my hand as we entered and went through the kitchen. Past a pile of chopped vegetables on the table. Tempted I was to put hand to and take and chew the healthy end of an un-chopped carrot. But instead snatched three grapes from a bunch in a basket. As Dru grabbed a bottle by the neck and briefly put it to her lips.

"Don't be shocked, Stephen. I often swig from the bottle."

Chew down my grapes as we pass ormolu-mounted mahogany commodes and go to the end of the longest hall and up the stairs where she led me to a spartan and nunlike bedroom, the windows looking out onto the East River below. And suddenly she retreated.

"Oh no. Not here. Let's go to the music room. We can listen and have some music."

Pulled by the hand I followed her back down the stairs and along the hall, over the splendor of rugs and parquet and past the paintings and a Canaletto scene of Venice I'd not seen before. The doors of the music room closing behind us. Out the windows the sky darkening with a storm and the glass streaked with rain. Dru going to her record player.

"I want to dance."

Bach's Suite No. 2 in B Minor. Then over by the window, Dru lifting her sweater over her head and undoing her skirt and casting them aside. Now her underclothing and stockings dropped to the floor, her lithe body twirling around in the middle of this room, in a sinuous dance. And a shiver of recognition of Sylvia. Then as the record ended and I was licking my lips watching her, she crossed to the piano to sit to the keys.

"Stephen, I've practiced and played from this whole pile of scores. I wish I could play as beautifully as you do."

"Ma'am you do, you do."

"Could you recognize the composer if I play a piece."

"I believe Ma'am, if I am not already distracted by other more pleasantly urgent matters, that you can play me any successive five or six notes or chords from any composer you like."

"Okay. Here we go, then."

"From the exquisiteness which comes when he lets go with his larghetto in his Oboe Concerto in C Major, that's Vivaldi."

"Oh, you are clever. Here we go next, maestro."

"Although great orchestral volume always provides the grandness, those four tinkling notes are from a Beethoven piano concerto."

"Well, I'll have to be more obscure. Try this."

"Ravel, Piano Concerto in G Major, adagio assai."

"Oh my God, how can one win. And one more."

"Rachmaninoff. Piano Concerto Number Four in G Minor, opus 40, allegro vivace."

"Well this one I'm sure you won't get."

"Sibelius, the 'Swan of Tuonela.'"

"My God, you are, aren't you, really clever. Which I always knew you would be. From the very first moment I clapped eyes on you and you first spoke, if a little bit pedantically."

"Ma'am, one does not regard this as any feat. It's just that I praise and love music in all its forms, harmonies, and rhythms."

"Khachaturian, then. Let me put on the record. While you dear sailor, take off your clothes. To have my need sated, it badly requires that Irish cock of yours stuck deep within me with plenty of percussion fucking to the 'Sabre Dance.'"

"Ma'am, outside of those motifs reptilian, you sure as hell do have some fine orchestral ideas for accompaniments."

"Inspired of course by having those arms of yours around me hugging and holding, that one day soon will have conducted some of the great orchestras of the world performing your first, second and third symphonies. And who knows, out of death perhaps the freedom of life doth come."

Dru pirouetting across the room to the window, turns, staring at me, her arms outstretched and undulating her breasts. Directed to sit on the piano, I sat. Waiting for her to come smiling on tiptoe. Slowly approaching, hips swaying, her winking eye winking.

"I come now to fuck thee, sailor."

And boy oh boy, who knows, maybe out of death the freedom of life really does come. Kissing me on the lid of each eye as she does. Her tongue burrowing like a corkscrew in each ear. Kissed then on the tip of the nose and at last on the lips. Then spreading her thighs she sits astride me. Haunches heaving to the rhythms of Khachaturian. Requiring astonishing syncopation. Bury my face in her soothing breasts. The bleakness of death to come again tomorrow. And wondering if we will break the goddamn stool which already felt as if it had gone wobbly and weak in one leg. Another's flesh against mine. Touch the beautiful, shun the ugly. Growing up I was told I was so good-looking that I would be welcome anywhere. And to try it out I walked the streets of Riverdale to see if I could find where there might be a party in progress. When I saw several lights on, I walked up the path to their door and knocked or rang. When the door was answered, I asked in all deep sincerity,

"excuse me, kind sir, is there a party going on in there."
I would nearly always be invited in and even was able
to test my looks further by beckoning to a couple of
friends hiding behind trees out in the road or across
the street and asking if they could be invited as well.
Only once did I hear a voice say, "Get the fucking hell off
this goddamn porch before I fucking well kill you." And
that bastard always flew an American flag on his front
lawn.

And now here was Dru. Her hair shrouding her face
and her head hung over my shoulder as she milked me,
she sang:

"My momma done told me
She didn't tell me much
But she told me not to do
To do such things like this."

A mournful hoot of a tugboat on the river and sound
of rain spattering windows as Dru released herself from
my lap and her voice dropped and seemed to fade away.
Her beautiful breasts seemed to hang lower.

"Oh God, Stephen, all these things have their repercussions. What have I done. Betrayed a daughter. A husband. Betrayed him."

"Holy cow, ma'am, you mustn't think like that."

"Don't you damn well tell me how to think. His memory should be sacred and it's betrayed. And he cares. I

307

know he does. He's somewhere, I know he is. And is mortified and horrified."

"Holy cow Dru, take it easy. As people die, they're no longer there to care."

"Well, maybe you don't care."

"Gee Dru. Give me a break, will you. At least from the new surprises, until I recover from some of the old ones."

My first nearly angry words spoken in the company of this rich woman. Innocent but carrying all the blame of all the millions dumped on her. And right at the moment I would love to get the sort of spiritual bliss that one can feel listening to vespers as I did once at King's College Cambridge, sung under the vault of the great chapel ceiling. And I suddenly imagined that in order to shock my Irish Catholic soul Dru might now hold out her hand in front of my face and say, Okay sailor you've had yours, pay me. But instead, her voice was plaintive.

"Although he loved Sylvia, I so disappointed him. That I wouldn't be a mother and he be a father of his own offspring. But I decided that with so many children already in the world, more coming would be too much. And I didn't want to bring any into the world myself. And still, even if I could, don't want to be a mother."

Dressed, we went out of the music room, past where I had pissed all over the powder room floor and up the stairs again to a different and sumptuous bedroom. Dru's private domain. A television set. Bookcases and books galore. Rugs deep as snowdrifts on the floor. Her diamonds which she usually wore around her wrists and neck, were on her dressing table. Portraits of her own mother and father on the wall. As she now lay on her back on the purple covers on her bed, staring up at the ceiling. A bottle in one hand and the other thrown across my stomach. She said it was time to think. Of Paris and next year's racing at Longchamp. And perhaps I thought she was even thinking of caressing my Irish cock to new endeavors as she always seemed to ethnically call it. And I was thinking of ole Max's occasional words of wisdom. "Pal, the world is where you make it, right in the close little space of the world around you. If you want more spiritual room, get back to old Europe, pal. Old Europe. That's where the solution is. Deep in the bowels of ancient traditions. And if what you're not doing is what you should be doing, then the solution is to have a roof over your head. Keep chickens. Fresh eggs for breakfast. Be careful of women. Trust none." And I said to Max, "Isn't that cynical." And he said, "You bet, pal, you bet." And then as she took a drink from her bottle, came Dru's words.

"Stephen."

"Yes."

"Do you want a swig of this sauce."

"No thank you."

"Well, Stephen, are you listening."

"Yes."

"You change your name by deed poll to mine. Swear fidelity to me under pain of discontinuance and renouncement. And I'll finance your career."

"Holy cow, ma'am."

"Is that your answer."

"No ma'am, just my expression of amazement."

"Well, what's your answer."

"You're buying me."

"In so many words. Yes. In certain circles it's called, 'singing for your supper.' "

"Well ma'am, you may be able to buy another world out beyond the sky. But I'm not singing for my supper. And while I still have a hand on the end of my arm and I can run and grab a hot dog off a hot dog stand, you're not going to buy me."

Waiting for a janitor to jump on me any second as an escaping jewel thief I went out the service entrance at Sutton Place. Just like the masturbating boy who probably wanted to do what I had just done. Gonads paining more than glowing, I walked every inch of my impoverished rain-soaked way down Third Avenue under the elevated train and back to Pell Street. Having thoughts enough that made it seem to take only a moment. Be adopted. Sing for my supper. Put on a butler's uniform. Announce, Madam, dinner is served. Then sing, "Bimba, bimba, non piangere" from Puccini's *Madama Butterfly*.

Wait for my own crumbs to be brushed off the table and fall into my upturned open mouth. She said as an aside one day, "We who buy people know those who can be bought." Well ma'am, not me.

Hanging clothes to dry I lay the night through in Pell Street, staring at a ceiling. Trying to make sure to wake in time for the funeral which gets more sounding like my own. Yet many great composers had patrons. And were bought and kept. And King Ludwig of Bavaria's largesse to Wagner never made his music any less beautiful.

In the early hours, down from the Adirondacks, a cold front descending on New York. A sprinkling of white on the street in the morning was the first sign of snow after one of the city's coolest summers. No frying eggs on the sidewalks or crisping your bacon on the steel manhole cover in the middle of the street. But it was after a snowfall that I first really learned how to spell when a bigger boy named Newt taught me while taking a pee, how to write my name with piss in the snow. Newt also said that it was knowing how to do things like that that held the Indians back and let the white man make our country great.

From the Bowery bar where now it seemed every other drink was on the house, I telephoned Amy again at the Pennsylvania Hotel, but she was out. Left a message to invite her on a ferry ride. At a nickel a head, a dime round-trip, it was the only thing that I could afford to do in New York. Smell of garlic on the subway train and a fume that

comes from wet wool. My shirt not the cleanest and covered up by a black chesterfield coat belonging to my older
brother who, like Max, worked on Wall Street before he
married a rich girl with money. But for it's being too conspicuous, I thought of coming in Max's motorcar. There
were the hearses and a line of limousines parked outside
St. Bartholomew's. And more around the corner with
their chauffeurs waiting across from the entrance to the
busy luxury of the Waldorf Towers. As I passed Ajello's
candle makers, a perfumed smell came out the doorway.

Brace myself. Cross the street, join as anonymously as
one can the elegant gathering. In the church, a flag on one
coffin and a posy of flowers on the other. Church nearly
full. Obsequies begun. The searing sorrow already an-
guishing through one's body. My lungs heaving to pour
out tears. Hold. Hold back. The despair. The hopeless-
ness. The dreadful guilt. Head up. Straighten the back.
Stand when they do. Kneel when they do. Sit when they
do. Recitation of the words from the Bible. Said to these
heads of the living and these coffins of the dead. "I am the
resurrection and the life, saith the Lord; he that believeth
in me, though he were dead, yet shall he live . . .

"For a man walketh in a vain shadow and disquieteth
himself in vain, he heapeth up riches and cannot tell who
shall gather them.

"The last enemy that shall be destroyed is death."

Voices of a choir. Sing "Now the Day Is Over." And

here I am at the back of this church in this last pew, the object of an occasional furtive look. It being nobody's business to care who I am. Or what I do or how I feel. But what I am is an outcast. An outsider. Who would not sing for his supper. Amid these mourners from near and far. Can nearly pick out the polo players. The society celebrities. Rustle of black silks. Yet perhaps silk doesn't rustle. But the scent of burning candles and fragrant perfumes is certainly aromatic. Dru in a front pew with relatives, family servants and retainers. And suddenly it's all over. The choir sings "Abide with Me." Triumphington had a great-aunt and -uncle who went down on the *Titanic,* stood on its deck in their evening clothes as it sank into the frigid Arctic waters.

Snow now falling heavily. The big white flakes melting on the church steps and sidewalk. Pallbearers, coffins on their shoulders, loading them back into their hearses. Odd nods, condolences and handshakes from the few familiar faces as they pass. Very very sorry about Sylvia. In one of the limousines, Ertha, Max's divorced wife. She nods her head about her. Sees me on the church steps just as she bends down to step into her car. She must now have Max's shell collection, all his silk ties and shoe trees. Plus his refrigeratorful of marvelous champagnes. Dru. There she goes. All in the bleakest but most luxurious black. On those wonderful legs carrying the rest of that slender wonderful body an out-of-work composer has got to know so well. For a moment I even thought I'd have to walk to take the subway to Brooklyn where the cemetery was. But on the sidewalk I was tapped on the arm by the chauffeur who took Dru and me to Valhalla when she was alias Mrs. Wilmington. He opened up the limousine door for me to step in to the comfort of this armored vehicle.

The cortege swept around the ramps of Grand Central Station and rapidly down Park and Fourth avenues. Funerals in New York always rush the fastest way away. Leaving behind all those familiar streets that I have so many times passed in my broke circumstances. Houston, Prince, Spring, Broome and Grand. Now travel in the luxurious comfort with my guts twisted in guilt and grief. I did and do love her. Her death now swept away over the Gothic majesty of the Brooklyn Bridge and down and along these stranger streets to the sudden oasis of open sky over this vast cemetery with its large buildings flanking its entrance. Triumphington's flag-draped coffin carried up the steps of the Triumphington family mausoleum. Sylvia's casket covered in flowers, waiting in the hearse parked on the road. So hard to believe that that once-lithe body is in there in its coffin, its living beauty scorched, seared and stilled in death. On the mausoleum steps, sailors in leggings, rifles at present arms. A commander in attendance, gold braid on his cap. Calling "Ready, aim, fire." The crack of shots echoes in the cold air. Bugler blowing taps. I raise my hand, stiffening my fingers to my brow in my best salute. Sailors take the flag from the casket and the Stars and Stripes is deftly and exquisitely folded and handed to Dru, and they too salute.

Sylvia's college chums assembled by her grave. High heels sticking into the ground. A pile of earth covered in artificial grass. The funeral director urging me closer to the hole. Elbow-to-elbow with Dru who draws away. And makes a distance which may be the closest we will ever be together again. The college chums standing behind me in force. Recognize a voice. Ertha pronouncing to her companions in her gossipy way clearly meant to be heard by my ears.

"Sylvia deliberately went back into the Doll's House, according to the workman. Before he even knew there was a fire she was standing on the drive in front watching it burn for fully three minutes and then as the flames took hold, she calmly walked back in."

Ertha's words dissipating in the chill air. Every silence now sounding like the end of my life. Straps unwind to lower the coffin. And whatever terrible burned part of her was left is gone. And Jesus Christ Almighty, thank God for the intervening voice of this refined Protestant clergyman. Who with faintly British vowels elegantly intones.

"Lord my God shall make my darkness be light. Deliver us not into the bitter pains of eternal death. But thy kingdom come."

Mourners retreating. Ertha stared at me and then as I

stared back, she looked away. One wants to say, What the fuck else did you do to Max, you bitch. Mourners reaching the roadway. Limousine doors opening and shutting. More snow falling. A blue jay squawking nearby in a tree. Dru in her black splendor accepting last condolences from relatives, staff, acquaintances. Making me feel as if I were some sort of trespasser. After someone for their money. Which is after all, the greatest tribute they can be paid. And now she's gone her way. And I'm gone mine. Walking down the gentle slope of this hill whitening in snow. As a figure sidles up. What more must I hear if I listen. The voice is asking would I chat with him at his office on the seventeenth floor of the Triumphington building on Madison Avenue at a time convenient. And now good God, a tap on my shoulder. What next. Another voice comes near as I turn. And this from a famous face in magazines and newspapers.

"I am so sorry and I apologize for intruding upon you at a time like this but I had, having only recently been able to meet with your wife Sylvia, been unable to reach you by telephone. I just wanted you to know that she gave me the score of your minuet sometime ago and which I regard as such a brilliant work of composition that I took the liberty of rehearsing it with my symphony orchestra. Might I just ask at this time if you would consider its being performed. Please telephone my office. I should like to invite you more formally to conduct its premier performance. I'll say no more except that Sylvia was one of the most brilliant and wonderful dancers, and she was too, such a princely girl. Again, please accept my most sincere condolences."

Dark pointed shoes of this famed conductor and composer who did not show up for our appointment when I was previously to meet him. Was the news of this event all over the newspapers. To bring him here in all his finery. Yet so courteous and pleasantly glittery-eyed, bracelets on his wrists. Amazing how when you meet people and they tell you something you want to hear, it transforms them from someone previously objectionable at a distance into someone delightful close-up. And even utterly charming and compassionate. But at least one thing is for sure. My name O'Kelly'O is going to go carved on a piece of marble over a grave dug near a socially registered Protestant mausoleum in one of the best cemeteries. And I've got to say again that when the chips were down, Jonathan Witherspoon Triumphington III, IV, or whatever he was, had plenty of guts after all. And some of Dru's words—or were they Sylvia's—come back to ring in my ears. "There will be one day in your life when you need not worry about the mundane anymore."

Workman at the pile of soil shoveling it into the grave. And then a figure in a tattered-looking brown coat who'd been lurking back at the side of the gray granite mausoleum, was coming down the little hill to walk away on

317

the road. And from the corner of my eye I saw just a flash of the face seen before behind a screen door in Syracuse. And I knew even now, cloaked with its veil, it was Sylvia's never-forgotten mother.

Dropped off on Pell Street, the heavy car door clunking closed, I hated to leave the warm secure comfort. Like being shoved out again into the cold world. And without even showing signs of wanting a tip, the chauffeur saluting me, and I realized he did so with a certain lack of precision distinctly naval. And I saluted back. Went into the hall, up these dusty stairs and back into the apartment. In an effort to prevent mess accumulating further in these shabby rooms I pulled out a drawer to place my clothes away. And there in the back corner of this depository was the sweater Sylvia wore when I first met her. The heavy wool folded on top of a pair of her black leotards. Gently, reverently, I lifted them up. There under the sweater was a brand-new twenty-dollar bill. Like the kind she used to give me for car fare. And a note.

Maestro, who knows, you may need this.

And the sob came up as if from the bottom of my feet and from the end of my toes. Unstoppable. Racking every part of my body. And clinging to myself I lay on the bed, my tears soaking the pillow. And next I knew, it was dawn and a pigeon standing in the snow outside on the windowsill.

I knew somehow that I had to get up out of this whirlpool of sorrow or be forever sucked down to no one's good. And get out into life again. I was sure I was being followed as I went to my familiar Bowery bar to call the Hotel Pennsylvania to ask Amy when I could take her, as I had promised, on a ride on the Staten Island Ferry which let you escape to a brief freedom and return with renewed confidence to New York. Remind myself again. That a nickel a head and a dime round-trip, it was something left I could afford to do in New York. And knowing the ferry was one of America's most incredible clubs, where each commuter could recognize a stranger and every other commuter's face and where they sat and what they read. But Amy was again out.

And so important now that I knew it was, to break the barren hold of all these buildings. To vigorously walk the rest of the streets right down to the tip of Manhattan Island. And past where in a twenty-five-cent lodging house Stephen Foster once lived. And who died abandoned and penniless in this city after creating such wonderful music and song.

At last at the end of Broadway the open park ahead, it was as if a whole new world was starting all over again after one had died and woke up living. Yet knowing one lost someone I must have loved. And the one who in death had saved my life. So that I and my music could live.

Remember again. It was my own decent hardworking parents who, even though they weren't invited to the wedding and with their own dire worries to think about, gave Sylvia and me a few hundred bucks as a present, and we were just able to afford to take the apartment with the big windows looking down on Pell Street. But they said I was moving back into a world that they had struggled to get out of all their lives. And it is true. Even as I go now, I feel disgust at the lack of human dignity along the Bowery streets. The pawnshops, bars and flophouses. A distinguished gray-haired gentleman who could have been my own father accosting me, begging. Asking him, "What has befallen you, friend." No answer. And I gave what coins I could. And now I know how the rich of the richest live. They have, while they're awake, appointments. And yet in these United States we live in, for many it was all falling asunder. Where once-respectable, dutiful, God-fearing people end up strewn in the gutter.

Trotted across the rest of the park on this very tip of Manhattan Island. The whistle blew. A Staten Island Ferry about to leave. Up the steps. Run. Run. Jump past as the gatekeeper closes the gates. The last passenger getting on board. Ferry pulling out, squealing against the greased great pilings. Go buy a hot dog adorned with bowel-moving sauerkraut, relish and mustard. Go out on deck. Eat it in the breeze. Stare out at this massive statue holding up its torch of liberty. Emblem of this city and America. Vessels anchored in the bay. Try to read the flags they fly. The wind beating upon the cold gray choppy waters. A tugboat plowing through the waves, foam up over its bow. Draw in a breath of chill air. Turn to go back into the warmth. Stop. And there she is, leaning on the railing. In a black beret, her blond hair being blown back by the wind over her shoulders. The delicate whiteness of that face. Amy from Knoxville. And I could hear Max's voice saying, How modern can life get, pal, how fast, and how surprising, to be even a bigger pain in the ass. And he also said, Amy was from a good family. That he had holed up with her without repercussions. And what a gal.

Then she turned, saw me. And smiles. Wide, beaming and wonderful. And welcoming. I smile. Go tell her now that I'll take her wherever she wants to go. Even on a jaunt in Max's ole Bentley, his legacy to me. With the headlights like two large bulging insect eyes. Knock this city for a loop. Sport, as he did, a crimson silk cravat adorned with black dots and stuck with a gold pin. Thumb my nose at those who jeer. And I know now Sylvia meant no harm when she said, "Throw that rag away." And even though death may never be put to death, let us ask that you who take the dead away always treat them kindly. And play music please.

Amy from Knoxville said she would stay on in New York and find a job. And it was on a day a month later that I'd gone to see the famed conductor and to meet him on

the steps of the Juilliard School of Music following his holding auditions and also to meet a cellist he had heard of there. But he had just learned from two girls, fellow students, about a girl named Sabrina, who had shot herself in the bus station and who at the school was considered one of their most brilliant young cellists. And as I stood there, still in my mind. That image. Of the girl in the bus station. "Excuse me, sir." When I was so near her. And who was she. And did it ever matter that I find out in this small city with its millions. And now had found out. On these steps where she once must have stood. And where she must have seen me at least once standing. For now I remember her features, posture and the warmth of her healthy glow. And I should have known of her life-threatening distress which was said in her words written all over her face. Just like the man who was also there and had just gone by. With his own face wreathed with concern.

To tell everybody
That wrong information
Is being given out
At Princeton